THE SEXY BILLIONAIRE

BOOK 2 - ITALIAN NIGHTS SERIES

JA LOW

Copyright @ 2024 JA Low

All rights reserved. No part of this eBook/paperback may be reproduced or transmitted in any form, including electronic or mechanical, without written permission from the publisher, except in the case of brief quotations embodied in critical articles or reviews.

This is a work of fiction. Names, characters, businesses, places, events, and incidents are either the products of the author's imagination or used in a fictitious manner. Any resemblance to actual persons, living or dead, or actual events is purely coincidental. JA Low is in no way affiliated with any brands, songs, musicians, or artists mentioned in this book.

This eBook/paperback is licensed for your personal enjoyment only. This eBook may not be re-sold or given away to other people. If you would like to share this eBook with another person, please purchase an additional copy for each person you share it with. If you are reading this eBook and did not purchase it, or it was not purchased for your use only, then you should return it to the seller and purchase your own copy.

Thank you for respecting the author's work.

Cover Design: Simply Defined Art

Editor: Ever more editing services

Second Edits: Book Witch Author Services

Proofing: More than words

Photographer: Wander Aguiar - www.wanderbookclub.com

Model: Leonardo

❀ Created with Vellum

1
PAIGE

"I can't believe she's gone," I sniffle through my tears as we lay my great-aunt to rest in the family crypt in the village cemetery. The sun is shining, the birds are singing, and a large crowd has gathered to say their goodbyes to a woman who loved them like they were her own family. One by one, they pay their respects to her and then to us before wiping away their tears and moving on. It's hard to hold it together while the procession of mourners passes by. I don't know how much longer I can stand here without collapsing into a heap, especially since my legs are wobbling like Jell-O. I wish my husband was here with me. I need his support at this time, but we've only just opened our restaurant back in New York months earlier, and as the head chef, he needed to be there. Thankfully, my girls, Callie and Savannah, are by my side, giving me the strength to get through this heartbreaking day.

Once the last of the mourners have paid their respects to her and us, we head back to my great-aunt's estate to celebrate her life with a huge Italian feast.

"It was a beautiful day, Paige," Savannah says, linking her arm with mine as we navigate the cobblestone lanes back to the car.

"She would have loved all the fuss," I tell her, which makes me smile while simultaneously making my heart ache.

"She never said no to a party," Callie adds, taking my other arm in hers.

That was the truth; she could out-party people half, if not a third her age. Losing her big ball of energy is going to be hard. I can already feel it about the place; something is missing, and it's her.

It doesn't take us long to get back to her estate, and when we arrive, I'm overwhelmed to see the entire village has come back and cooked, producing an amazing meal for all the mourners and placing it on an array of tables that have been set up in the gardens. A band of older men have set up in the corner and are playing traditional music, which has people singing and clapping.

"Girls, you look like you need a drink." Mario, the winemaker from next door, hands the three of us glasses of wine and tells us all to drink up. Before I know it, the somber mood of earlier has been replaced with one of celebration as everyone sings, chats, drinks, and eats. Lucia would have loved all this; she's probably looking down on the party as we speak, dressed in head-to-toe designer threads, dripping in diamonds, probably internally cringing that we are using the wrong wine glasses for everyone's drinks. But she would be saying, "Life is too short to not enjoy it," and enjoy it she did. She was the coolest woman I knew. Great-Aunt Lucia was an over-the-top, uninhibited Italian spinster who never got married because she never wanted a man to tell her how she could live her life. She balked at the social conforms of women of her era, and she was a force to be reckoned with.

There's a giant hole left in my heart now that she's gone. She was my ride-or-die, and we would speak for hours about everything. Each summer, my parents would send me and my brother, Smith, to her estate in the Tuscan countryside to soak up our Italian heritage. Unfortunately, my mother's parents had both passed before we were born. Lucia was the link for my mother and us to the Italian blood that flowed in our veins.

I loved Italy. It was always my happy place—the sunshine, the rolling hills of vines, the food, the culture, and the fashion. I was a die-hard Italian junkie; so much so that I chose to attend college in Florence instead of back home. I studied at the American University of Florence and received a Bachelor of Arts degree in food and wine studies. I love food and wine; *who doesn't?* My great-aunt had a little apartment in the heart of Florence right near the school that I lived in during the week, and on the weekends, I would drive out to her estate and spend most of my time with her. I did this for four years.

She loved it when I asked if I could bring some friends with me for the weekend. She was in her element, hosting everyone, filling us with food, and plying us with wine from her neighbors' vineyard. My friends loved hanging out with her; she was a larger-than-life character who wore diamonds while cooking up a big batch of homemade pasta. She was eccentric, but also badass.

And now, those times are over. When we found out she was sick, we all flew out as soon as we could. We had a couple of days with her before she passed peacefully in her bed at home. Ever the diva, a ray of moonlight shone on her as she took her last breath as if God himself was calling her to the heavens. I don't know how I'm going to go on without her being a phone call away.

She was my rock.

The celebration of her life continued well into the evening; it's been hard putting on a brave face in front of everyone. The wine has helped, but I need a moment by myself; it's all too much for me.

Why did you have to get sick? Why did you leave me? What am I meant to do without you?

The tears stream down my face as I stare out across the darkened land, the twinkling lights of distant houses illuminating sporadically across the vineyards that have disappeared, along with the sun's gaze.

"I'm sorry to disturb you. I wanted to pay my respects." The deep, velvety voice startles me, making me jump, and I pour wine all over myself.

"Shit," I curse as I drop my glass and jump up, my private moment broken.

"I didn't mean to scare you," the voice says.

Turning around quickly, I'm seconds away from giving this well-wisher a piece of my mind when I look up into those dark chocolate eyes, ones I haven't seen in a lifetime, ones that used to know every inch of my body and could read my soul.

"Giorgio." I gasp as I take in the man standing in front of me. He's not the shy eighteen-year-old boy he once was. This is a man full of confidence, comfortable in his skin. My eyes trail down over his black tailored suit cut to perfection across his broad shoulders, before returning up to that face, the one that I'd spent all my summers staring at from beneath our sheets, across the table, underneath our favorite tree, and snuggled up in the back seat of his car. "You've grown up." I gulp as the air around us thickens. The boy I once loved has turned into one of the most handsome men I've ever laid eyes on.

"So have you," he says, giving me the once-over, clocking the changes the past fifteen years have had on us.

A flush starts to rise along my chest as he stares down at me. I'm a married woman. I shouldn't be feeling like this; it's the wine, that's all. It's been a horrible day, and I'm shocked to see him here.

"I'm sorry about Lucia. I know how hard this must be for you."

The air is sucked out of my lungs and tears start to well in my eyes over long-lost memories that are floating to the surface. The next thing I know, I am wrapping my arms around the man from my past as I start to break down. He stiffens against me before hugging me back. We stand there in dark silence as I try to compose myself. Eventually, I pull away and realize I've smudged mascara across his white shirt.

Shit.

"I'm sorry," I say, staring at what looks to be a designer shirt—it probably cost more than I have.

"It's fine. Only fair seeing as I made you spill your wine," he states, giving me a small smile.

That's right, he did.

"Guess we're even," I say, giving him a shrug.

We stare at each other in silence for far too long before my anxiety kicks in. I hate that seeing him after all this time has stirred up something inside of me. I need to escape, I can't be here. Not with him, not when I'm so vulnerable.

"It's been great seeing you, Gio. Guess I'll see you in another fifteen years." And with that, I turn and head inside.

"Paige," he calls after me, but I ignore him, my feet picking up speed the further I move into the light.

"Paige?" Savannah calls out, noticing me emerging from the darkness with haste. As my best friend, she can tell when I'm not myself, and seeing Giorgio again after all these years and today of all days is too much for me. Ignoring her, I race up the stairs and head toward my old room; she is only moments behind me as I throw myself onto the bed and scream.

"Are you okay?" she asks.

"No," I answer. It's muffled thanks to my face being pressed against the bed. The bed dips beside me as she takes a seat and starts rubbing my back.

"Today has been tough. It's okay to not be okay," she explains.

Rolling over, I sit up and look at her. "Today has been tough and I'm not okay."

"I know," she says, reaching out and wrapping a reassuring arm around me.

"Might have also done something incredibly stupid," I confess to her.

She raises her brows at me. "Not like anyone would blame you."

"I ran into my ex."

Savannah's eyes widen at my confession.

"Then I cried in his arms. His strong arms. I hate that he still smells so fricken good too."

"What? Why would your ex be here?" And as soon as the words leave her mouth, she gasps, remembering the stories I've told her about Giorgio. "I need to see this man. Show me," she asks.

"Hold on," I say, getting up and rushing over to the window that I know looks down over the garden as she follows behind. I point out

Giorgio, who's talking to his parents, his mother, wiping his shirt with a hanky. *That's mortifying.*

"You're not talking about that sublime creature in the dark suit, are you?" Savannah asks.

I nod. "He's that good-looking, isn't he?" I turn and ask as I nervously chew my nails.

"Can't believe you've had that man inside you."

"'Savannah,"' I squeal as I playfully slap her before falling into fits of laughter that I so desperately need. I can't believe she said that. She shrugs my protest away. "I'm embarrassed. He said hi, I haven't seen him in fifteen years and the next thing I know, I'm crying in his arms and have wiped mascara all over his white shirt."

"The man looks like a god, Paige. I'd use my sadness as an excuse to get in his arms, too."

My eyes widen at my bestie. "You're messed up." I smirk as I point my finger at her.

"I'm saying it's what I'd do, not you," she says, giving me a wink.

"I'm married."

"And he's not here," she quips before realizing what she's said.

My face falls because it's true my husband isn't here at a time when I need him the most. He knows how important Lucia was in my life—in our lives—she was our biggest supporter for the restaurant, and he couldn't have taken a couple of days off to be by my side.

"I'm sorry, PJ. I didn't mean to say that," she says, walking over and hugging me.

"It's the truth though, he's not here when he should be," I say, bursting into tears again.

2

PAIGE

It's been a couple of days since the funeral, and I'm still thinking about Giorgio Fiorenzo. *I shouldn't be.* He doesn't deserve my thoughts. I'm still mortified over my interaction with him and that's the only reason why he's still on my mind. The first time seeing him in all those years, and I crumble into his arms. I can't believe I cried on him like I did. He must think I'm an idiot. *It was nice of him to come and pay his respects, though.* It was. My great-aunt loved Giorgio, she thought he was a good boy. *He wasn't.* He and his younger brother spent every summer working at his family's vineyard, which backed onto Lucia's. They were one of the reasons I was always excited to come back to Italy. Giorgio was best friends with my brother, as was his younger brother, and the three of them would hang out together all summer long.

I wonder what he's been up to all these years. *He looks good.* Guess over the years, I've blocked all thoughts of him from my mind until now. Is he married? Does he have kids? Is he working for the family? *Does it matter? Why do you need to know? You're happily married.* I'm curious, that's all. Why am I arguing with myself? I've lost it. *If you want to look, look, if not, leave him in the past where he belongs.* This is all true, but he did make an effort to come to Lucia's funeral, and that means a lot *because Michael didn't.*

Grabbing my phone, I type his name in to search on the socials.

Shit.

He pops up as verified. He's engaged. *Of course he is, look at the man.* I continue to scroll. And he's engaged to Giada Rossi, the Italian actress who is sexy, gorgeous, and rich.

They look happy together, photos of them on yachts looking carefree, photos of them walking the red carpets, they look gorgeous together. Giada looks like she belongs in his world. *You never did.* I know. I'm not aristocratic like him. I'm just a girl from upstate New York, living in the city, trying to make it big in the culinary world, who owns a French restaurant and is in debt up to her eyeballs.

"No, no, no," I scream as my fat fingers accidentally hit *follow* on his account. He's going to know I've been thinking about him because I haven't in fifteen years. I've been fine not knowing what he's been doing. He's been living his glamorous life here in Italy and I've been living my perfectly fine life in New York. Then my phone vibrates with a notification, *Giorgio Fiorenzo Official is now following you.*

"Fuck," I curse at the screen.

"You ready?" Smith calls into my bedroom.

I'm so wrapped up in my phone that I scream and drop it on the floor. "You scared the hell out of me!"

My brother's eyes narrow on me, and I can see he is using his detective face, the one he gives people he's arrested. *I'm not a criminal, don't look at me like that.* I just did something stupid.

"You okay?" he asks tentatively.

"Not really. I accidentally followed someone I wasn't supposed to, and they saw and followed me back, and now I can't unfollow them because it will look weird," I blurt out.

My brother stares at me, possibly surprised over my honest admission. "Wait a week, and then unfollow them," he suggests.

Right. Of course. I could do that.

"Can't you like, go in and do something?"

Smith frowns at me. "Like what? Arrest them for following you?"

"You could do that? That would be helpful. But he doesn't live in the States, so I don't think that would work."

"He?" he asks, raising a brow at me.

Dammit, me and my big mouth. Note to self, don't ever get arrested, you will spill the beans instantly. "I ran into Giorgio Fiorenzo at the funeral."

"Wow, that's a blast from the past. It has been years since I've seen him. Damn, I missed him. I would have loved to catch up," Smith says.

"Yeah, it's been a long time," I mumble.

"Why were you looking him up?" he asks.

"Curious, I guess. We had some great summers together."

"We did and so many girls." He chuckles.

Rolling my eyes at him, of course, that's what he remembers.

"He kind of vanished after high school. But to be fair, so did I. Guess we all grew up. It was nice of him to show up to the funeral, though."

"Yeah, it was," I agree.

"What's he up to then?" Smith asks.

"He's engaged to a famous actress now," I tell him.

"No way," my brother answers as he pulls out his phone and looks him up. "She's hot, lucky guy," he states as he starts scrolling on his phone.

"You two ready?" my mom asks, popping her head into the room.

"I guess."

And we head to the lawyer's office for the reading of Lucia's will.

"Thank you all for coming here for the reading of the last will and testament of Countess Lucia Francesca Chiara Borghese. Let us begin," the stuffy lawyer explains.

It's strange hearing Great-Aunt Lucia being addressed as a countess; she was just Lucia to my brother and me. I look over at where my brother is seated, dressed in a dark suit as he stares forward, listening to the lawyer. He's struggling to keep his emotions in check as a single tear falls down his cheek. My brother is one of the strongest people I know. He's a detective in the NYPD, just like our father was. Smith's used to seeing the worst of the worst and is a vault when it comes to his emotions, so seeing him struggle today breaks my heart.

I peer over at my parents; Dad is holding my mother's hand tightly in his as she dabs her eyes with a tissue, leaning on him for strength. I wish my own husband was here beside me, giving me the strength I need to get through this.

"Firstly, Bianca Johnson, formally Leone, my niece, I bequeath five million euros."

My parents gasp, and my brother and I look at each other. Holy hell, that is a lot of money. I had no idea she was that rich. I assumed the title was in name only, not that it held anything of significance; obviously, I was wrong.

"Next, we have my great-nephew, Smith Johnson. I bequeath five million euros to you, too."

"Holy shit." My brother gasps beside me.

"And my apartment in the Upper East Side and my home in the Hamptons," the lawyer adds quickly.

Smith and I look at each other again, our eyes wide. That is crazy, no way; that apartment is insane with views over Central Park, and my brother loved that house in the Hamptons. It was his refuge from the city and his job when he needed to get away from his world for a moment.

The lawyer then turns his attention to me. "Next, my great-niece, Paige Johnson. What I am about to leave to you is a lot and I know you are going to say it is too much and that you aren't the right person for it. But I have always believed in you, and I know that my decision is the right one. If you don't take it, I will haunt you from the grave until you do."

As the lawyer reads out Lucia's comments, the room erupts with laughter despite the sorrowful time. What on earth does she have planned for me?

"I bequeath the title Countess and all that comes with that title."

What in the hell? Countess? No.

"That includes the estate outside Florence, an apartment in Rome, an apartment in Paris, a villa in Sardinia, as well as twenty million euros cash for the upkeep and staff of the estates. Additionally, family heirloom jewels worth five million euros. Then there are the investments, stocks, and bonds as well as my businesses that I own. Please see my financial advisor, Antony, for the full list of everything that comes with the name," the lawyer explains.

Wait, what?

This cannot be happening right now.

"Holy shit, Paige," Smith curses under his breath as he stares at me in bewilderment.

"This is too much. That doesn't seem fair to the rest of my family," I say, looking at my parents who only received cash compared to my brother and me.

"Sweetheart, these are Lucia's wishes. She wants you to be the next countess, she's entrusting the family's legacy with you," my mother explains.

"But what about you?" I say to them.

"Lucia knew what my parents left me when they passed. They set us up, it is the reason we haven't had to worry about our retirement. Please, sweetheart, we have more than enough."

What was Lucia thinking, making me a countess?

"But …" I begin to argue, but my mother shakes her head.

"Before she passed, Lucia explained to me her wishes of handing over her legacy to you. She spoke about how you always felt at home here in Italy, that it brought out the best in you. She believed your destiny was always to come back and create a life and a family here," my mother explains.

Of course, I love Italy; it's in my bones, my essence, and I would give anything to live here, except my husband doesn't have the same love for Italy as I do. In fact, he hates it, probably because he's French.

"My life is in New York. Michael and I have our restaurant."

"As a chef, you think Michael is going to say no to moving to Italy?" my father asks.

"Michael isn't a fan of Italy," I mumble, which pulls gasps from my family. It's something I've never confessed to them before. "We can't run a restaurant from halfway across the world."

"You can hire people," my brother adds.

"We've only been open six months …" I argue.

"Sweetheart, you don't have to do anything now. It will be here waiting for you when you're ready. Wait until you get home to talk to Michael about it, you two have a lot to discuss," my mother states wisely.

How can I leave all that real estate sitting there? Is this what rich people do? They leave empty homes and never use them?

The meeting soon wraps up. I'm exhausted, my anxiety is through the roof, and panic is lacing my body. I'm a freaking countess …. What the hell does that mean? All I know is tomorrow I have a meeting with Lucia's financial advisor, and he is going to explain everything else she has left to me. How did I not know she was this rich? I knew she had generational wealth because of the gorgeous home, and I knew about her apartment in Rome, and of course, the apartment in New York, and we would use the house in the Hamptons for Christmas most years, and I lived in the Florence apartment but everything else …?

Our parents say their goodbyes as they, too, are exhausted and head up to their rooms, leaving my brother and I standing in the living room in disbelief.

"What the fuck, Paige?" my brother curses as he walks over to the bar set up in the corner of the room and opens the glass cabinet, pulling out a crystal bottle and two matching glasses. He pours us two generous glasses and takes an enormous gulp of his, and I do the same.

The amber liquid slides down my throat, burning on its way, but it feels good.

"Did you have any idea how rich Lucia was?"

I shake my head.

"This is life-changing money and real estate for me, but for you …" He lets the sentence hang as he throws back another large gulp of alcohol.

"I'm literally freaking out, Smith. Like, what the hell, I'm a countess."

Smith turns and then proceeds to burst out laughing, clutching his stomach.

What the hell is so funny?

"Does that mean I have to curtsy to you now?" he teases.

My eyes widen in surprise before the first chuckles start to fall past my lips. "You better start addressing me correctly. Otherwise, it's off with your head," I joke, and we both continue to laugh at the absurdity of the entire situation. Me, royalty.

Once our laughter has subsided, silence falls across the room again as reality sets in.

"I'm going to miss her," I say, my voice hitching with emotion as the tears of laughter turn into tears of sadness.

"Come here," my brother says, holding open one arm, and I rush into his embrace. I bury my face in his chest and sob. "I'm going to miss her, too. She was a funny old bat," he whispers.

"I don't want to let her down, all this seems like a lot. I don't think I can do it," I confess, the suffocating fear of letting Lucia's legacy fail tightens around my chest.

"She wouldn't have given it to you if she didn't think you were the right person for the job."

I hiccup on my emotions as I take in my brother's words. "My life is in New York. What happens if Michael doesn't want to move?"

Smith is quiet for a bit, absorbing my question. "Then he's not the right person for you."

Instantly, I pull out of my brother's arms; I know Smith hates my husband. He's never forgiven Michael for breaking my heart when we first started dating and he cheated on me. We had only been together six months, and he'd gone to Vegas with his boys, and I found out that he'd drunkenly hooked up with someone. We were not in a good spot at that time and were constantly fighting. We broke up after that, and eventually, he won me over again, worked on himself, promised he would never betray me like he had, and with therapy, we were able to get back to a good place. My brother doesn't forgive or forget as easily and has held on to that grudge ever since.

"You always say that. When will you understand that I love him? I mean, the man is my husband. We have a restaurant. We are building an empire in New York together," I yell at him.

Smith doesn't waiver at my words. He's dealt with worse people than his little sister. "All the things he wanted to do. You compromise all the time and yet he would never do the same for you."

My brother's words sting because it's a fear I have deep down inside of me. I know I'm the one to compromise more than Michael ever could, but the man is French; he's passionate about his culinary arts. He's the creative genius behind the menu and I'm his support system to help make sure everything is perfect for him to do what he does best, which is cooking. *And yet when you need him, where is he?* He's working. Michael couldn't leave our new business, the kitchen staff aren't fully trained, all our hard work would go down the drain and in the competitive world of restaurants, the slightest dip could topple us.

"I love my life, Smith. Just because you're unhappy with yours doesn't mean everyone else is," I bite back.

My brother rolls his eyes at me; we've had this argument before, usually when he is telling me I can do better than Michael.

"I think you're jealous of my life, Paige. I don't have to answer to anyone. I have the freedom to do whatever the hell I want. I'm not tied down."

It's the same response he gives, the perennial bachelor of Manhattan, sleeping his way through the never-ending supply of badge bunnies that chase police officers.

"Why would I be jealous of your one-night stands? There's more to life than sex," I say.

"That's something someone who isn't getting good sex says," my brother teases.

I flip him off. I'm not going to defend my sex life to my brother. Has it dropped down significantly? Yes. But that's because starting a business is stressful, every couple goes through a dry spell. This dry spell has spanned months, but neither one of us has the energy after working sixteen-plus-hour days to come home and get it on. I wish there was more intimacy in my marriage, but I know that all marriages have ups and downs, and this, too, shall pass. *I hope.*

3

PAIGE

It was hard to say goodbye to Italy; it felt like a piece of me was missing as I stepped onto the plane and headed back to New York. I was happy to be getting back to my life, but in the same breath, I felt unsettled as if heading back to the States wasn't the right thing to do. It's probably because every other time I left Italy, I knew I'd be seeing Lucia again, but this time, it's goodbye, the first time I'm leaving not knowing when I'll come back again, and even if I do go back, she isn't waiting for me. I don't want our connection to break because it will be broken when I step off on the other side of the world, and I'm not ready to say goodbye, even though I must.

"You want me to wait?" my brother asks, having arrived back in New York.

I wave his concern away. "Michael said he's stuck in traffic," I lie. Michael isn't waiting for me at the airport like he said he would; why am I surprised? He's obviously lost track of time while in the kitchen and is probably at the restaurant prepping for the day.

"You sure?" he double-checks.

"Yes, go," I tell him.

He nods, eventually leaving me to it. Mom and Dad had decided to stay on in Italy for a couple of weeks more to do some exploring in

Europe. I pick up my phone and call Michael to find out where the hell he is, but his cell is switched off.

What the hell?

There was a small part of me that hoped he would be here, greeting me at the airport with a bouquet of flowers, telling me how much he missed me and that everything was going to be okay. Instead, I'm heading to our restaurant to see my husband for the first time in a month. I never got a chance to tell him he's married to a countess now, that we're rich and don't have to struggle anymore, especially after speaking with Lucia's financial advisor. Antony explained to me all about the businesses she had invested in and that I was now the proud owner of multiple enterprises across Europe. Including, the co-owner of the vineyard next door to Lucia's estate, which I had no idea was partly hers. Lucia owns the land that they grow the grapes on, and the Fiorenzo family owns the wine-making business. Apparently, the two families have worked together for generations, creating the wine. It was quite shocking to discover that Giorgio and I are now in business together. Antony went on to explain that the Fiorenzo family live in Rome and don't come down much to see it as they employ numerous people to run it for them. Mario, who I always assumed was Lucia's neighbor, not her employee, being one of them.

She'd also invested in another winery in France, in the Champagne region, and owns her own champagne brand. Why had she never told me any of this? There are also boutique hotels in the Amalfi Coast, Cinque Terre, Venice, Santorini, St Tropez, Marrakesh, and Hvar in Croatia, as well as ski chalets in the Dolomites, St Moritz, and Chamonix. I always assumed when we went to these places on holidays that she chose them because she wanted to go there, not because she was visiting her hotels, but now it makes sense why everyone was falling over themselves to assist us every time we stayed—because she was the fricken owner.

Then there were other generosities like supporting up-and-coming artists and fashion designers with scholarships and grants in her name.

That she is a silent partner in the world-renowned brand Yvette Sanchez, whose head office is in Paris.

And now, it was all mine. *I don't want to let you down, Lucia.*

Antony also explained the huge charity organization that she founded, helping to raise millions for various charities that were dear to her. Every year there is a ball in Rome that she co-hosts with the Fiorenzo family; it's a huge fundraiser for their charity. It's horrible to realize you didn't know parts of someone you were so close to. I should have done better.

Another stunning revelation was Lucia also has a classic car collection which is housed in a garage somewhere on the outskirts of Florence, not at her home as she didn't like the clutter. Smith is going to freak when he finds out. This woman was an undercover multi-millionaire, and we had no idea. I feel so stupid not realizing, but I guess you're only looking at what people are showing you and she never showed me the countess side of her. Now I wonder what she was really like when I wasn't around. I imagine this outspoken, assertive, ballbuster countess wrapped in fur, dripping in diamonds, driving classic cars between her estate in Italy and who the hell knows where else. She was a boss bitch, and I didn't even know it, and yet she thinks I can continue her legacy when my own life is a hot mess.

The taxi pulls up out the front of my own legacy, the restaurant Michael and I opened together. Maybe I can do this; I just need to have faith. Lucia saw something in me that I never did—until now. As I grab my suitcase and tip the driver, a sense of calm slides over me; I've got this. I, too, can be a badass boss bitch; I'm a fricken countess now.

I straighten my back and hold my head up higher than I normally would as I turn down the side alley and head into the restaurant via the back door. Opening the door, I walk through the back area and toward the kitchen, placing my suitcase down beside the fridges before continuing through. It's awfully quiet, I assumed a couple of the chefs would be in early prepping. Maybe the time difference has messed me up and it's earlier than I think it is. Then I hear grunting coming from the main kitchen. My heart skips a beat as the strange sounds echo around me. What on earth is that?

As soon as I turn the corner, I freeze as the source of the grunting becomes abundantly clear. My husband is fucking someone over the stainless-steel kitchen bench. *That's not hygienic. If the city found out, we would be closed down,* I think as I watch his white bare ass piston into someone that is not his wife. The woman lets out a moan as she moves her head to the side, and that's when I realize it's our sous chef, Amelia. A slew of French curse words fall from his lips as he slaps her ass a couple of times until his grunting ends with a long moan. I can tell that he got what he needed, not sure if Amelia did though.

Her eyes open and they land on me; her face instantly pales, and she quickly tries to push Michael off her.

"Hey, what the fuck?" he curses as his limp condom-covered dick falls from her. I should be happy that he's at least practicing safe sex.

"Paige," Amelia whispers as she quickly pulls her pants up.

"Why are you worried about Paige now? It's never bothered you before," he states, sounding annoyed that his sous chef has brought up his wife. He ties off his condom and throws it into the bin before pulling up his pants and turning around; his face drops as he stares disbelieving at me.

"Surprise. Guess you didn't miss me then?" I say before storming out of the kitchen. *Be strong, Paige, do not let this man see you cry, he doesn't deserve it.*

"Paige, wait, please, let me explain," Michael calls out after me.

Let him explain? There's nothing to explain. I turn around and furiously grab a baguette from the pile to my left and start hitting him with it. "You fucking cheating bastard," I scream as I hit him with the French breadstick.

"Paige, ouch, stop it, would you, ouch." He groans as he blocks the bread.

"Here I am mourning Lucia a world away, and you're fucking the staff. I needed you and you weren't there for me," I scream at him. The tears begin to pour down my cheeks as humiliation sets in.

How could he do this to me? Why did *she* do this to me? Who else knows at work? Because they sure as hell didn't seem to be hiding their cheating.

"Babe, please, let me explain," he pleads as he dodges more of my wrath.

"There's nothing to explain. I hate you," I yell as I pick up a new baguette and proceed to assault him with it.

"Would you stop it? I need them for tonight," he yells at me angrily.

"Of course, you're more worried about your precious food than you are about breaking your wife's heart. Fuck you, you piece of shit," I rage as I pick up the entire delivery of baguettes, throw them on the ground, and start jumping on them to be a petty bitch. "Fuck you," I scream, losing my mind. How could I have been so stupid? He promised me he would never do this again, and yet here we are. He chose to stay home and sleep with the staff over helping his wife mourn the loss of her favorite person in the world. What an asshole.

"Paige, stop it! Have you lost your fucking mind?" Michael yells as he pulls me from the mountain of bread that I have turned into dust.

"Of course, I've lost it! You've been fucking our sous chef for who the hell knows how long, while refusing to sleep with me. Guess now I know why you don't, you're too fucking tired from screwing the staff."

"It's not like that," Michael tries to reassure me. "Baby, I'm sorry, it was just sex, it meant nothing. I've been so stressed about making this restaurant a success, and you weren't here, and she offered, I tried so many times to say no, but …"

Asshole.

"Just sex! If I knew I could be having *just sex* with anyone I liked to help relieve my stress, I would have been. Thanks for forgetting to give me the fucking memo."

Michael stills and stares at me in bewilderment, as if the thought that I could be sleeping with someone else was the craziest thing he's ever heard. Misogynistic dick.

"You're being ridiculous."

I'm being ridiculous? He thinks that he's the only one that can pull a side piece.

"You don't think men find me attractive anymore? You think this ring stops them from wanting me?" I scream, holding up my ring finger, the image of Giorgio Fiorenzo flashing across my mind. "Let me assure you it doesn't, but somehow, I seem to be able to say no to their advances."

Not that Giorgio made a move. He's engaged and not a cheating asshole like my husband, he was the perfect gentleman. Michael's eye twitches at my statement and his left hand curls into a fist as if the thought of a man wanting his wife enrages him. "Men have needs that women don't."

Wow. I didn't think I could be any more speechless or shocked than I was and then he quotes some alpha male wannabe's bullshit he heard from one of the dumbass podcasts he listens to.

"And you think women don't want sex?" I'm literally shaking with anger right now.

"It's different for women," he argues.

I can't believe I'm arguing with my cheating husband that men need sex more than women, and that is why he is cheating on me.

"Let me explain something to you about women, we are simple creatures, most women want a hard, thick dick to fulfill their every need so they don't have to use their vibrator to finish off because their cheating scumbag of a husband can't get the job done," I spit at him.

"Fucking bitch," he curses under his breath.

"I'm the bitch?" I rage. "Fuck you." I point at him, then turn around and find an onion and peg it at him, missing him completely, which is rather unsatisfactory.

"Stop throwing things at me, you fucking crazy bitch," he yells at me.

"Not only am I a bitch but now I'm crazy too? Stop fucking the staff and maybe then I wouldn't be acting like this," I yell as I try to find something else to throw at him.

"Paige, I'm sorry, okay? We can get through this. Baby, please," he pleads with me.

"How long?" I scream at him as I pick up a tomato and roll it between my fingers.

"Baby, put the tomato down."

"No."

"I won't tell you then," he bites back.

The audacity of this motherfucker. I hurl the tomato at him and miss. Again.

Dammit.

"Paige, stop it."

"No, you stop it, Michael. You're the one who is cheating on me. You deserve all the tomatoes."

"We won't have anything left for service tonight," he yells back.

This stills me for a moment and my eyes narrow on him. He's right, I'm throwing away good produce, and that's not good for the bottom line.

"Would you rather I throw knives instead?" I bite back.

Michael stills, unsure if I mean it or not.

"You're safe. Orange doesn't look good on me, so it's your fucking lucky day."

"I'm sorry, Pea," he says, using his pet name for me. It always made me cringe.

"How long?" I ask him again.

"Does it matter?"

"It matters to me. You owe me that," I tell him as I wipe away my tears.

"On and off for a year."

My stomach does somersaults. A year. One whole year. I can't. How could he do that to me? One fucking year. We've only been married for two. Half our marriage.

"Have there been others?" I question him.

"Paige, I think we should talk about this at home." He tries to steer the conversation away from answering the question.

"No. You will answer me now. Have there been more?"

"Yes," he answers reluctantly.

Of course there have been. "Who?"

"Lucy."

I'm going to be sick. He's fucking our head waitress, too. No wonder he doesn't have time to fuck me; he's got two other women on the go.

"And there's been others over the years," he confesses.

Others, as in multiple.

"Who the hell are you?"

"Paige, I need a release to help me be great. I'm an artist."

Is he serious right now?

"You're sick, Michael. You have a problem. I loved you. You were my world and I'm realizing I never was yours," I say as the truth finally sets in. There was only ever one of us in this marriage, and it was me. My shoulders fall as the heaviness of that truth weighs me down. "I'm done, we're done," I tell him, then turn on my heel, grab my bag, and walk out of the kitchen.

"Paige, wait, please, let me fix this," he says, grabbing me.

I slap his hands away from me. "Don't touch me," I scream at him. "You will never touch me again." And with that, I storm out of the restaurant and into the alley. I hail the first taxi I can find and head home.

Do I even know where home is anymore?

4
GIORGIO

"Just breathe," my brother reassures me. "If you're this stressed out at your engagement party, what are you going to be like at the wedding?"

I turn and glare at my younger brother, Luca. "Fuck you."

This makes him laugh.

The audacity of the man to tell me to breathe when he did the runaway groom years ago and hid in the Scottish Highlands to escape his reality. He's happily married to Lilly, the beautiful woman he met while hiding out in Scotland, but that's beside the point. When they got engaged, their party was an intimate gathering of friends and family, something that I wished I could have done. Instead, I have five hundred well-wishers at mine. *Do I know all five hundred?* No, of course not, but as the heir to the family name, there was going to be no other option than to have an extravaganza complete with heads of state, royal family friends, celebrities, and other distinguished guests.

"I want this circus to be over with," I moan to my brother.

I think I know maybe eighty people here, unlike my fiancée, Giada, who knows everyone, and if she doesn't, she soon will. Guess it comes with the territory of being Italy's sweetheart, the beautiful woman that's beamed onto our nation's television screens every night starring in a successful drama; everyone loves her. If I'm honest, I've never watched the show, I don't understand what the fuss is all about.

The who's who of Italian television is here tonight celebrating her —*I mean us.* Our engagement is so big that Italian Vogue is photographing the entire event. They are doing an article leading up to what they're calling the society wedding of the year with a six-page spread in the magazine. I don't think anyone cares what I'm wearing tonight. *Armani, if you're wondering,* but what I do know is my fiancée cares and at the end of the day, that is all that matters.

My brother's brows pull together, listening to my complaints. "You can't say that at your engagement party. It's supposed to be the happiest moment of your life. You're celebrating that you've found your soulmate."

Soulmate? Giada is great, but soulmate? Do they even exist? Maybe for other people, but not me.

Luca pauses as he notices that I don't answer right away. He steps closer to me and leans in. "She's your soulmate, right?"

I roll my eyes at my younger brother. "You're the romantic, Luca."

He frowns at me, not understanding that not everyone has what he has.

"She understands my life, and doesn't want to change me, so I'm guessing that's the same," I try explaining to him.

He winces at my words. I never thought I would be marrying an actress, their need for the spotlight was previously a turnoff for me. I like living my life quietly, discreetly. I don't strive for the glitz and glamor. Underneath the designer clothes, I'm a simple man who likes his home comforts, his small group of friends, and who just happened to be born into an unordinary family. It's something I've always struggled with—the limelight, the pressure of being the first-born son. Luca is better suited for the role than I ever could have been. *If only he was born first.*

Having grown up in this world, I'm not fooled by the illusion it creates and the people it lures. I've met plenty of inauthentic people over the years, which has made me retreat into my hermit shell even more than I already do. Giada was born for all this and has worked hard to achieve the success she already has. I'm not sure how she's going to fare when she must give up her old life on television for her new life as a socialite once we are married. The attention will be different to what she's used to. Giada promised after she accepted my ring that she will look at starting a family in the next two years. My parents would like to have grandchildren soon. And honestly, the thought of becoming a father fills me with excitement, which is surprising, as children used to irritate me. I never thought it would happen, but now that I'm building a future with someone, the idea of little versions of us running around sounds nice, especially if Luca and Lilly start having children, too, and the cousins can grow up together.

I take a sip of my wine while we wait for my fiancée to make her grand entrance. "My relationship is different to yours, Luca."

How did two people who are complete opposites like Giada and I meet? I can thank my sister Allegra for introducing Giada to me; she suggested I take her to a society dinner as my date to shut our parents up about my love life; they have been hounding me about my marriage prospects ever since Luca met Lilly. *Thanks, brother.* They had been setting me up on near-weekly dates with their friends' daughters; some of them were not good matches.

I sat on the sidelines watching my brother stubbornly deny his love for Lilly, all because of pride and a broken heart. *A bit like you and Paige.* No. *I will not be thinking about her at my engagement party.* Then I watched my brother literally raise hell when Lilly was kidnapped by the Russian mafia. He moved heaven and earth to get her back because the thought of living another day without her in it ruined him. Not gonna lie, it melted my ice-cold heart, *a little*. I saw the pain that he went through, thinking he had lost the love of his life. I'd never experienced that kind of love before. *Yes, you have, but you lost it.* I was young. I shake those wayward thoughts from my mind. During Luca's darkest days fighting for Lilly, watching him struggle to survive, I didn't know if I ever wanted to love someone that much —*again*. Remembering the feeling of having your heart ripped out while you're still alive feels like, the agony is unbearable. But your heart heals, not perfectly, a little jagged, but eventually you learn to live with the scars. Deep down inside, I'm jealous of my brother. I want what he has found with Lilly. Guess that's what he means by soulmates.

It may not have been love at first sight, like my brother. *I don't live in a fairy tale*, but what we have suits us. It's not that I don't have feelings for Giada, I do, and my feelings are slowly blossoming the more time I'm spending with her, but is it love? *No.* If I'm honest, we've only been together five months. As harsh as it sounds, I looked at my proposal as a business arrangement because, really, that's all marriage is two people merging their lives together.

It was Giada's independence that swayed it for me, it's refreshing. I'm busy working in the family business as well as coordinating all our philanthropic endeavors. I don't have time for a needy partner who wants me to call them every day, *I've had those before and it's not fun.* Is that selfish? Probably. My workload is never-ending, but I love it like that. I'm making a difference in the world and that should count for something. She is also fantastic at walking a red carpet and working a room at a black-tie event, something that is a constant in my life. She's able to talk to anyone on an array of different topics at those events, which takes the stress off me. I've taken some women that have been nothing more than glorified arm candy and they were happy being that. They liked being seen and not heard, but after a couple of dates, it's not sustainable for any kind of long-term future. So, when Giada came along to these events with her alluring confidence, it made things easier for me. *Is it wrong to think like that?* I don't know, but isn't companionship supposed to be two people working together to make their lives easier? Maybe that's not a traditional way to think, but passion only lasts for so long before the reality of spending the rest of your life with this person sinks in. And if you are not compatible in other areas besides passion, how will it work? I don't have a normal nine-to-five job; my life is constantly surrounded by people either wanting something from me or talking about me. I need someone who can handle the personal scrutiny of my family, as well as the public one that my family name brings.

That's why Giada is the right woman for me. She doesn't want to change me, *unlike some*. She's comfortable in this world, she doesn't care what some gossip columnist writes about her or what some troll on social media says. She courts the cameras, loves the attention, and is happy to bask in it, which means I don't have to. Also, she was insistent on keeping her apartment as she likes her own space to be creative. She isn't offended if I don't want to go to an event with her, because she has a long list of friends who are only too happy to go. How could I not fall for all that?

"I know it is, it's just … I don't want you to be getting married for the wrong reasons," my brother confesses.

Giada and I may not look gooey-eyed at each other like Luca and Lilly do, but that doesn't mean we won't eventually. Luca and Lilly's relationship was dramatic, chaotic, and passionate; not everyone likes nor wants that for theirs.

"I like Giada in my way, why is that not enough?" I ask him.

Luca places a reassuring hand on my shoulder. "It is but I also know you're under a lot of pressure to find a partner due to Father's ill health and Mother's desperate need for grandbabies."

He's not wrong.

If our father hadn't gotten sick again this year, I'd probably have waited another year or two to propose to Giada; we have only been together for five months. It's my father's greatest wish to see all his children happily married, and my mother's to have us popping out grandchildren. As the oldest, my mother has told me that I should have gotten married first, not my younger brother. It's not like I wouldn't have been marrying Giada eventually, because I would be. I just would have waited a little longer to propose.

"Are you getting the grandchildren talk, too?" I ask him.

He nods in agreement.

"And?" I say, turning to him.

"And, well …"

I still as a smirk falls across his lips. "No way," I say.

He nods enthusiastically. "I'm going to be a dad."

I pull my brother into a tight hug. I'm so incredibly happy for them. "Why didn't you say something sooner?"

"Because of all this," he says, waving his hand around the lavish room. "Lilly and I decided we would wait until after your engagement party to announce it. Tonight is your night," he tells me.

"Do Mamma and Papà know?"

He shakes his head.

Shit. "Mamma is going to lose her mind when she finds out," I say, which has me chuckling; she is going to want to be a part of that pregnancy as if it were her own. "Who else knows?"

"Only Natalia as she's so close with Lilly."

Our youngest sister and Lilly hit it off from the start, unlike our other sister, Allegra. I understand Lilly and Luca are not her greatest fans, seeing as Allegra tracked Luca and Lilly down on New Year's Day years ago and presented his ex to him on their doorstep. All while knowing her best friend at the time was cheating on her brother with his best friend; Allegra even helped them hide it from Luca. Since then, everyone is civil with each other, but that's where it stops. Allegra's just cut from a different cloth than Luca, Natalia, and me; even growing up, she never hung out with us, preferring to be with anyone else. It is what it is with her.

I can't believe my brother is going to have a baby. This is wild. I'm so happy for them and relieved that this might stop our mother from harassing me.

"Congrats, man, this is the best news."

He gives me a wide smile, and I can see he is happy that he's finally told me.

"She's just gone three months. We wanted to wait to make sure everything was okay before telling anyone. She's had a miscarriage before this one, right after we found out the first time, she lost it which devastated her."

"I'm sorry, I had no idea," I say.

He shakes his head. "We didn't want to say anything, it all happened quickly, but everything is good now and that's what we focus on."

"Hey, losers, what are you doing hanging out here?" Natalia asks, joining us in our secluded corner of the party.

"I just told him about Lilly," Luca adds.

Our sister's face lights up. "Isn't that awesome? We are going to be an aunt and uncle."

Uncle.

I'm going to be a freaking uncle. Those words hit me square in the chest and nearly take my breath away.

"Yeah, it's cool."

"Sure is. So anyway, where is Giada and why is it taking her so long to join her engagement party?" my sister asks.

I shrug my shoulders. "However long it takes *Vogue* to get whatever they need, I guess."

My sister rolls her eyes. She's not the biggest fan of Giada, mainly because she is best friends with our sister. Natalia and Allegra are chalk and cheese and there is no love lost between the two of them. "Can you hurry her up? People are starting to talk about her and not in a good way."

What does that mean? I frown at my sister, who rolls her eyes again.

"People think she's not going to show up because she's doing a runner."

They think what?

"Why the hell would they think that?" I ask her.

"Because she's an hour late." She shrugs.

"Fine, I'll go find her. This is ridiculous, it's fucking *Vogue*, she's just getting the right photos," I grumble to myself as I put my empty champagne glass down on a passing waiter's tray and grab a new one as I storm off to find my fiancée.

"Just trying to help," Natalia calls out after me.

As I make my way across the elaborate ballroom, I'm stopped to chat with well-wishers but quickly excuse myself by letting them know I'm on a mission to hurry up my fiancée, which eventually stops them from continuing their conversations. I take one of the back ways to get to Giada's apartment where she is getting ready. I nod and smile at the dozens of staff rushing back and forth along the corridors.

I head up a flight of stairs away from the pandemonium and make my way to her room. I don't even knock, she won't hear it anyway with all the people who usually help her get ready. As I walk in, I hear moaning coming from her room. *Is she okay? Has she hurt herself?*

I round the corner and still when I notice someone is kneeling between my fiancée's legs, underneath her ballgown, making her moan. Giada's head is thrown back in ecstasy as she thrashes around against the bed and comes loudly, something that she doesn't do with me. Not that we have sex all that often, as we are so busy. But I've never seen her so animated before. What the hell are they doing that I'm not?

Seconds later, she notices me standing there and screams.

"Gio, fuck." She clutches her chest, her dark eyes wide with surprise, her cheeks pink from her orgasm. "It's not what you think," she quickly adds as the person slowly emerges from between my fiancée's thighs.

My face falls when I realize who it is.

5

GIORGIO

"Allegra?"

"It's not what you think," Giada quickly states as my sister fully reveals herself.

Shaking my head, I take a step back, trying to process the fact that my fiancée is cheating on me during our engagement party. With my own fucking sister.

"Gio, I'm so sorry. You weren't meant to find out like this?" Allegra tells me.

"How could you do this to me, both of you?" I roar, which has them both slinking back.

"I'm sorry," my sister mumbles as tears well in her eyes.

"It was my fault. I was nervous after *Vogue* and then I looked downstairs at the party and saw how many people were there and I had a panic attack and Allegra came to my rescue," my fiancée explains.

"By making you come?"

Allegra looks down at the floor and Giada doesn't answer my question because it's a bullshit excuse.

"How long has this been going on?" I question them.

"Four months," Giada answers.

"First time," Allegra adds at the same time.

"Four months?" They have been fooling around the entire time we've been together.

She nods in agreement as my attention turns to my sister who blatantly lied to me.

She sighs. "Yes, it started after you had gotten together," she finally confesses.

I'm blown away.

"How could you do this to me?" I ask again.

"We didn't mean to hurt you, Gio," Allegra tries to explain, but I don't want to hear it. I'm disgusted, humiliated, embarrassed, hurt, and blindsided.

"But you did," I tell her honestly, which has her bursting into tears again. I pull out my phone and quickly type away.

"Who are you messaging?" Giada asks nervously.

"None of your business," I bite back.

"My guess is he's messaged Luca and Natalia." Allegra sniffs through her tears.

My eyes widen at the disdain falling from her lips.

"Why?" Giada asks frantically. "I'm sorry, okay? We don't have to make any irrational decisions. We can go downstairs and pretend this never happened. Enjoy the night for our families and then break up after," she suggests.

"You're seriously wanting me to go downstairs and pretend I didn't catch you with someone else?"

"It was only a woman, Gio. It's not a big deal," Giada suggests.

Not a big deal? Am I in the twilight zone or something?

"She's my sister, not some random. The two of you are best friends," I yell at her, and then the sinking realization hits me.

"We came as quickly as we could. What's the SOS?" Natalia asks as she enters the room. She stops and looks between the pissed-off faces of her sister and my fiancée. "What did you do?" she asks our sister.

Allegra rolls her eyes and folds her arms, refusing to give her an answer as if we are the ones with the problem.

"Apparently, the two of them have been having an affair for four months," I explain, pointing between the two of them.

"What the hell?" Luca states.

"An affair? The two of them? Giada and Allegra?" Natalia questions.

I nod my head.

"What the hell is wrong with you?" Luca yells at our sister.

"Wrong with me? Nothing," she defends.

"You cheated with your brother's fiancée; how can you not see that's wrong?" Natalia adds.

"It wasn't my fault. I've been in love with Giada for years. I had no idea she felt the same way, too," she screams.

The room falls silent at her admission.

Love?

"How could you do this to Gio?" Luca questions.

Giada and Allegra look between each other but don't answer him.

"You don't care about anyone but yourself, do you?" Natalia sneers.

"Fuck you," our sister retorts.

"No, fuck you. You've always been a selfish bitch. How could you do this to Gio? He's the one sibling that likes you," Natalia adds.

Allegra looks over at me as tears fall down her cheeks. "You weren't supposed to fall in love with her," she confesses.

Her words shock me. That's the thing, I'm not in love with Giada.

"I wasn't supposed to have fallen for him either," Giada adds.

Turning, I look over at where she is standing, wiping her tears away. "You don't love me, Giada."

Her eyes soften. "I fell in love with both of you."

What? I'm shocked. We have never said I love you before.

"Are you fucking serious?" Allegra spits, looking at Giada angrily.

Giada nods.

"I don't understand. You told me you didn't love him," Allegra questions her.

"I lied," Giada tells her. "I didn't want you to know that I was falling for him, while I was falling for you, too. What kind of person falls in love with a brother and sister?"

"The same kind of fucked-up person that accepts the brother's proposal while continuing to sleep with his sister. This is bullshit," Natalia barks as she folds her arms, not believing anything my fiancée is saying.

"I thought you agreed it was a marriage of convenience and you weren't even sleeping together," Allegra asks Giada.

Giada's eyes fall to the floor as she's unable to look at Allegra.

Why do I feel like I'm the side piece in this fucked up situation?

"I lied," Giada confesses as tears fall down her cheeks.

Allegra's face falls, hurt and betrayal etched onto it.

"You're upset because she slept with her fiancé?" Natalia asks.

Allegra turns and narrows her eyes as she glares at her younger sister.

"I'm sorry I didn't tell you. I didn't know how. This entire thing is one big mess," Giada says.

"You can say that again," Natalia adds, rolling her eyes.

"This is all my fault. I should have been honest with them both," Giada states.

"You should never have said yes to Gio," Luca adds.

Giada looks over at Luca and nods. "I know, but Gio and I had an understanding, didn't we?" she says, turning to me.

The room falls silent.

"That you could sleep with other people?" Natalia questions as she looks up at me.

"Yes."

Natalia gasps, while Luca shakes his head.

"Guess you didn't mean your sister though," Natalia snips.

She would be right there.

"Gio, when we got together, there was nothing but friendship between Allegra and me. She set us up because she truly thought we would be a great fit. She knew you didn't want to marry for love, and I needed the exposure," Giada explains.

Luca looks over at me and his face says it all, he's disappointed in me.

"So, you're a gold digger?" Natalia snaps.

"I have my own money, I don't need his," Giada bites back. "I didn't want to marry someone who was after my money and fame. Women can fall for gold diggers, too."

Natalia huffs.

"Was this your plan all along?" I ask my sister.

She shakes her head. "I know I can be a bitch, Gio."

"Yep," Natalia adds.

Allegra ignores her. "But I never meant for this to happen."

"How did it?" I ask.

Allegra turns to Giada and then looks back at me. "It happened when we were on that group ski trip to Gstaad when you first started dating. We were drunk, and I confessed my feelings for her, and things escalated from there."

"Why didn't you break up with me then?" I ask Giada.

She twists her hands together nervously. "Because I liked you and …" she lets out a heavy sigh, "because if I came out to the world, my career would have been over. There is no way everyone would have accepted Allegra and I being together."

"You used him as your beard," Natalia states.

"It wasn't like that. I was confused," Giada explains.

"So, you used my brother while you sorted out your confusion. You accepted his proposal, you planned a life with him all the while knowing you were sleeping with his sister," Natalia argues.

"Yes," Giada agrees.

"You both make me sick. How could you do that to him?" she yells at them.

"I'm sorry," Allegra says quietly, her head down, unable to look at me. "You know Mamma and Papà would never allow me to date a woman, let alone marry one."

"That's not an excuse to do this to Gio," Natalia yells at her.

"You should have spoken to me, both of you," I say.

"Why are you not more upset, Gio? Why are you not throwing things? Cussing them out?" Natalia whirls around and glares at me.

"Because I didn't love her." The words come out and my hand flies up to my mouth and covers it. I look over at Giada and see her eyes well with tears.

"G, I'm sorry. I didn't mean it to sound like that."

She shakes her head. "It's okay. I understand. Your feelings didn't match my own," she says through her sniffles.

Now I feel bad. How the hell does this happen? I'm the one cheated on and now I'm being made to feel like the bad guy because I wasn't in love with my fiancée.

"That's not fair," I tell her.

"You were cheating on Gio. You don't get to be upset because he didn't love you," Natalia says, glaring at Giada.

I love that she has my back on this.

"I'm sorry I hurt you, Gio," Allegra says.

"Me too," Giada adds.

"Fuck you both," Natalia says, pointing her finger at the two of them.

"This has gotten fucking complicated," Luca adds.

It certainly has.

"Guessing we should probably tell everyone the engagement party is over," Luca suggests.

"No," Giada exclaims as does Allegra.

"This is going to be a huge scandal if we do," Giada explains.

Yep, it sure is—one you created.

"Think of our father's heart," Allegra adds.

I still, my own heart constricting at the thought that this news could do something to his heart.

"You are a disgusting piece of shit. How dare you say that to him. You should have thought about our father when you hooked up with Gio's fiancée," Natalia yells at her.

"I know, Nat. Okay. I get it. I'm the devil. You hate me. You all hate me. But please don't do this to father, his heart won't be able to take it. I fucked up badly. I fell in love with someone I shouldn't have. But please, I can't hurt, Papà. I know you owe me nothing, Gio, but please, can we keep this a secret until we can sort it out?" Allegra begs.

The room falls silent at her request.

"You want Gio to pretend none of this happened? That he didn't catch the two of you together during his engagement party?" Luca asks.

Allegra nods. "Yes, until we work out a solution."

"What do you mean *a solution*?" Luca questions.

"I don't know. All I know is I can't be responsible for killing our father." Allegra cries.

She's right. We all know she's right.

"Fine. I won't say a word about tonight. But we are done, both of you." I point to them both as I turn and walk out of the room.

"Fuck," Luca says as he follows out after me.

"This is a shit show," Natalia adds as we stand in the middle hallway, shell-shocked.

"I need to get out of here. I can't be here. How the hell am I going to get out of this place without being detected?" I ask my siblings.

The palace is swamped with partygoers, paparazzi, and a film crew.

"Follow me," Luca says as he weaves his way through the back passages of the palace that we grew up in—the easiest way to move around the home as kids, especially as teens when we wanted to head out to a party without getting caught. It's a maze behind here; you could get lost and be missing for days if you didn't know your way around.

The three of us head along the last tunnel, which brings us out into the garages and my car. We pause as my adrenaline starts to subside. "What do I do? Where should I go?" I turn and ask my siblings. For the first time in my life, I don't know what to do.

"Go home. I'll call you once we've cut the event short," Luca tells me.

"People are going to wonder what happened. Why I'm not there."

Luca shakes his head. "I promise you, I'll work it out. Just get out of here."

"It's going to be a shit show, Luca. He should get out of town, get out of the country even," Natalia states.

She's right. This entire event has eyes on it. Every major paper, magazine, and online site is following it, the melding of royalty and celebrity, it's a huge money spinner for everyone. They are going to notice when the groom doesn't come back.

"Go home. I promise I'll sort it out. Allegra is right though, we can't cancel the engagement party. It will damage our family's reputation and that is going to hurt our parents. Papa's heart won't be able to take it. The media will have a field day with the news."

"It's not fair though," Natalia adds.

"No, it's not. And none of this is your fault, Gio. You've been thrown into the middle of a shitshow not of your making."

He's right. I let out a heavy sigh as I run my fingers through my hair. "I'll do whatever you need me to do, to make sure Papà is okay."

Luca nods before he turns and heads back into the party.

6

PAIGE

I press the buzzer to my brother's apartment repeatedly until he finally answers.

"What the hell, Paige? What's going ... oh shit, why are you crying? What happened? Quick, come up. I'm going to fucking kill him, aren't I?" he curses as he presses the button to let me into his complex. I shuffle into the foyer and head toward the lift, then press the button to his floor and slowly head on up. As soon as the doors open, he's there.

"Paige, what happened?" he asks as he looks me over for any visual damage, but it's all internal; that man ripped my heart out and threw it in the trash in the alley at the back of our restaurant. I drop my suitcases and wrap myself around him, and he does the same, hugging me tightly. He's not normally this huggy with me.

"It's going to be okay, I promise. Whatever he did, I'm going to make him pay," he whispers into my ear.

"Don't hurt him," I mumble as I know Smith will make good on his threat toward Michael; he'll probably get his brothers in blue to help him.

"Everything would be above board. I'm a cop," he says, giving me a smirk as he grabs my suitcases and ushers me into his apartment. "Go take a seat and I'll get you something strong to drink," he says as he slides my suitcases to the side before ushering me toward the sofa. I curl myself up into a ball, hoping to wake from a terrible dream, that what I witnessed earlier didn't happen. *I can wake up now, universe. Enough is enough.*

"Here, drink this," Smith says, shoving an opened bottle of wine into my hand. I take a swig and let the fruity concoction settle me. "Do you want me to call in reinforcements? They might be better at all this. I mean, I'm good, but you know," he asks.

"Yes, please."

He gives me a nod as he pulls his phone from his pocket and starts calling my two besties, Callie and Savannah. I take another sip from the bottle; I don't know if there is enough wine to erase how I feel, but I'm sure I can try.

"It's an emergency. I think Michael fucked up. You need to drop everything and get here, and tell the other one," I hear my brother say before hanging up. "The girls will be here soon," he says, walking into the kitchen and grabbing himself a beer from the fridge before coming back and taking a seat on the sofa beside me. He cracks open the beer and takes a large swig before reclining back and placing his arm along the back of the sofa, not quite touching me. I can see he's a little out of his element. "I love you, Paige. Whatever it is I'm here for you," he says gruffly before throwing back half his drink.

"I know," I say as I roll over and curl into his side. "Why do men suck?" I ask him.

He lets out a sigh. "Not all men, sis, just French dickheads."

We both sit in silence, drinking our drinks.

Twenty minutes later, his door buzzes and relief falls across my brother's face. Smith doesn't do well with female emotions, or maybe it's just mine he can't handle. He walks over and buzzes in my girls. Moments later, I can hear talking and my two besties come rushing in.

"I'm going to fucking kill him," Callie states angrily.

"Maybe don't say that in front of an NYPD officer." Savannah chuckles.

"I'll make sure the crime scene is spotless," my brother adds, giving Savannah a wink as he throws back the rest of his beer.

I've known Callie Campbell my entire life; we grew up together, both from the same town in Upstate New York. Her mom and my mom were teachers and our dads both worked on the police force together, so it was inevitable that we would be friends as we were always around each other. Her older brother, Lane, is best friends with mine. We bonded as we both hated that we had older brothers who annoyed the hell out of us.

Then we were introduced to Savannah King, this gorgeous, radiant, wild Australian girl, who had moved to New York with her family as they built their bar and nightclub empire. Her older brother, Owen, was friends with Smith and Lane and introduced us to Savannah as Callie and I were looking for an apartment to rent. I had moved back from Italy and Callie had moved down from upstate to go to law school in the city. Owen was worried about his younger sister living in her apartment by herself. He also didn't like the fact that a lot of girls would try and befriend her so they could get closer to him and his cousins, who were famous in the city for being the party boys. So, he asked if we were interested, knowing we were not like some of the girls she had met; it was going to be free rent as they owned the apartment. *Who could turn that down in the city?* He wanted us to take her under our wing and keep an eye on her; little did we know what a full-time job that was going to be. When we met her at her multi-million-dollar apartment in Tribeca and she welcomed us in with a glass of champagne in one hand and vegemite toast in the other, her blonde hair pulled up in a messy bun, T-shirt and sweatpants with fluffy slippers, we knew she was our kind of people. We lived together for years, right up until I met Michael and Callie bought her own apartment.

"What happened?" Callie asks, taking a seat beside me on the sofa, grabbing the bottle of wine from my hand, and taking a large swig. I grab it off her and do the same, needing the alcohol to help me get through the story. And so I tell them how I came home from Italy and found my husband fucking the sous chef.

"I can make this fucker disappear," my brother says angrily.

"I think you should take your brother up on it," Callie adds with a smirk.

Smith paces up and down the room. I know he's trying to calm himself down, so he doesn't go off and do something that could land him in jail.

"Would you stop pacing, Smith, it's making our heads spin," Callie snips at him.

"If I don't pace, Callie, then I'm worried I'll shoot the fucking weasel and that isn't going to benefit anyone, is it?" my brother argues back.

Callie rolls her eyes, and huffs before she holds out the bottle of wine toward Smith. "Drink this, it will calm you down."

My brother stares at the bottle of wine in disgust. "It's too early for wine."

Callie shakes her head at him.

"I'll grab another beer instead," he adds before disappearing into the kitchen.

"Sorry, his nervous anxiety was doing my head in." Callie chuckles.

I give her a small smile, knowing anything my brother does annoys the hell out of her; it's been this way since forever. Those two always seem to be able to get on each other's nerves.

"Why did he do this to me?" I ask, turning and looking at my two best friends before bursting into tears. They both cuddle me on either side as I sob.

"It's not you, it's him. It's always been him. That man has always had an overinflated ego for someone so mediocre," Callie states angrily.

"You didn't deserve this, you're too good for him," Savannah adds.

I had no idea they all hated him so much. I mean, I knew Smith wasn't Michael's biggest fan, but my girls never let on at all that they hated him.

"You all hated him?"

Savannah and Callie look up at each other and they both nod in agreement.

"Not at first, but like a true narcissist, he showed us what we wanted to see and as the years have gone on, that façade has slowly slipped. He was slowly dimming your light to make his brighter," Callie explains.

Wow. I had no idea.

I guess when you're right in the thick of the relationship, you don't see what someone on the outside might. I thought because Michael was such an extrovert, a creative, an artist, he deserved the limelight more than I ever did, but maybe that was his goal all along, to be the face of our business, to keep me hidden, so everyone thought he was the genius behind it all. He needed me as he couldn't have done it by himself. Was I truly that blind?

"What am I supposed to do now? We have the restaurant and our apartment together," I ask.

"That restaurant was more his dream than yours, you never wanted to do French cuisine," Callie reminds me.

"I know, but all that money we sank into it, all those debts. I can't go back and work there. Everyone must have known about the affairs; he didn't seem to be hiding them. Why did no one tell me?" I sniffle. They could have saved me so much heartache.

"They probably didn't want to lose their jobs," Savannah suggests.

Smith bursts out laughing. "You're seriously worried about that restaurant after everything Lucia left you in her will?"

Callie and Savannah look between Smith and me.

He's right, I kinda forgot, and then I burst out laughing, too.

"Is she having a breakdown?" Savannah asks.

I shake my head. "No, the complete opposite. That moron has no idea how much he has fucked up, nor how much that dalliance today has cost him. I'm fucking rich, ladies," I scream as reality starts to set in.

I'm rich.

I don't have to worry about where the hell I'm going to live because I have a home, multiple homes actually, and hotels and vineyards, and cars and a million and one other things.

I'm a countess!

"Rich?" Callie questions me as if I've lost my mind.

"And she's royalty," Smith adds.

"Wait, what?" Callie asks.

"Like Downton Abbey?" Savannah questions.

"Kind of, sort of; I don't know how it works or where I am in the scheme of royalty," I answer with a smile on my face.

"Shit, we didn't curtsy when we arrived." Callie chuckles.

"It doesn't mean anything. I don't think?"

"Um, yeah, it does, you're royal," Callie says.

"I'm already the Party Princess, you need to find me a prince to make it legal," Savannah jokes.

"Does that mean you can introduce us to all the hot, single royal men of Europe? It has to be better than the dating pool in Manhattan." Callie grins.

"Maybe stop dating lawyers, that might be a start." Smith grunts before throwing back the rest of his beer. "Never met a lawyer I liked."

Callie places a hand on her chest and pouts at my brother. "Smith, you wound me, and here I thought I was helping you get over your lawyer allergy," she teases him.

"I tolerate you, for Paige," Smith grumbles over his bottle of beer.

"Oh, I thought it was because you loved my sparkling personality and witty banter," she throws back at him.

He rolls his eyes at her. These two have always bickered; I joke it's because they secretly love each other, but Callie says she just likes sparring with him.

My stomach sinks at the realization that I'm rich and I'm about to ask my husband for a divorce. Does that mean I'm going to have to give half of everything I now own to that good-for-nothing asswipe? Fuck no, how is that fair?

"Are you okay?" Callie asks, seeing my sudden mood change.

"You're the lawyer, can I ask you a question?"

Callie nods in agreement.

"Do I have to share my inheritance with Michael?"

Callie is quiet for a moment. "I'm not a divorce attorney, Paige, but I can put you in touch with some great ones who could answer the question better, but no, the inheritance remains yours, from my memory."

Oh, thank fuck. If Michael found out exactly how much I'm worth, he would be changing his tune and I would have a fight on my hands.

"The sooner you file, the quicker you can start freeing yourself of that man," Callie explains.

She's right. That man is never going to change. He doesn't love me, that's if he ever did. I think I was the chump that came along, fell for his French charms, and listened to his bullshit.

"Can you set something up? I want to make sure I have everything I need. I don't think Michael thought I was serious when I told him we're done. He thinks because of the restaurant and our apartment, I can't go anywhere, but now it doesn't matter. I don't have to worry about a thing, Lucia has set me up for life. A life that I should have been living instead of a life Michael demanded we live. Let's get the ball rolling while I'm still so angry, and Michael hasn't had a chance to try and sway me with his lies."

"I'll organize it right now," Callie states as she stands up, pulls out her phone from her pocket, and starts dialing someone.

"You sure this is what you want?" Savannah asks.

I nod. "How can I stay with him after all this, Sav?"

She gives me a small smile. "I don't know, but it doesn't mean you don't still love him."

Tears well in my eyes as I furiously brush them away. "I love me more, I have to love me more," I tell her.

She reaches out and hugs me tightly. "Whatever your decision, I am here for you," she says, reassuring me.

"Right, you're all booked in with one of the best divorce attorneys in Manhattan. She's a real bulldog and she's going to make sure that you are looked after," Callie explains.

"Thank you. I don't know how I would get through this if I didn't have you all."

"We've got your back," my brother tells me.

I sniffle, trying to hold the tears back as their support warms me.

"So, like, how rich are you?" Savannah asks, which makes me laugh.

Then I go on to explain what the will said and the two of them stare at me in disbelief.

"I know, it's insane right?" I say, looking between them.

"Um, no, this is amazing, we are so going to explore Europe this summer," Savannah squeals excitedly.

"Does that mean you're going to move back to Italy?" Callie asks.

Her question makes me pause. Does it? I mean, there's nothing here for me now other than my friends and my family; I don't have a job or a place to live.

"Move back to Italy?"

Callie nods. "You've always talked about how much you love it there and when you talk about it, your entire face lights up. Michael hated Italy, and he always refused to go back every time you asked him. Remember how you had always envisioned a gorgeous Italian wedding at Lucia's estate, and he refused because he was French, and no Frenchman would ever get married in Italy," Callie explains to me.

She's not wrong. I had always dreamed of getting married at Lucia's estate and it broke my heart when Michael refused; he also said that he would rather we spent the money opening our own business than on a wedding and we ended up getting married at a courthouse in Manhattan and Savannah's family lent us their bar for the reception. It was a low-key, no-frills wedding, not at all where I thought I would ever get married. I guess it was about the people surrounding us, not the location at the time. Even when it came time to choose a theme for our restaurant, I wanted a fusion of Italian and French, but Michael ranted that he was the chef and was trained in French cuisine, not Italian, even though I was. Again, I gave in and he got his way, like he always seemed to do. How was I so blind to all his red flags?

"I didn't mean to make you sad," Callie says, noticing my mood dipping.

I wave her concern away. "I'm realizing how much of myself I'd given up in this marriage. I don't know who I am anymore. All my dreams, wants, and needs were never met, I gave in to him all the time. He got everything he wanted while I sat on the sidelines and then he has the audacity to cheat on me."

"We could never say anything, Paige," my brother states.

"You wouldn't have listened even if we had," Callie adds.

They're both right. I was blinded by what I thought love was. How wrong was I?

"We love you, and you seemed happy with Michael, and who are we, the single trio, to tell you what a marriage should be," Savannah explains. "Michael did you a favor today. You might not see it, or feel it, but there will come a time when you realize that if he didn't show you exactly who he truly was, you would never have made the decision to leave."

I grab the open bottle of wine and throw it back. Today has been a roller coaster ride and I'm not sure what is up or down anymore. My entire existence has been ripped from me and now it feels like I'm about to morph into a different person. Firstly, I'm a countess and secondly, I'm rich.

"I can get you on the next plane to Florence if you need," Smith tells me.

"Why would I leave?" I ask him.

"To get away from Michael," he adds.

"You think I need to disappear halfway across the world, I'm not a coward. I can face that cheating bastard head-on," I tell him angrily.

"I know you can, Paige, but you don't have to," he says, giving me a reassuring smile.

"Oh no, I want that man to see exactly the woman I am, and what he gave up. I want him to realize that cheating on me was the biggest regret of his life and I want him to regret it every day."

"That a girl," Callie calls out.

"Does Michael even know you're a countess?" Savannah asks.

I burst out laughing. "Nope, I went there after getting off the plane to tell him that we were rich but instead …" I shake my head, trying to get the images of him and the sous chef from my mind.

Savannah bursts out laughing. "That is brilliant, that is the best revenge, being a rich bitch, sorry, a royal rich bitch." This has us all cackling. "Now let's get fucked up and put all the thoughts of Michael out of your mind," Savannah says, holding up a new bottle of wine.

7

GIORGIO

"I'm worried about you," Natalia states as she chews on her bottom lip before walking over and giving me a hug. "You never deserved this. You're a good guy, Gio. Allegra is such a bitch. How are we related to her?"

I hug my sister back, enjoying her concern. As the oldest sibling, I'm used to being the one that the family relies on to be steadfast and stable. I'm the pragmatic one, always looking at both sides of a problem, understanding where the two parties are coming from, especially when making decisions, but this time, I don't understand what happened. I don't want to feel empathy for my sister, who is obviously hiding her sexuality because how she went about it is messed up. I can't imagine what that must be like, to not have a chance to be who you really want to be. Might explain why she's such a bitch all the time. Why didn't she come to me, especially after I proposed, before I had announced it to the world? She should have said something then and there. It would have saved the fucking mess we are in right now.

"I'll be okay. Please don't worry about me."

Natalia looks up at me. "It's my turn to look after you. You've always been there for me, let me do the same."

I give my youngest sister a small smile and hug her back.

"I'm worried about Papà, his heart can't take this news," Natalia says tearfully as she buries herself into me even more.

This is my worry as well. "He's going to be okay. Luca will make sure. Plus, Lilly is a doctor, she will be right beside him if anything happens," I try to reassure her.

"That's true, Lilly will be there. She's a great doctor, he will be fine." She sniffles. "Sorry, I'm supposed to be cheering you up, not the other way around." She chuckles.

"You are, just by being here. How about we get out of here and head back to my place? We can hang out on the sofa eating ice cream just like we do when you have a breakup. How does that sound?"

"Perfect," she says, nodding and wiping her eyes.

We walk over to my car and unlock it. Thankfully, I have tinted windows on my car, so if anyone does spot me escaping, they shouldn't get a photo of me. I put my sports car into drive, press my foot flat to the floor and get out of there. We zoom out and head through the busy streets of Rome. The hustle and bustle of the city simmers my tension.

"I'm sorry this happened to you, Gio," Natalia says as we stop at a red light.

"I know," I say as there isn't much else to say.

"She was the wrong woman for you."

"Clearly," I joke, trying to lighten the mood.

Natalia rolls her eyes at me. "I'm being serious, Gio. You're a catch. All my friends think so."

I turn and give her a look.

"I mean it, or maybe my friends have daddy issues and like older men," she jokes, which makes me smile. "I know you're not as romantic as Luca is or are up for public displays of affection like I am, but that doesn't mean you can't love someone in your own way."

She's right; I am a little more reserved when it comes to my relationships. I reach out and give her hand a squeeze. "Thanks."

"I think the universe had other plans for you. Maybe you weren't listening to the signs it was giving you until it gave you a big one. Marrying Giada was a mistake."

I love my sister, but she believes in fate, star signs, tarot cards, and other hocus pocus stuff. When really, it's just that my fiancée is a cheater. It wasn't the universe telling me I was making a mistake; it was two consenting adults making bad choices.

"If the universe had other plans, I wish I didn't have to see my sister going down on my fiancée to tell me it was a bad idea."

Natalia lets out a scream, nearly causing me to have an accident.

"Nat, what the fuck?" I curse as I right the car again and try to still my racing heart.

"I'm sorry. But, Gio, what the fuck? You've scarred me for life."

"How the fuck do you think I feel? I saw it. It's seared into my brain. I need the *Men in Black* guys to come and wipe my mind," I confess to her.

"That's messed up. No wonder you're traumatized. Just the thought of it has me wanting to book a late-night session with my therapist. Maybe I should make a booking for you, too." She chuckles.

"If they can hypnotize me to forget what I saw, I'm in," I tell her.

"Allegra is the one that needs therapy."

Can't argue with that.

"You sure she's not adopted or was swapped at the hospital? Did Mamma have an affair with a psychopath? It would explain her."

This makes me laugh.

It's not long until we are driving into my underground car park and heading up to my penthouse. Home sweet home, my sanctuary, my serenity, my happy place. I can pause the noise of the outside world, and no one can bother me when I'm in here.

"Hey, can I borrow a T-shirt or something? I need to get out of this dress," Natalia asks.

"Sure, let me grab one," I tell her as I head down the corridor to my bedroom. Pushing the door open, I throw my suit jacket onto the bed, then pull my tie off and it lands next to it. I kick off my shoes and take off my belt as I head into my wardrobe. I grab a T-shirt for myself and a pair of sweatpants and get changed and then grab a shirt for my sister before heading back out to the living area.

"Here, you need this," she states, handing me a shot glass. I take it and throw it back, letting the tequila ease my soul. I hand her the shirt and she rushes off to get changed. I walk into my kitchen and start to rummage in my freezer for any pints of ice cream in there. Picking up a vanilla chocolate chip one for Natalia and a tiramisu flavor for me, I grab two spoons and head back to the sofa and take a seat.

"Thanks for this, I can breathe now." My sister sighs, walking back into the living room with my T-shirt on, but it's more like a dress on her. "Oh, you did have ice cream," she squeals, rushing over and grabbing her pint from my hand.

"What do we do now?" I ask, taking a spoonful of ice cream.

"We usually bitch about the boy who broke our heart. My girlies tell me he was no good for me, that I can do better. Then we down a bottle of wine and talk shit about the boy. Oh, then we usually plot revenge," she informs me.

"I think I have wine," I tell her with a smile as I get up and walk over to my wine fridge and grab a rosé.

"Screw the glasses we drink from the bottle," she yells from the living room. I stiffen. What, no glasses? She wants to drink straight from the bottle. "I can see that sentence is freaking you out, Gio. Trust the process."

Fine. I can do this. *Trust the process.* I turn and take a large swig from the bottle.

"Hell, yeah, that's how you do it," Natalia squeals.

I wipe my mouth with the back of my hand. Very liberating. I walk back into the living room and retake my seat beside her. She reaches out, takes the bottle from me, and has a drink.

"How did I not see it?" I ask as I dig into my ice cream again.

Natalia contemplates her answer. "None of us saw this happening, Gio. Honestly, Allegra and Giada looked like friends; whenever I saw them together, there was nothing that appeared inappropriate. I'm not sure if that is better or worse."

They are both good liars.

"You and Giada did live separate lives. It's not an excuse, but maybe it was easier for them to go undetected."

Probably. And here I thought it was great that Giada was so independent; the joke's on me.

"Maybe the universe is telling me that I should never get married," I say, scooping more ice cream into my mouth. Gosh, this is so good.

"Don't you dare say that. You just haven't found the right woman yet," Natalia protests.

"I'm okay with playing the fun uncle role," I tell her.

She takes another swig of rosé before handing it back to me, and I do the same. "Never thought I would see you give up."

I raise a brow at her. I'm not giving up. I just know my strengths and obviously, it's not being in a relationship. Most of the women I have been with have cheated on me; that says as much about me as it does them. I don't give them what they need, so they have to go somewhere else to find it.

Except Paige Johnson.

Huh.

I haven't thought about her since …. Who am I kidding? I haven't stopped thinking about her since her great-aunt's funeral. It was good seeing her again after all these years. She's still as beautiful as she always was with her cocoa-brown waves, chocolate eyes, curves still in all the right places, and a smile that could light up the darkest of rooms. Not going to lie, seeing her there by herself in the darkness looking so despondent over losing Lucia, all I wanted to do was wrap her in my arms and protect her from the pain. It felt nice when she recognized me and the first thing she did was walk right into my arms, when she buried her face against my chest it felt like it always did with her—right. We were kids when we met. Every summer, Paige and her brother, Smith, would stay with Lucia, and my parents would send us to the vineyard to learn the work. I think I was ten, and she was nine when we first met, and instantly, Luca and I hit it off with them. We had a blast spending the summer holidays running through fields, swimming in the dams, and sneaking grapes off the vines. It was idyllic and after that first summer, Luca and I wanted to go back and sure enough, they were there again. From then on, I'd look forward to seeing them both every year.

It wasn't until I was sixteen and she was fifteen that things changed. Smith and Luca had discovered local girls and were hanging out with them. We were invited to a party in a field by the locals; we were drinking, smoking, and doing things that teens do. Paige was sitting by the campfire; the light must have hit her at the right angle and my heart went *thud* in my chest and my dick tightened in my pants.

"Hey, what are you doing all alone here?" I ask Paige.

"Everyone has paired off except me. None of the boys are interested," she confesses, but I can see the sadness on her face.

Are those other boys blind? She's the most beautiful girl at this party.

"They are stupid then. I think you're the most interesting person here."

Paige chuckles and then playfully hits me. *"You're only saying that because we are friends. I'm interesting, but not pretty like the other girls."*

How can she say that?

"I think you're the prettiest girl here."

Paige stills beside me. Did I say the wrong thing? I shouldn't have said anything. I'm too scared to look at her.

"You do?" she asks.

I gulp and turn my attention to her. "I do."

A frown forms on her face. *"You're just being kind, Gio, I appreciate it. But don't you have to get back to Chiara? She's been eyeballing you all night."*

"And yet here I am with you."

"Because you're a good friend."

"Should a friend think about what it would be like to kiss another friend?" I confess.

"Gio."

I look up into her confused eyes. Her cheeks have turned a pale shade of pink; she keeps licking her lips and all I can think about is what they would feel like against my own. Should I kiss her?

We continue to stare at each other, the tension thickening with each second until gravity starts to pull us together and the next thing I know, our lips are touching and the world explodes into fireworks.

From that night on, we spent the rest of the summer kissing and slowly exploring each other until the last night when Paige asked me to take her virginity. I was a virgin at the time, too, and she was who I wanted my first time to be with. So, I agreed. I set up rugs in one of the stables, with only the light from my cell phone, not wanting to set the hay on fire with candles. And that night, under the stars, we made love. The next morning, she flew back to the States. We agreed that what we had was only for the summer and that whatever happened during the year, neither of us wanted to know about. Yes, I'd kissed a couple of girls that year but never went further. The next year she was back, and we had both blossomed. I was now a strapping seventeen-year-old boy, and she had developed so much in that year. As soon as we saw each other again, it was as if no time had passed, and we fell right back into our routine of sneaking away from our brothers and meeting up under the cover of darkness. Those last two summers we were together were the happiest time in my life.

"Are you okay? You look lost in thought," Natalia asks, pulling me from my memories.

Shaking my head. "I'm okay," I tell her, then take another large gulp of rosé. I shouldn't be thinking about another woman while my life is imploding, especially not a married one. After the funeral, I may have looked her up, trying to see what she had been up to over the years. She looked happy, thriving. She had a successful French restaurant in New York and a great group of friends. Her socials showed how happy in her life she was. It was funny because at the exact moment I was stalking her, it seemed she was stalking me, as a notification came up. *PJ NYC started following you.* Next thing I know, I'm following her back and that was it, until the panic hit me. I thought I shouldn't be following my ex when I'm an engaged man and she is married. But I couldn't also turn around and now unfollow her, that would be weird, so I left it and tried to forget all about her, until now.

"It's okay to not be okay, Gio. You don't have to be strong for me," Natalia tells me.

She's right; I shouldn't have to hide how I feel about the situation, but the thing is, other than feeling numb and shocked, deep down inside I feel free. Is that bad? That's bad. I shouldn't feel like that.

"I don't know how I feel."

"Relief is what you should be feeling. Marrying her would have been the biggest mistake of your life," Natalia states.

Maybe she's right.

We continue with our ice cream binge and drinking rosé until I can't see straight, and I'm belting out the words to "You Oughta Know" by Alanis Morrisette as the next song on the *Best Revenge Breakup Songs* playlist.

"What the hell is going on here?" Luca asks as he and Lilly walk into my apartment. Both are staring at me as if I've lost my mind, and maybe I have, but the rosé has given me a buzz and the ice cream has given me a sugar rush so when Natalia suggested we dance, I thought hell yeah, let's dance and here we are.

"We are dancing tonight out of Gio's mind," Natalia explains to our shocked brother.

"Yeah, fuck her," I scream as I continue to thrash around my apartment as if I'm in an imaginary mosh pit.

"This is healthy, I guess," Luca states.

"I created a dart board with your face on it when we broke up," Lilly chuckles at Luca.

Once the song is over, I come back to earth and take a seat. Luca hands each of us a bottle of water, which I throw back instantly, only now realizing how much I needed it.

"Shit, congrats, on the baby, Lilly," I say, rushing over and scooping up my soon-to-be sister-in-law and spinning her around happily.

"Thanks, Gio. Ew, you're all sweaty," she says as I place her back down.

Luca shoots me a glare. "Don't ever do that again. She has precious cargo," he warns.

Noted.

"How did everyone take the news?" Natalia asks.

Luca and Lilly stand there in silence. What the hell happened?

"We thought it would be better if we took your parents into a private room and told them that way," Lilly adds.

And?

"Papà didn't take it very well when he heard the news. He was pretty angry with Giada and …" Luca explains.

"And what?" I ask them.

"Your father didn't feel so good. I checked him out, he was all good, but his heartbeat was erratic, and I thought the best course of action would be to go home and get his doctor to do a late-night house call to double-check on him. I believe it was just shock and he let his anger get the better of him. He needs to rest," Lilly advises.

"Fuck," I yell as I run my fingers through my hair. "I knew this would happen. It's all my fault."

"Hey, no, it's Allegra's. None of this is on you." My brother tries to calm me down.

"She could have killed him," Natalia yells as tears stream down her face, while Lilly goes over and consoles her.

"We announced that due to our father having a health emergency, you would have to leave your party early to attend," Luca explains.

"Papà would not like that."

"It was his idea."

Wow. That's surprising. He is so stubborn he has never wanted anyone to think he is frail, but he did for me.

"Then what happened?"

Luca sighs. "Giada showed up like a professional, gave a speech saying that the party would wrap up early as family comes first, and she thanked everyone for their well-wishes."

"No one knows the real reason?" Natalia asks.

Luca and Lilly both shake their heads.

"People think I'm still engaged to her?" They nod in agreement.

"Maybe it's for the best. You can discreetly break up and no one would be the wiser," Luca advises.

"When? A week? A month? Day of the wedding?"

"It's not ideal, but at least you won't be hounded by the paparazzi," my brother suggests.

True.

"Do our parents know about Allegra?" I ask.

They both shake their heads. "We didn't want to out her to them. She needs to do it when she's ready," Lilly explains.

That's fair.

Instead, I'm now stuck in limbo, waiting for them to sort their shit out.

8

PAIGE

"Thanks for coming with me today, I'm so nervous," I tell Callie as we walk into the attorney's office.

"It's going to be okay, I'm here to help you. She will want to run through your options. Unfortunately, it's not as easy to get divorced as you might like," Callie warns me.

I want this entire situation over with. It's been a week since I found Michael screwing the sous chef. I texted him to say I'm moving out of our home and in with my brother. He didn't like it but said he would give me the space I needed to calm down. Like he has a choice in the matter. I'm done. We are over, and in the words of the great Taylor Swift, "We are never, ever, getting back together."

Thankfully, Smith and some of his boys from the station helped me get my things and within a day, every trace of my existence in our marital home had been erased. I got an angry text later that night when Michael had finished at the restaurant about how empty the house was and *why did I take everything of mine*. I reminded him I needed space, but I reassured him that it was only temporary as I needed him to think there was still a chance, so I had time to visit with my attorney and file for divorce before him.

"Hi, Paige Johnson for Abigail Spence," I say, greeting the receptionist.

She gives me a warm smile and tells us to follow her to the conference room where Abigail will meet us in about five minutes. She places a bottle of water and a couple of glasses in the middle of the table for us. I grab the bottle of water with shaky hands and pour Callie and myself a glass. I need something to do with my hands while I wait.

"It's going to be okay. I promise you," Callie tries to reassure me.

I nod but my insides feel like they are on a constant loop-de-loop. My anxiety is flooding the room, and I'm chewing my nails nervously. It's the unknown that is freaking me out. What happens if Michael wants to fight this divorce? Especially if he knows about my inheritance. I don't want to be locked in a battle with him for years. I want him out of my life for good.

Moments later, the glass door opens and in walks a sophisticated woman, not much older than us, with short black hair, dressed in a designer black suit with a red shirt and red sky-high heels.

"Callie, it's so good to see you," Abigail says, greeting Callie with a firm handshake. "And you must be Paige," she says, offering her hand to me. "I'm sorry we are meeting under these circumstances," she states, taking a seat on the other side of the conference table.

"I told Paige you were the right woman for the job," Callie says.

"You're too kind, but she's not lying," Abigail says with a chuckle, turning her attention to me. "Why don't you explain to me why you are here today."

Taking a deep breath and handing over the folder of paperwork Callie told me to bring, I start explaining to Abigail what has happened over the last month that I've been away in Italy and what I came home to find. She takes notes of everything that I've said and nods her head in places. I then explain to her about my inheritance and how I would like to make sure that he doesn't get a cent of it. She continues scribbling before she starts talking again.

"Right, firstly, I'm sorry for your loss and having to go through all of that alone, and secondly, I'm sorry you came home and walked in on him with another woman. You are a stronger woman than me, I would have stabbed him in the nuts." She chuckles.

"The closest thing was a baguette," I say with a smile.

"Better than a weapon; someone was looking out for you that day." She smiles. "Back to business, regarding your inheritance, your husband doesn't have access to that, it's not considered marital assets. Can he bitch and moan about it? Yes. Can he try to file a claim over it? Also, yes. But legally, he doesn't have rights to it. Now regarding your assets, is it just the home and restaurant?"

"Yes, both. I borrowed the deposit for both from my great-aunt. I insisted it be a loan, and we had papers drawn up regarding it. Callie told me to do it that way, probably guessing she knew that this day would happen," I say, turning and looking over at my best friend, who reaches out and squeezes my hand.

"Callie's a brilliant lawyer. Even if she didn't have her reservations, she would have still suggested it. It's smart. Now as you were the main beneficiary of your great-aunt's will, the loan would be voided for you but not your husband, as I see, he too, has signed this document," she states, flipping through the paperwork.

My eyes widen at her comment, the realization hitting that Michael might owe me some money; not that I need it, but the pettiness in me is feeling gleeful.

"You're missing your marriage license in here," she states, flicking through more papers.

"I assumed it was in the box of paperwork. Everything important was in there, but it wasn't. I left in such a hurry that I didn't have time to search for it," I explain to her.

She nods in understanding before picking up the conference room phone and telling the person on the other end to get a copy of it to place in the file, then hangs up.

"Now, regarding the restaurant, I see you have set up an LLC with it, but the loan contract was as individuals. This is his own personal debt, not the restaurant's. I'm assuming you do not want to be a part of that company anymore?"

I shake my head.

"Right, we will need to look at him buying you out of the restaurant if he wants to keep it or you would have to sell it. It would be the same with your marital home. Do you think this is going to be a problem?" she asks.

Turning, I look over at Callie to answer that.

"If Michael wants to be a dick, and he will be, knowing him. He's going to fight for the house and the restaurant, just to mess with you," Callie answers.

Abigail scribbles down some more notes in her file. "I would suggest we file for a no-fault divorce, it means if you both can come to an agreement easily, then the divorce could be done in about three months, depending on how busy the courts are. Otherwise, we would file for infidelity, and that is going to take a lot longer, it's hard to show the court. Yes, you caught him in the act, but that could be hearsay," she explains.

Shit.

I don't want to be married to him any longer than I have to be. "If we go the non-fault route, he can still fight me, right?"

"Yes, it can still get complicated, but we can show the courts that you are willing to be reasonable with your requests and it won't look good on his part if he doesn't," Abigail states.

Just then, the phone rings, and Abigail picks it up and listens intently to whoever is on the other end before hanging up.

"Well, things just got interesting. Paige, did you know that there is no marriage filed in New York for you?"

My mouth falls open. What does she mean there's no marriage? My heart begins to thunder in my chest.

"What do you mean no marriage? I was there as a witness," Callie adds.

Abigail's perfect brows arch. "A marriage license was purchased, but it was never filed. Which usually means you didn't send back the paperwork within fifteen days of the wedding to get it validated."

Wait, what? I remember signing it. Michael and I had a fight about it, as it was still sitting on the hallway table for days after our wedding. I remember being annoyed because it was the one thing I asked him to do while I was working and he wasn't. We had a huge argument, and he grabbed the paperwork and stormed out of our apartment, saying he would do it right away just to shut me up, and when he came back, he smugly told me he had. I relay this to Abigail.

"If the city doesn't have a record of your marriage, then legally you aren't married," she informs me.

Wait, I'm not married.

"Does that mean Paige doesn't need a divorce?" Callie asks.

Abigail turns and nods. "There is no marriage to dissolve. There is a relationship to dissolve, which we can help with because it's looking like you're going to need a whole heap of mediation to untangle yourself from the business and the home, but there's nothing to file, you're already free of him."

I don't understand.

Callie bursts out laughing. "That useless idiot fucked himself, but this is good. That man has no control over you, Paige. Don't you see, you're free to a certain extent."

Free.

My mind can't seem to wrap itself around that word. It can't be that easy.

"This ... I ...?"

Abigail nods. "This is highly unusual, but you're not my first client to find out she's not technically married. In those cases, it's been bad for the woman, but in your case, I'd say it's the best outcome. Your ex will still fight you over the joint assets you have, but most men will because of their egos. I can't imagine he is going to be happy to find out what's happened. What I'm going to do is write a letter to your ex, letting him know that you would like to call in the debts owed to your great-aunt regarding your home and the restaurant. That you would be happy to set up a meeting once he's sought counsel to work out how to proceed next."

"Do we have to tell him about the not being married bit?" I ask.

Abigail chuckles. "We could, but legally, we don't have to. It's up to his lawyers to work that out. We don't need to make it easier on him."

Sneaky and petty, I like it.

"I'm all in," I tell her.

"What the hell is this?" Michael yells at me, stepping out of the alley beside my brother's apartment, scaring me half to death.

"Michael," I squeal, trying to catch my breath.

"How did you do this?" he asks angrily, shaking papers at me.

"We shouldn't be talking. It's best we wait for a meeting," I tell him as I struggle to grab my keys out of my bag.

"Can't believe what a bitch you're being about all this. It was sex, Paige, fucking sex. I wasn't in love with anyone else. I didn't marry anyone else. I don't have a business with anyone else. It was always you I wanted. And what I did with them was stress relief. Men have fucking needs."

He still doesn't get it. "Lucky, now you can have all the stress relief you need."

His face turns red over my comment. "You're such a bitch. No wonder I had to fuck other women to put up with you."

Low blow. I hate how his words hurt me. I'm trying to be strong, but I can feel my throat closing as my emotions begin to get the better of me.

"Talk to my lawyer, Michael. I have nothing left to say to you," I tell him as I head toward the door to Smith's apartment.

"I'm going to make you pay if you don't stop what you're doing," he warns me.

My veins turn to ice. When I turn back, his blue eyes are narrowed on me.

"Do you seriously think threatening me is a good idea? You do remember who my brother is?" I toss back, trying to sound confident, but inside I'm shaking like a leaf. I've never seen him so angry before. He's scaring me.

"I mean it, Paige. Don't push me," he says, pointing the papers at me before turning on his heel and storming away.

"Are you okay? What did he do to you? I'll kill him," Smith says as he walks through the door, ready to murder Michael.

I shake my head as I stay curled up on the sofa, tears streaming down my cheeks.

"I pulled the security footage, he's on camera threatening you. There's no sound, but you can see by his face what he is doing and how scared you looked. I'm so sorry, Paige," he says, pulling me into his arms and hugging me, while I continue to break down. "I swear I won't let him hurt you."

A while later, Callie and Savannah come in to check on me.

"Did you send it?" Smith asks Callie.

Send what?

Callie looks over at me, then to my brother. "I passed on the footage to Abigail. If you want to get a protective order against Michael, she can take over the talks between her and Michael's lawyers."

"I can get you that order. Just say the word, Paige," Smith tells me.

"I'm sure he didn't mean it, he's been served the papers, and he let his emotions get the better of him. I'm sure his lawyer will be pissed that he did it, it doesn't help his case," I tell them.

Smith lets out a frustrated groan and Callie reaches out and tries to settle him down, pulling him out of the living room.

"Your brother is worried about you, that's all," Savannah says.

"I know, but if I get a protective order, it could make him angrier. Can I tell you something, but you can't tell Callie or Smith? I don't need them worrying," I ask her.

She gives me an unsure look but eventually nods in agreement.

"Michael threatened that he would make me pay if I continue this 'revenge'," I say, doing air quotes. "And I believe him."

"Paige, then you should get the order against him. He could do something bad," she tells me.

I shake my head. "I don't think he would kill me. I think he would try to ruin my reputation in New York though, making it hard for me to get a job."

Savannah looks at me, dumbfounded. "Paige, you never have to work another day in your life ever again. Lucia set you up, there's nothing Michael can do that will ruin you. You don't need to work in New York, not for anyone else, that is."

Oh. She's right. A hiccup of a giggle falls from my lips. "I keep forgetting that."

Savannah gives me a bright smile as she pulls me into a hug. "Girl, you are a hot ass, rich bitch countess who can spend her days sunning herself at one of her many hotels around Europe, sleeping with the pool boys, and drinking champagne from your vineyard. Do you even understand how awesome your life is? And no pin-dicked, cheating Frenchman can change that," she says, waving her hand around the room. "You don't have to answer to a man ever again. You can do whatever your heart desires, Paige. Live in Italy, France, Greece, and move to Australia or Antarctica if you want. The world is your oyster," she tells me firmly, which has me smiling widely.

"Thank you," I tell her before hugging her again.

"Any time, babe. Remember me when you meet any eligible billionaires while away," she says, giving me a wink.

"You have yourself a deal," I tell her.

9

GIORGIO

Why do I feel like I've been hit by a truck? I roll over in my bed and the room spins while my stomach groans. What did I eat last night? Oh, that's right, a pint of ice cream and two bottles of rosé —not a good mix. I was hoping last night was a dream, that I didn't witness my fiancée and sister together.

In this moment, I'm so thankful that we haven't told anyone about our breakup. I couldn't possibly deal with the media fallout with this hangover. I reach over and grab my phone to see if I've missed anything important and notice a message from Paige. I quickly sit up in bed and regret it instantly, so I lie back down again and turn onto my side. I swipe my phone open and am met with a whole message thread.

> Giorgio: Just walked in on my sister going down on my fiancée at my engagement party.

> Paige: Who is this?

> Giorgio: It's me, Gio.

> Paige: Have you been hacked?

Giorgio: Wish I had been but no. I've drunk a lot of rosé and eaten a pint of ice cream, trying to forget what I've seen.

> Paige: Oh shit, I'm so sorry. That would have been horrible.

Giorgio: My sister, like what the fuck?

> Paige: I got off the plane after the funeral and walked in on my husband fucking our sous chef at work.

Giorgio: No fucking way.

> Paige: I hit him with a baguette. Wish it was something harder.

Giorgio: Lucky it wasn't. You're too pretty for jail.

> Paige: I hate orange more than I hate him.

Giorgio: What did that color ever do to you?

> Paige: I don't know, but it gives me a visceral reaction. Past life trauma, maybe I was murdered by a bunch of oranges.

Giorgio: Oranges don't have arms.

> Paige: You really are drunk.

Giorgio: I really am.

> Paige: Why did you message me?

And I must have fallen asleep at that point because I've left her last message unanswered.

Shit.

Also, why the hell did I message all that shit to Paige? *Lucky, you did because now you know she's in the same boat as you.* How is it lucky that she caught her asshole husband fucking the sous chef?

That's messed up. *She's single.* No, she's not. She's *it's complicated* at best, like me.

> Giorgio: Hey, I'm sorry about dumping a heap of emotional baggage into your DMs like that. I fell asleep right after I sent you the message. If it helps, I'm suffering from the mother of all hangovers this morning. Hope you're doing well, and I'm sorry that you're going through the same shit as me.

Then I throw my phone away from me; I've done enough damage. I've apologized and she can do with it what she wants. I'm not even sure what the time is in New York; I think it's early. Either way, I need a shower to feel human.

"There he is," my mother says as she rushes up and embraces me after my shower. She smothers me with kisses, which is too much for this level of hangover.

"Mamma, please," I tell her.

"No. I need to make it all better. You used to love it when you were little," she explains.

"I'm an adult," I say, which falls on deaf ears. "Hey, Papà, how are you feeling?" I ask, seeing him sit down.

"Don't worry about this old man. How are you, my son?"

"I've been better," I tell him honestly.

"I can't believe Giada did this to you. I called her, but she refused to answer my calls," Mamma states.

Natalia chuckles from the corner. How the hell does she look normal when I feel like shit?

"And where is your sister? Why is she not here?" Mamma asks.

Yeah, I'm not touching that subject at all. "Your heart okay?" I ask my father.

He waves my concern away. "The doctor said all good."

That's something, I guess.

"What do you need from me?" he asks.

"Nothing."

"Oh," Natalia exclaims from the corner as she stares at her phone.

My heart sinks. This is it. The moment the world finds out that we've broken up and the mayhem starts.

"Oh, what?" Mamma asks her.

Her eyes widen as she stares down at her phone, then back to me, then to Mamma and back again. "Fendi is having a sale."

My mother rolls her eyes at my sister's lie, guessing it's not something she wants to say in front of her.

"Sorry, we're late. Lilly wasn't feeling well."

As soon as the words are out of my brother's mouth, he clocks our parents sitting in the room, and I can see he is internally cursing himself for letting the news slip like that.

"Are you pregnant?" Mamma asks, rushing over to where they are standing.

"Yes, we just—" Luca starts to explain but doesn't get far, as she starts screaming and rejoicing as she gives Lilly a huge hug, then smothers Luca in kisses like she had just done for me.

"A baby. My baby is having a baby. This is the best news I've heard. We needed some good news," she says, looking over at me.

Like I had any control of what's happened to me.

"Thanks, Mamma, we are so very excited," Luca says.

"Congratulations, my son," Papà says as he gets up from his chair to give his well-wishes to the happy couple.

"Sorry," Luca says.

I shake my head. "They needed some good news, especially Papà. He doesn't need the stress of my doomed relationship on his mind."

"Might keep Mamma out of your hair, too." He chuckles.

Isn't that the truth.

"Allegra and Giada are in fucking Mykonos," Natalia whispers as she joins us.

"They're in Greece?"

She nods.

"Doesn't that look bad? After we said we were finishing the engagement party early because of family health issues," Luca adds.

"As if those two selfish bitches care, please," Natalia says with a huff.

This isn't good.

"There is already chatter on some of the blogs saying the timing is weird. But Giada said she had already been booked to DJ at some club in Mykonos over the summer and couldn't get out of the commitment."

News to me, but to be fair, I never asked many questions about what she was up to. That sounds bad. I should know where my fiancée is working, shouldn't I? How the hell did I think Giada and I were ever going to work? I've been delusional about this relationship. I was focused on making everyone else happy except me.

"What about Allegra?" Luca asks.

"She posted that she was there for work, too. That her family were the ones to tell her to go to Greece, and everything was okay. Like what the fuck is that bullshit? She's a cold-hearted bitch," Natalia explains.

"It's probably for the best that she's away. Papà doesn't need that stress," Luca adds.

"Wish I was on an island somewhere running from my problems."

"You could be. I'd be down for lying on a beach somewhere, obviously not Greece." Natalia nudges me, which makes me smile.

That sounds fantastic. Then the thought of New York pops into my mind. *Are you fricken crazy?* Paige doesn't need you there with your baggage at a time when she is going through her own shit.

My phone buzzes, and I look down to see a notification from Paige. What the? That's freaky. I was just thinking about her, and then she messages.

> Paige: No need to apologize. It's nice to know that someone else is going through the same thing I am. I love my family and friends, but they don't get it.

Giorgio: You can message me anytime.

Giorgio: And I get it.

"Why are you smiling?" Luca asks as he tries to peer over my shoulder. I snatch my phone away from his snooping.

"I wasn't smiling."

"Um, yeah, you were. Don't tell me you are already DMing girls."

I glare at my brother. "I was chatting with a friend if you must know. Someone who is going through the same shit as me, actually."

"Who?" Natalia asks.

"I'm not telling you who."

"Do I know her?" she asks.

"Why do you automatically think it's a woman?"

"Because I don't smile like that when one of my boys DMs." Luca grins.

"Fuck you both, and no, you don't know her."

"A new friend?" Luca questions.

"An old one."

Luca's eyes widen, and a smile falls across his face. "No fucking way, you're talking to that American girl. What's her name …?" he says, clicking his fingers.

"Wait, what the hell, who is this? I don't know this story." Natalia pouts.

"Shit, was that the funeral you went to?" Luca asks.

"Wait, Gio's first love died?" my sister pipes in.

"No, she didn't. And yes, it was the funeral I went to, it was her great-aunt that passed." I hiss at my nosey siblings.

"You didn't tell me you ran into her," Luca states.

"It wasn't anything."

"But it is something now?" he questions.

I let out a sigh. "I messaged her last night when I was drunk telling her what happened. I don't know why, but I did. She came back and said that when she got off the plane in New York after the funeral, she caught her husband screwing the sous chef at their restaurant."

"No way, that's horrible." Natalia gasps.

I nod my head.

"I sent her a message this morning apologizing for dumping my drama on her in a DM and she said it was fine, that it was nice talking to someone going through the exact same thing as each other."

Natalia and Luca look at each other and burst out laughing. Why is this so funny?

"That was who messaged you?" Luca questions me.

"Yes, she messaged me."

"And?" Natalia adds.

"What? And nothing."

Her eyes narrow. "What did you say her name was?"

"I didn't."

"Paige, shit, what was her last name?" Luca says, scrambling to work out her last name.

Natalia pulls out her phone and starts scrolling. What is she doing?

"Is this her?" she says, turning the phone around and showing me a picture of Paige. How the hell did she do that? "Judging by your lack of response and shock on your face, that's a yes. Oh my gosh, she is gorgeous. A natural beauty, not like these women you normally date."

"I'm not dating her." I hiss, making sure our parents don't hear this conversation.

"Ew, her husband is French, explains why he's a douchebag," she adds.

"Please, leave this alone. She's an old friend. There's nothing wrong with me talking to someone who is going through the same thing, is there?" I ask them.

"No problem at all." Natalia grins.

"It's fine, as long as you don't start jerking off to her pictures at night," Luca adds.

"Ew." My sister screws up her face.

"Fuck you," I say and punch him hard in the arm.

"Hey, you two, no fighting," Mamma yells from across the room where she is talking Lilly's ear off.

"What happened between the two of you that you haven't spoken for that long?" Natalia asks.

"We lost touch," I say, which isn't the truth. I broke her heart, but she doesn't need to know that.

"And the first time you'd seen her since you were kids was at that funeral?" she asks.

"Yeah, first time in fifteen years. We were best friends growing up, and then, you know, you grow up," I add.

"But now that you've seen her again, you can't stop thinking about her?" Natalia questions.

"Ye—I mean no," I say, tripping myself up.

My siblings burst out laughing at me.

"Stop being assholes. I've just been left by my fiancée for my sister at my own engagement party. I deserve to talk to someone who isn't family about it."

They both shut up quickly. "We're just playing," Luca says.

"Paige has enough baggage of her own. There is no way in hell either one of us would be looking for anything more than shared heartbreak," I explain to them.

"Are you really that heartbroken?" Luca questions me.

I glare at him. That's not the point.

"Doesn't matter how deep your feelings were for her, what they did was appalling. You should have a friend to talk to, Gio. She's not going to sell the story, is she?" my sister asks, concern written all over her face.

"Doubtful, our families are in business together."

"They're what?" Natalia says, her voice raising with confusion.

"The vineyard near Florence, her family lent us the land to plant the vines for our wine. I think it was like a hundred years ago or something like that," I explain.

Natalia's mouth falls open. "Why have I never heard of this?"

"It's not something you needed to know."

"You were too young, but we used to go to the vineyard every summer growing up. We had the best time there, I miss it," Luca explains to our sister.

"Me too. When I was down there it was like time had stopped, nothing had changed," I tell him.

"This trip down memory lane is nice, but can you trust her?" my sister pushes.

"Yes," I say, not like I know Paige now, but she's had ample opportunity to sell her story and has never done so. But Natalia doesn't look convinced.

"Just be careful, Gio," she warns.

10

PAIGE

> Giorgio: Hey, I'm sorry about dumping a heap of emotional baggage into your DMs like that. I fell asleep right after I sent you the message. If it helps, I'm suffering from the mother of all hangovers this morning. Hope you're doing well and I'm sorry that you're going through the same shit as me.

I wasn't expecting to hear from him again after his drunk texts. But his apology is sweet. He didn't need to, but it was nice to get one. It's wild to think we are both going through the same thing. I thought my betrayal was bad with someone I considered a friend, but your sister, a family member, doing that to you seems so much worse.

> Paige: No need to apologize. It's nice to know that someone else is going through the same thing I am. I love my family and friends, but they don't get it.

I have an amazing support network around me—they have been brilliant—but they also never liked Michael, so their level of disdain for him is at an all-time high. I can't vent to them that I miss him, that I miss how we were building a future together, that the dreams we once had will never come true, not together anyway. I miss being in a relationship. They are all single and happy being single, so to them, being a twosome isn't something any of them are into. I'm now going to have to navigate this new world alone. Add in the insane pressure of now being a countess, as well as getting my head around the fact that I have financial freedom—immense freedom—it's daunting, especially by myself. What does my life look like now? Is it in New York? Do I have to spend more time in Europe? And if I do, then I'm leaving all my family and friends and embarking on a new life on the other side of the world, alone. It's a lot to think about, what I want out of my new life. Yes, it's exciting, but I'm fearful of the unknown. Will anyone ever want me again? The thought of starting over on the single scene is terrifying, especially listening to the stories Callie and Savannah share with me.

My phone buzzes.

> Giorgio: You can message me anytime.
>
> Giorgio: And I get it.

I notice myself staring down at the phone and smiling. Does he really mean it, or is he being polite? *Or like you, he has no one else to talk to except a virtual stranger.* Guess we really are strangers; it's been so long since we've seen each other. Yet if you had asked me fifteen years ago who knew me the best, I would have said him. There was no one in my life, besides maybe Callie and Smith, that knew me better. Then he messed it up.

I've flown in tonight to Florence, and the first person I want to see is Giorgio. A year between seeing each other is too much. Yes, we talk all the time online, but I miss being in his arms, I miss his kisses. I miss his ... you know. Not like I haven't dated anyone since the last time I saw him, because I have, but none of the boys back home can compare to Gio. I was so excited that my parents let me travel by myself to Italy for the first time. My brother just graduated high school and he wanted to hang out with his friends instead of spending the entire summer in Italy, so he's coming later in the holidays. After eating dinner with

Lucia, I head on down to the vineyard to say hi to Giorgio and Luca, who should have arrived by now. I knock on the door and eagerly wait to see him. I can barely contain my excitement.

"Paige, what a surprise. Welcome home," Mario, the winemaker, greets me happily, kissing my cheeks.

"It's good to be back in Italy," I tell him.

He nods and gives me a wide smile, then movement behind him catches my attention.

"Paige," Luca says, greeting me warmly. "When did you get here?"

"I've just arrived and thought I'd come say hi," I tell him as I nervously look around for Gio.

"I'll leave you kids to catch up," Mario says, disappearing from the room.

"Is your brother here?" Luca asks.

I shake my head. "He's coming later."

He nods in understanding.

"Where's Gio?"

Luca's face falls at the mention of his brother, which has my stomach doing the same. "He's in his room."

"Oh great, I'll go say hi," I tell him.

Luca's arm reaches out. "Don't, he's sleeping," he states, but I notice his cheeks have gone bright red. Pulling my arm from him, I storm off through the house toward Gio's room. What is he hiding from me? "Paige, please."

I ignore him and continue to storm through the house until I reach Gio's door. I don't even bother knocking before storming in.

"Noooo," Luca calls out behind me, but it's in slow motion as the full impact of what he was stopping me from hits me. I see Gio in bed with Bella Gallo, one of the local girls who is always a bitch to me. I know she's slept with my brother and has made out with Luca. She always had her sights on Gio, but he never gave in ... until now.

"What the fuck?" Gio curses as he tries to scramble off Bella, who squeals and pulls the blankets up over her naked body.

"Surprise, I'm back," I say, then hear Gio let out a hundred curses.

Think I've seen enough. I turn and exit his room and head back out of the house. We were never exclusive, so I can't be mad at him, but her? He promised me he would never go near Bella because of the way she treated me.

"Paige, wait, please, let me explain," Gio calls out after me.

I've made it to the path that winds its way through the vineyard back to my place.

"Why her?" I turn around and yell at him. "You could have had anyone, and I wouldn't have cared, but her," I say as tears stream down my cheeks.

"I'm sorry, okay?"

"You're sorry I caught you."

He rakes his hand through his hair, causing his biceps to flex. Shit, I hate that I checked him out. I hate that even when I'm so mad at him, I notice him standing in the darkness in his low-slung shorts that show off the deep V of his hips, and the impressive six pack, the one that I used to run my hand over every summer.

"I'm sorry, I didn't tell you."

"That you're messing around with Bella Gallo." Ew, saying her name makes me want to gag.

Gio's face falls. "No, sorry that I didn't tell you she's my girlfriend."

Everything in me stills. He is dating my enemy. I thought we were friends.

"Her? You're dating her?" I spit, pointing in the direction of his home.

He nods his head.

"Why her?"

"Because you live on the other side of the world, Paige," he says, raising his voice at me.

"I know, and every summer I come back to you."

"Maybe I want more than that," he argues. His words are like a knife to the chest. "Bella's family moved up to Rome. She joined my school, and we started dating a couple of months ago," he explains.

"There were no pictures of her on your socials."

He shrugs. "I don't put everything on there."

Bullshit, we are teens, everything goes on our socials. "You never wanted me to find out about her."

Gio remains silent.

"After everything we've been through, you didn't have the balls to tell me you were dating my mortal enemy. Fuck you, Gio Fiorenzo, for being too chickenshit to tell me the truth," I yell at him.

"You weren't supposed to be here," he says back.

"I came early to surprise you. To celebrate your graduation and your eighteenth birthday. I'm an idiot," I say, raising my hands in the air.

"I'm heading back to Rome tomorrow with Bella. We're going away with friends to celebrate." He was hoping that when I turned up, he'd be long gone and never had to deal with the confrontation.

"You're not the guy I thought you were," I say, my eyes narrowing on him.

"You weren't supposed to find out like this."

I wipe the tears away from my cheeks. "I wasn't supposed to find out, period. I'm glad I did because now I know who you really are. I wish I'd never met you." I cry as I turn and start to run back home, my heart breaking with each step I take.

He doesn't follow me.

When I make it home, Lucia is there, and I confess that Gio and I have been seeing each other and that I thought I loved him but he's dating a bitch called Bella who hates me, and I don't want to be here anymore. And the next day, Lucia packs us up and we head to Paris, helping me forget all about Giorgio Fiorenzo.

Until now.

The next time I saw him, he was standing in Lucia's garden, looking as handsome as he did all those years ago. I continue to stare down at my phone and contemplate if I want to reply or not. *Would be rude not to reply.*

> Paige: You might regret that offer.

> Giorgio: There's a lot I regret, but that offer isn't one of them.

I bite my lip as I read his text. What does that mean? What does he regret? What am I doing? I have to get ready as I have mediation with Michael later on today. I need to be focusing on that, not an old acquaintance.

11

PAIGE

"I don't like this," my brother tells me as I get ready to leave for my mediation.

"I'll be in a room full of lawyers, it'll be safe," I try to assure him.

I love my brother, but he has been in full protection mode since my run-in with Michael a week ago. I get it. He sees the worst of humanity on a daily basis and he's only trying to keep me safe, but he's smothering me.

"I'll be in the room with her. She's going to be okay," Callie reassures him.

"I'm a phone call away, and I can be down at the lawyer's office in twenty minutes if you need me, okay?"

"I'll be fine, I promise, and I'll call you as soon as it's over."

He gives me a nod and reluctantly lets me leave the apartment with Callie in tow.

"He's worried, you know," Callie tells me.

"I know he is, but he needs to understand I'm an adult and that I also know Michael. He has always been nothing but hot air."

Callie doesn't look convinced, but she doesn't say anything more when we step out of the apartment and into the waiting taxi. We ride in silence all the way to Abigail's office. Then we get out and head upstairs to the conference room, getting there before Michael and his team. As we walk into the room, I nervously start to play with my hands.

"It's going to be okay," Callie reassures me as we take our seats. "Be calm and rational, you know Michael is going to lose his shit because of his temper. That will be a win for you with the mediator. Put all emotion aside, deal with nothing but facts, and think about things logically," Callie reminds me.

Easier said than done. I can do this. *I have to do this.*

Abigail walks in with her staff and gives me a wide smile. "You ready for this?" she asks.

"Yes, no, kind of," I answer.

"It's going to be all good, especially if his lawyer has told him to play nice."

He has no power over me anymore. We aren't even married. There are only two things we need to agree upon, and then I can move on with my life.

Movement outside catches my attention, and I can see the receptionist ushering Michael and his lawyers into the conference room.

This is it.

When Michael's eyes land on me, a sneer pulls on his upper lip, and I can see the venom behind those blue eyes. *This man hates me.*

Oh no, this isn't good. But also, how dare he hate me. I hate him. He's the one who's been cheating on me. I've done nothing wrong. I shouldn't be surprised, he's always been self-absorbed. I was too stupid to realize he wasn't some cooking genius, just a Frenchman with an ego.

Michael steps further into the conference room, his blond hair slicked back, and he's clean-shaven. I can smell his cologne from across the room, the same one I got him for our wedding, the one that used to give me butterflies every time I smelled it, and now it does nothing but repulse me. Nice try, but that won't work on me anymore as I pretend to sneeze.

"Something's irritated my nose," I whisper to Callie, who nods and pretends that she doesn't know exactly what I'm doing.

Michael glares at me when I look back over at him. Two can play that game, I made sure that I looked good today, too. Not because I want him back, but because I want him to see the consequence of his actions, that he's never going to get all this ever again. He probably doesn't care because he never has, but it's made me feel more confident and that's the whole point. I've gone for a gorgeous white shift dress that hugs my curves and black heels. My chocolate-brown hair is pulled up into a high ponytail with natural makeup except for a pop of red on my lips, a color he said he hated me wearing; he said that I looked like a hooker.

He takes his seat across from me, those blue eyes trained on mine; he's trying to intimidate me, but I no longer care. Callie squeezes my hand underneath the table, giving me strength.

"Shall we start?" the mediator asks.

Michael's lawyer nods and starts talking. "We all know why we are here today, to dissolve the marriage of Ms. Paige Johnson and Mr. Michael Nelson," his lawyer starts his opening monologue.

"Sorry, can I interrupt for one moment, please," Abigail asks as she looks over at the mediator, who nods while wearing a serious frown. "We aren't here to dissolve a marriage, as there isn't a legal marriage between Ms. Johnson and Mr. Nelson."

A collective gasp falls from Michael's camp as the junior lawyers share confused looks between them.

"I'm sorry, what did you say?" the mediator asks as Michael and his lawyer frantically whisper between each other.

"Oh, I'm sorry. I assumed due diligence had been done before today, because we found that there were no papers filed on behalf of Ms. Johnson or Mr. Nelson. If you search for their marriage certificate, there is not one registered with the city or anywhere, for that matter."

"What the hell are they talking about?" Michael turns and asks his lawyer loudly. His lawyer tries to reassure him that everything is okay as he turns and asks the junior lawyers for their input. One of the lawyers pulls out some paperwork and places it on the desk in front of the mediator.

"See here," one of the younger lawyers states, pushing the paper toward him. The mediator grabs the piece of paper and starts to read it.

"It looks like their marriage license," the mediator states with another frown.

"True, it is their marriage license, except it wasn't filed. And the reason we know it hasn't been filed is, if you see here," Abigail states as one of her team pulls out paperwork and their laptop, showing that our marriage doesn't exist in New York State.

The mediator adjusts his glasses and looks at the evidence presented before him. "She's right, Mr. Cannon, there doesn't look to be any filed marriage by your client."

"She's lying," Michael pipes up, while his lawyer orders him to hush.

Abigail adds, "My client remembers asking Mr. Nelson to file the paperwork after their marriage, and he assured her that he did. She even remembers there being a disagreement about it. Does that ring a bell with your client?"

The lawyer turns and looks at Michael who is spluttering, trying to find an answer, knowing full well he never filed it.

"But … I don't understand … how can this be?" Michael stutters over his words.

"Ms. Spence, do you mind giving me and my team a moment to discuss this latest development?" the lawyer asks Abigail.

"Of course, we'll just be outside," she states, indicating for all of us to get up and follow her. One of the staff takes the mediator to another room. I can feel Michael's eyes burning into my back as we walk past. As soon as we leave the room, the curtains are closed in the conference room, and I can hear Michael losing it inside.

"Someone didn't do their job." Callie chuckles beside me.

"What does this mean though?" I ask. Will we have to postpone this entire meeting? I was hoping this would be it.

"It means that Michael is fucked, and he doesn't have a case. That he needs to accept that what you're going to offer him is a generous deal," Callie explains.

Twenty minutes later, the blinds are back up and a fuming Michael is sulking in the corner, clearly not happy with the news that his own incompetence is his downfall.

"Showtime, ladies," Abigail states before we walk back into the room.

"Thank you so much, Ms. Spence, for letting us convene with our client. It seems your records are correct. That there was no filing of the marriage between your client and mine," he states, with Michael looking on furiously. "It seems there is no marriage to dissolve, so I am happy for us to get into the de facto separation of assets."

The mediator nods in agreement at the change.

"Very good, Mr. Cannon. Let's start with the loan your client and mine took out with her great-aunt. As you can see here in the paperwork, it was the down payment to purchase their apartment, and an amendment added regarding the restaurant with a deposit amount borrowed for that venture," Abigail explains to the room.

"What loan?" Michael turns and argues with his lawyer, who tells him to be quiet as he takes the paperwork from the mediator. He scans it and you can see on his face that he is not getting paid enough to deal with whatever Michael had been telling him.

"Is this your signature on the paperwork?" the mediator asks Michael.

"Yes, it looks like it, but I never signed it. She forged it, she used to do it all the time," he stammers.

My heart skips a beat; what in the hell is he saying? I never forged it.

"Ms. Johnson, could you please elaborate for us?" the mediator asks.

"I would never forge someone's signature. We had come back from our honeymoon at my aunt's place in the Hamptons, as we couldn't afford to go anywhere else. Lucia was staying at her Manhattan home when we got back. We had dinner with her and asked if we could borrow the money for the apartment," I explain.

"She said it was a wedding gift," he argues.

"And I said that it was too much money. That it should be as a loan, and you agreed, reluctantly, as you didn't want to be indebted to my family."

Michael glares at me; he knows that's how the conversation went.

"We then went into Callie's office, and she had another lawyer draw up the paperwork, and we both signed it. Callie was there when you did," I say, pointing to my best friend.

"Is this true?" the mediator asks.

"Yes. As I knew them both, I didn't think it would be right for me to do the paperwork, so I had someone else do it. I was a witness to the signing," she explains.

"What about the loan for the restaurant?" the mediator asks.

"When Lucia came to visit again, we had dinner with her and told her our vision to open our own restaurant, but we needed a loan to set it up. She was very excited and offered to loan us the money," I clarify.

"She said she would be our first investor, it wasn't a loan," Michael argues again.

"Then why did you sign the loan paperwork, Mr. Nelson?" the mediator asks.

Michael has nothing to say; he keeps searching for the words, but nothing comes out and I can see he is fuming over it.

"You know Lucia gave us that money as a gift. She never expected us to pay her back. Why are you lying? You're doing this out of revenge because I fucked someone else. You're being petty, Paige," Michael spits. His lawyer turns and glares at him, unhappy with his outburst.

"As per the paperwork you signed, the contract states that it was a loan from her family and that you would be paying off the debt together," the mediator explains to him.

"My client wishes for her name to be taken off all paperwork relating to the restaurant. She would also like to be taken off the

LLC, and she wants no liabilities regarding the restaurant," Abigail adds.

Michael's mouth falls open at my request. See, I'm not a bitch.

"What would your client want in return?" Michael's lawyer asks.

"That Mr. Nelson's name be removed from the ownership of their apartment. She is not seeking any other monetary compensation. We believe what is owed on each asset is about the same amount and would be a fair swap," Abigail explains.

"Are you fucking serious? You want to turn me out on the streets?" Michael argues.

"Calm down," Michael's lawyer says, chastising him.

"No, I won't calm down. This woman here has inherited a fortune. That's right, I had someone investigate you and find out what happened in Italy, because I'm sure you were cheating on me the entire time you were there."

Is he serious right now? He had someone investigate me.

His lawyer throws up his hands at his outburst.

"I'm sure they found my client was faithful the entire time," Abigail answers, staring Michael down.

"Yeah, whatever. What was even more important was he found out she's been crowned a countess and inherited a multi-million-dollar fortune. She's rich. Stinking fucking rich. With houses and businesses all over the world and now she wants to take my home when she has so much. Were you ever going to tell me, Paige? Or was that your plan when you came back from Italy? You were going to leave me and take everything I worked my ass off for."

Is he serious?

He thinks I planned for him to not file our marriage papers all those years ago. That I planned to be named Lucia's heir. That somehow it was all in my master plan that I would catch him cheating on me. For what? To get our crappy apartment?

"You are throwing me out on the street to get revenge on me for sleeping with Amelia. That's pretty fucking low, Paige," he curses at me.

How is this my fault?

Callie squeezes my hand under the table trying to calm me down, as she can tell my temperature is rising with every word out of his mouth.

"Mr. Nelson, please calm down, I will not have you raising your voice in this meeting. Mr. Cannon, I suggest you remind your client of where he is," the mediator intervenes, then Michael's lawyer whispers into his ear and tries to calm him down.

"My client is being very fair. Under the law, she is entitled to call in the debt. My suggestion so that you both don't waste your money on lawyer fees is that we resolve this today or Mr. Cannon and I would be only too happy to continue this fight. There's a new Mercedes that I have my eye on," Abigail suggests.

"Paige doesn't need the apartment. She has three in Europe that she can live in. I have nothing," he yells.

"You could also have no restaurant, too, if you look at it like that. The choice is yours, Mr. Nelson," Abigail states.

"But it's not fair. She has everything, and I have nothing," he moans.

He should have thought about that before sticking his dick in every woman that works for us.

"Mr. Nelson, this is a good deal. If the relationship is over, then it is for the best to move on and this way you can," his lawyer explains to him.

"She has so much already," he continues to argue.

"What she inherited has nothing to do with what you two have built together. I'm sorry if you feel that it's unfair, but if you do not resolve this, then you are both going to be tied up in court cases for the next year and the only people who will win will be the lawyers. A court will rule that everything should be split, which means she will get half of your restaurant. Is that what you want, Mr. Nelson?" the mediator asks him.

"No," Michael snaps.

"Today has been quite a surprising day and I think it would be best if I talk to my client and we reconvene regarding the matter," Michael's lawyer asks.

"I think that would be a great idea, Mr. Cannon. One week, will that be enough time?" the mediator asks.

"That would be perfect," his lawyer says in agreement.

"Right, well. This mediation is over, and we will reconvene in a week's time, hopefully with a resolution," the mediator states as he gets up from his chair and starts gathering his things. Michael's team does the same, when suddenly, Michael lunges toward me, his hands hitting the conference table with a thud.

"You're going to pay for this, Paige, mark my words," Michael says, pointing at me.

I'm in shock as I stare at my very pissed-off ex.

"I don't think it's very smart of your client to threaten my client in front of all these witnesses," Abigail says, looking at Michael's lawyer who is trying to drag his client out of the room, but he's refusing to budge. "This isn't the first time he has threatened her either. Luckily for us, it was caught on CCTV outside the front of her residence. I will suggest you have a chat with him, otherwise he's going to end up behind bars if he continues this behavior."

"We will be in touch, ladies," Michael's lawyer says, nodding in our directions as he ushers Michael out of the conference room.

"I'm sorry, Paige, but that man is unhinged," Abigail tells me.

"After the first time, she refused to get a protective order," Callie adds, and I turn and glare at my best friend.

"This isn't him. I've never seen this side before."

"It's now the second time he's threatened you, and this time, it's in front of his lawyers. He doesn't care," Abigail states.

"I know, but he's clearly upset that I've taken so much from him. Of course, he's going to be angry. What happens if he does more?

"I think you should talk to Smith about getting that order," Callie adds.

"Won't that affect the meetings?" I ask.

Abigail shakes her head. "We can have it without the two of you."

Right. I guess then it might be a good idea. "I'll talk to my brother."

"Good. Today went well. Michael's theatrics are a win for us. If his lawyer is smart, they will tell him to take the deal, it's the best offer he will get. But today proved he doesn't like to listen, so we shall see. I'll be in touch with the new meeting time. Stay safe and let me know if you need anything," she says, shaking our hands before leaving.

"How are you really doing?" Callie asks as we take a seat at a nearby bar.

"I'm shaken but okay," I answer, perusing the drinks menu; after today, I need something strong. "Why does Michael hate me so much? I've done nothing to him other than love and support him."

The waiter interrupts us, and we give him our drink order before continuing. "His ego is bruised. Especially since he knows he's fucked up and because you're rich."

"Wasn't that weird when he said he had someone investigate me?" Callie nods. "He thought I would be cheating on him while I was looking after my dying relative, like what the hell?"

"He wanted to find any excuse, in case you found out about his infidelity, then he could throw it back in your face," Callie adds.

Tears well in my eyes. "It's been a lot, all of this has," I tell her, trying to hide the fact I'm crying in a bar.

"Hey, it's going to be okay," she reassures me, reaching around to squeeze my hand. "You've had a really hard time recently. I'm so proud of how well you have been dealing with it. So, a few tears in a bar after a horrible meeting with your ex, you're doing pretty well."

"Today was brutal, and I wonder if it was worth it. Maybe he's right, do I really need the apartment when I have so much from Lucia?"

Callie's brows pull together. "It was your home, too."

"I know, but it's tainted now. I don't want to go back there. I have so many homes I could live in, do I really need that one?"

"You plan on leaving New York?" she asks.

I shrug my shoulders. I don't know. Before I have a chance to say any more, the waiter brings our drinks. I pick it up and take a large sip. Ah, that feels better.

"You seriously thinking about leaving the city?" Callie questions me again.

"I have no home or job here anymore."

She remains silent for a little while, thinking over what I've just said. "You would be okay giving everything to him?"

I turn the glass in my hands. "If I didn't have so much, I would be fighting harder, but if I'm honest, I want nothing more to do with him. I want him out of my life."

"I get that, babe, but don't you think he wins if you give in?"

"Callie, I'm a fucking countess. I have twenty million dollars in my bank account, I don't think I'm losing," I say with a chuckle.

My best friend's eyes widen, and then she bursts out laughing. "Fucking hell, bitch. You are rich, rich."

"Right?" I say, holding my glass up to her. She does the same and we clink glasses.

"If you think you will feel better about moving on, then don't fight it. Let him have the apartment and restaurant. I'm a petty bitch so I would fight tooth and nail, but with the way he's acting, I don't blame you for wanting to walk away. You don't need to worry about that man any longer than you need to."

I knew she would understand. "I want a fresh start. Having a shitty apartment isn't going to make or break my fortune."

"You're too good. I would want to make him pay." She smirks.

"Me living the life Lucia's given me is the best payback. He could have been living this life, but he chose to screw other women instead. That's the price he must pay, seeing me thrive without him."

"Ain't that the truth," she says, raising her glass again and we clink it together.

12

GIORGIO

Thankfully, my family finally left me alone and have gone back to their homes, happy in the knowledge that I seem to be doing okay after last night. Guess most people wouldn't be doing so well after finding out their fiancée is cheating on them. Normal people would be sitting on the sofa crying; I'm not sure if I've even shed a tear. Something is wrong with me, isn't there? That's not normal.

As I stare out of my home, looking over the gardens of the Villa Borghese, my mind wanders back to this morning when Paige messaged me back.

> Paige: You might regret that offer.

My reply was instant.

> Giorgio: There's a lot I regret, but that offer isn't one of them.

I realize I haven't heard back from her since my last text. I swipe up the international times and it's late afternoon for her. Was the text too much by bringing up the past? I thought it might be playful. Because I do regret choosing Bella Gallo over her. I don't know why I did it; I knew Paige hated her, but Bella joined our school, hung out with my friends, was hot, and wanted to do all the dirty things to me. I was a young guy. How was I going to say no to that? Seeing the pain on Paige's face when she discovered us ripped my heart out; never in my life have I ever felt more of a jerk than I did in that moment. And what does an idiot do when they are confronted? They double down on it. I hurt her and I just hope that my stupidity didn't mess her up over the years. Should I have reached out as soon as Bella and I had broken up and apologized to Paige for messing up? Yeah, I should have—especially after finding Bella screwing one of my buddies only a couple of days into our vacation, but I didn't want Paige to think I only did it because Bella messed me over. I did go back once that summer, but Paige had fled back to the States. After that summer, she stopped coming to her aunt's place. Instead, they would head off to Greece, or France, or wherever, and I hate that there's a chance she stopped coming to the place she loved the most because of me. So yeah, I have a lot of regrets when it comes to Paige, and I guess I've shoved them deep down inside me, and it wasn't until I saw her again that they decided to bubble to the surface.

>Giorgio: Hope your day was better than mine.

As soon as I send it, my anxiety gets the better of me, and I quickly swipe up to delete it, but then I see bubbles appear underneath it and I still.

>Paige: I's drunk to escape mi day.

A smile falls across my lips at her jumbled text, then a frown sets in when I realize what she's said, *to escape her day.*

>Giorgio: What happened?

>Paige: French penis

Not sure what that means. I'm going to assume it has something to do with her ex-husband.

> Giorgio: That explains a lot.

> Paige: They shuck with there stupidt accents.

I can just imagine she is typing away furiously on her phone; I can feel her anger coming through.

> Giorgio: Can an Italian man help?

> Paige: U accent is

Is what?

> Paige: Mayb I feel for a a French 1 becus I hated the Italian 1.

> Paige: Italian remindded me of U.

Oh.

> Paige: Ignore me ims drunk.

> Giorgio: You're hard to ignore.

I shouldn't have said that; she's obviously going through something heavy, just as I am. Dredging up the past isn't going to help the situation. Maybe it's best I leave her to it. She doesn't need me adding baggage to her already overloaded plate.

> Paige: U found it eazy years ago.

Shit. Like I said, I shouldn't have brought up the past, not while she is in a fragile headspace.

> Giorgio: Like I said, I have many regrets.

Paige: like finding ur siss with your fiancée. LOL.

Paige: fuk that's mean. Soz,

Giorgio: It's true though.

Giorgio: I've just found out they have fled to Greece together.

Paige: 2gether

Giorgio: Yeah

Paige: Shit, that's bed

Giorgio: No one knows they are together. It's a secret. I couldn't out them.

Paige: That's nise. I'm sorry

Paige: sshhh I wont say

This makes me smile.

Giorgio: Thankfully my brother announced he's going to be a dad this morning, taking the heat off me

Paige: congrats

Giorgio: Yeah, that's helped keep Mamma from stressing about my love life. Except I've had to hear all day how excited she is to finally have grandchildren, she thought after last night, all hope was lost. That this might be her only chance

Paige: Ouch

Giorgio: Italian mammas

Paige: LOL

Paige: That's not as bed as my day.

Giorgio: What happened?

Paige: Meditation with ex.

She went and meditated with him? Weird. Maybe it's an American thing.

Paige: and lawyers

Oh, she means mediation.

Paige: he fond out we not married

Giorgio: You're not married?

I thought she said she was married.

Paige: No he forget to fill papers

Paige: I told him 2 do it so many times

I burst out laughing; what a moron.

Giorgio: Guessing he isn't happy about this.

Paige: No. He blew a beret offs his head

Giorgio: He was wearing a beret?

Paige: No. That was a joke.

Giorgio: Good one.

I smile down at my phone as I type.

Paige: I'm hilarios when dunk

Paige: we go back in a week cuz they didn't know we wernt married

Giorgio: Wouldn't that be your job as a divorce lawyer to know if your client is married or not?

Paige: yep

Paige: he's not happy

Giorgio: His fault

Paige: Right?

Giorgio: That's why you're out releasing stress.

Paige: Yep

Paige: Hey can I asks u something?

Giorgio: Sure

Paige: You're rich, right?

Um, not sure what that has to do with anything, but I'll go along, she's drunk.

Giorgio: I'm doing okay, yes.

Paige: OK for rich peple? Or Normal peple?

Giorgio: What's your question?

Paige: Im rich now to. Its weird

That's not at all what I thought she was going to say.

Paige: Im rich, rich. Not sure how that is to u but it's loads 4 me

Paige: Soz. Rich peple don't talk $$$

Why am I finding this adorable?

> Paige: I now have loads my ex dosnt should I give him our home and restaurant?

> Giorgio: Do you want them?

> Paige: No

> Paige: I don't need the crappy apartment. But my girls think I need to be petty.

> Giorgio: Do you want to be petty?

> Paige: yes and no

> Paige: I want him gone more

> Giorgio: Sounds like you know your answer, then.

> Paige: My friends think he needs to be taught a lesson.

Maybe he does. The man is an idiot for letting her go.

Giorgio: The lesson should be that he lost you. If he cares more about the material things than losing you, then that's your answer.

> Paige: I ahte him.

> Paige: He broke our future

> Paige: Now im alone and don't know what to do

> Giorgio: You're not alone you have your family and friends and now me

> Paige: You left me alone once

My stomach sinks.

> Giorgio: And I regret it.

> Paige: Not enough to find me

She's right. I wanted to but didn't because I thought too much time had slipped between us.

> Giorgio: I know.

> Paige: Its good to chat to u

> Giorgio: It's good chatting with you too

> Giorgio: I'll be here whenever you need it.

> Paige: Same

> Paige: Can I ask u sumthing?

> Giorgio: Sure.

> Paige: R u Ok about being an uncle now youre not getting married?

> Paige: I remember you said you're gonna b an uncle

> Paige: And I remember u always wanted kidz

Did I? I don't remember that.

> Giorgio: I'm so happy for them. He's going to make the best papa.

> Giorgio: And I'll be the best uncle.

> Paige: Did you still want kidz?

> Giorgio: I always saw my life with them in it, but now I'm not sure. Uncle Gio has a good ring to it.

> Giorgio: What about you?

> Paige: Yes but my ex never wanted them

> Paige: Not sure if it will happen now

> Giorgio: You're still young.

My stomach sours at the thought of Paige dating again. I don't have a claim to her. She isn't mine anymore.

> Paige: yes but eww dating

This makes me chuckle.

> Paige: Having 2 start over again

She's right. How long until Mamma starts setting me up again?

> Giorgio: Don't need a man to have a baby. You can do it by yourself instead?

> Paige: maybe never thought of that

> Giorgio: Do you think you will ever marry again?

> Paige: didn't get marry the first time. LOL

I laugh at her joke.

> Paige: no and u?

> Giorgio: My family will hate it, but I don't think so.

> Paige: baggage sucks

> Giorgio: Yeah, it does.

> Giorgio: Can I tell you something?

> Paige: Of course, Bestie

Bestie? What the?

> Giorgio: I feel relief that I was able to get out of the engagement

> Paige: Oh

Giorgio: That's bad isn't it?

Paige: did you not love her

How do I answer this?

Giorgio: It was more about making my parents happy.

Paige: Oh

Paige: They were pressuring you to get married?

Giorgio: My father has been sick

Paige: Is he ok

Giorgio: Yeah, he's okay.

Paige: that's good

Paige: Did she not make u happy?

Giorgio: I'd convinced myself that she did.

Is it wrong that I'm talking to my ex about this? *You were kids when you dated, it was such a long time ago.* That is true.

Giorgio: She was independent, she didn't beg for any of my time, she loved a red carpet.

Paige: Most actresses do

My brows pull together.

Giorgio: How did you know?

Silence falls between us.

Paige: I saw online

This makes me smile.

> Paige: It was after the funeral. I curious. It had been years

Giorgio: I did the same.

> Paige: U did?

Giorgio: I saw you were married

> Paige: I saw u were engaged tp the most beautiful woman

Giorgio: It was her job to look like that.

> Paige: She stunning.

> Paige: You looked good together.

Giorgio: Looks can be deceiving.

> Paige: I know.

> Paige: Do you regret her?

I let out a heavy sigh because I don't know what I feel.

Giorgio: No. What I do regret is the embarrassment. That I didn't see the signs. Who knew about them? Was everyone laughing behind my back?

> Paige: I get it. My own staff was sleeping with my husband. Every day I walk into restuarant and no one tell me. How could they stand there an knowing what he was doing behind my back.

Giorgio: I'm sorry.

> Paige: I'm sorry for u 2 it was your sister not some random

Giorgio: But you loved your husband

Paige: I did

Giorgio: It sucks

Paige: It does

Paige: U think it gets easier?

Giorgio: Hopefully

Paige: I don't know what2 do anymore

Paige: My life is wide open. I have so much freedom yet I feel isolated I'm on this island by myself

It hurts my heart hearing her say this. Wish I could give her a big hug.

Giorgio: I'm here

Paige: U R

Paige: Thnx 4 listening

Giorgio: Thanks for the free therapy

Paige: Anytime

Giorgio: Same goes for you too

Giorgio: Night

Paige: Night

13

PAIGE

"I'm surprised this is what you want to do," my lawyer exclaims. "He deserves a fire poker to the balls, but he is right, my inheritance has set me up. I don't need that crappy apartment or the restaurant, which are nothing like I envisioned, it was all him."

"Just because you got a good inheritance doesn't mean you don't deserve your half of what you built together."

"If only it was what I had wanted to build. Michael was very adamant that it had to be a French restaurant because he hated Italian food. I thought it might be fun to fuse French and Italian together. That caused a huge fight, and, in the end, I gave in to his demands because it was easier to, rather than fight. I know if I hadn't got this inheritance, I would have ended up being miserable, resented the hell out of him and probably would have stayed because there was no other option."

Abigail nods in understanding. "What are your plans, then?"

I shrug my shoulders. "For the first time in my life, I have nothing planned. I don't know. I've been given freedom, and that is scary when you have had everything controlled for so long."

Abigail smiles. "As cliché as it sounds, the world is your oyster."

Her comment makes me chuckle. It's the truth though; the world is my oyster, and I have to work out what I want it to be.

"What I wouldn't give to spend the summer in Italy," she says, giving me a wink.

Giorgio's face filters through my mind. I didn't remember half of our chat the other night. My head was sore the next morning and when I woke up, I thought I'd dreamed it, so I opened my phone to check and reread all the messages. There was a lot. I really let it all out, which is kind of embarrassing, but he was super honest with me, too. I was surprised by his comments saying he was relieved that his ex cheated on him so that he wouldn't have to go through with the wedding. That's sad that he would have married her, knowing he wasn't in love with her just to make his family happy. Sacrificing your happiness for others, while it sounds noble, isn't. The only person who loses in that situation is you. I'm sure his parents wouldn't want him to sacrifice his happiness for them.

It's kind of weird that I'm even talking to Giorgio again after all this time, but if I'm being honest, it's hardly like fifteen years has passed, the ease in which we have been able to slip back into our friendship is astonishing. But that's all it will ever be, friendship. It's nice having someone to talk to about all this that isn't Smith or my parents or even the girls. I love them all, but they are too close to it. *No.* If I go to Italy in the summer, I will not be going to see him. There will be no trips down memory lane physically between us. It's best when there's an ocean between us, where he is kept far, far away. I'm not emotionally equipped to deal with Giorgio in the flesh, my walls are too cracked for that.

"It does sound nice, but the reason for me going is no longer there," I tell her, emotion making my voice crack.

She gives me a small, understanding smile. "Well, this is it. He's already signed his side, now you need to sign your side of the paperwork, and it's all done."

I take her pen and sign goodbye to my old life, and with a couple of quick strokes, it's done.

"Hopefully, this will simmer his anger toward you, and you don't have to worry about Michael bothering you ever again."

I don't like the person Michael has turned into, or maybe he has always been like that, and I've been too blinded by love to notice.

"Fingers crossed we can move on and put this all behind us."

"Good, now go out and celebrate, you deserve it," she says as we stand up, shake hands, and she wishes me luck on my new journey.

A sense of calm floats over me as I step out of the office, my back straightens, and I feel my confidence start to come back. I always thought if Michael and I ever broke up that I would be a heartbroken mess, and don't get me wrong, I have been, but somehow, I've found an inner strength I didn't know I possessed. Maybe it's the financial freedom that's helped, maybe it's that Michael doesn't have any control over me anymore, or maybe I'm back on the path I should have been on before getting married.

I suck in a deep breath before pushing the glass doors open and stepping out onto the busy street as a newly single woman. It's lunchtime and the crowds have swollen as they all busily try to get to where they are going. I head into the crowd and walk straight into someone, bouncing off their hard chest.

"I'm so sorry," I say to the stranger; I was obviously in my own little world and didn't see them. As I look up, familiar blue eyes stare back at me. Ice runs through my veins when I see my ex-husband standing before me, not looking very happy. What the hell is he doing here? "Leave me alone, Michael," I say as I try to sidestep him, not in the mood for his theatrics. He reaches out and grabs my arm, gripping me tightly. My brows pull together as pain shoots up my arm. "Ouch, you're hurting me," I moan.

"Look at you," he says, disgust dripping from his words, "walking out with a smug smile on your face, thinking you've won."

Won what?

"I gave you everything you wanted," I spit back.

"Because you think I'm a charity. I don't need your pity, Paige," he sneers.

This man is unbelievable. His ego is hurt because I gave him everything.

"I can't fucking win with you. You have a house, so you won't be on the streets and a business. Why can't you be happy with that?" I scream at him.

"Because you have so much more."

"You could have had more, too, but you chose to stick your dick in your employees instead. That's not my fault. You ruined us, Michael, you," I say, pushing back at him.

"You think you're too good now, don't you?" He hisses as his grip tightens even more.

"You're hurting me," I say, trying to tug my arm from his.

"You're hurting me, Paige. You've broken my heart and ripped it right out of my chest," he screams.

"I broke your heart? You're the one that ripped out my heart and stomped all over it. You constantly cheated on me throughout our entire marriage."

"It was just sex, Paige. Jesus, how many times do I have to tell you? I loved you. You were my wife."

What in the hell logic is that? Having sex with random women who aren't your wife isn't loving me. *Bullshit.* He wanted his cake and now, he can have all the cake he wants.

"What you did isn't love," I argue back as people stare and push past us on the busy sidewalk.

"You're so fucking hard to talk to sometimes, Paige."

"If I'm so hard to talk to then contact my lawyer," I tell him, trying to pull away, but he grabs me again. "Michael," I scream.

"Hey, man, she doesn't like that," a young guy stops, noticing what's happening, and glares at Michael.

"Are you fucking him? Is he your new man?" Michael screams at me.

"Hey, don't talk to her like that," the guy interjects as he steps closer to my ex.

"Fuck off, this is my wife. I can talk to her any way I damn well like," he snips at the stranger.

The man looks down at me, and I shake my head. "Ex, he's my ex-husband."

"Doesn't look like she wants to be anywhere near you," the stranger states, moving even closer, making Michael take a couple of steps back and let go of my arm. I move away quickly and start rubbing the bruises I can feel forming under my skin.

"This isn't over, Paige, you will listen to me," Michael warns as he storms off into the crowd.

"Are you okay?" the young man asks.

Am I? I don't know. I'm shaking, tears are welling in my eyes, and my chest is tight.

"Where do you need to go? I can walk you there," the guy states.

"My lawyers are here," I say, pointing behind me. He nods and escorts me back into the building, then he asks reception to call Abigail. That's when I start to crumble, the shock setting in. The stranger catches me as I stumble and makes me take a seat.

Thirty minutes later, my brother arrives to escort me home. When I see him walking through the doors, I stand up and rush over to him. He wraps his arms around me and hugs me tightly as I break down again.

"Did he hurt you?" he asks, looking down at me.

I shake my head. "Just bruises on my arm." I feel him stiffen against me as anger radiates from him while he inspects my arm.

"Let's get you home, where you are safe," he says, escorting me from the office.

"Say it, I know you're dying to," I say once we're in his car, beating him to the punch.

"Damn right I'll say it. He could have hurt you, Paige," he says as his hands grip the steering wheel tightly.

"I know, okay? I get it," I argue back.

Smith takes a couple of deep breaths beside me. "You're my sister, Paige. I want to protect you."

Turning my head, I look over at him, and I can see the stress of the day on his face. "I know you do. I'm still shocked that he did it."

"I'm not," my brother grumbles.

He's concerned for you, give him a break. "Guess I'm naïve then. I thought I knew this man. I was supposed to spend forever with him. You're going to have to give me a moment to realize he's nothing like I thought he was."

"Anger can manifest. He is unhinged, you need a protective order."

Okay, I get it now. The person standing before me today was not the man I used to love.

"Why does he hate me so much? I didn't cheat," I ask my brother as I try to hold back my tears. That man doesn't deserve them.

"Because he's a controlling son of a bitch and he knows he no longer has control over you. That you don't need him anymore and that thought has sent him mad," he explains.

"Was he really that controlling of me? Why did no one tell me?" I ask him.

"Paige, you loved him. You would never have listened to any of us," he answers.

Does love make you that delusional? I thought I was a levelheaded girl.

"I didn't think I was stupid though?"

"Hey, you weren't stupid. He didn't want you to see who he truly was, he's a master manipulator," he adds.

"I feel stupid. How did I not see him cheating on me with my staff or whoever else he cheated on me with? There would have been signs."

"Paige, seriously, the guy was a professional at it. I'm sure he's done this his entire life," my brother explains.

"What if it happens again?" That's what I'm truly afraid of. What if he's broken me and now, I'm so damaged that I can't see red flags, even if they are waving in front of me?

"We won't let it happen again," he states.

"How can you be sure?"

"You have to have faith in yourself that you can spot these assholes from a mile away."

My shoulders slump. "See, that's the thing, I don't trust myself," I confess.

My brother looks over at me and gives me a small smile before returning his eyes back to the road. "You need to give yourself time to heal."

The thought of jumping into a relationship again frightens me, but so does dating. The whole awkward stage, working out what the other person is about, sleeping with someone new; ew, this is all too much for me.

"Things will get better, I promise. It hasn't been long and look how far you have come already. Imagine how good your life will be in three, six- or twelve-months' time. You will be saying *Michael who?*"

Maybe he's right. Can I fast forward to that moment?

14

GIORGIO

My phone buzzes, and it's a message from Paige, which makes me smile. I find myself looking forward to hearing from her; the time difference sucks though, as it's usually when I'm going to bed or when I'm waking up that she writes.

> Paige: Today sucked!

> Giorgio: What happened? I thought you just had to sign some papers.

> Paige: Yeah, until my ex grabbed me and started yelling at me in the street.

What the fuck? I sit up in my bed as anger radiates off me. Who the fuck does this guy think he is? Why would he touch her like that?

> Giorgio: What the fuck. Do you need me to come over there and tell him to leave you alone?

Because I would, I would hop on the next plane to New York if she asked me to. *That's not strange, is it?* Maybe it is.

> Paige: Appreciate the sentiment, but Smith has it covered. I've filed for a protective order against him.

Thank goodness.

Giorgio: That's good. Hopefully, that will make him think twice.

Giorgio: What the hell was he thinking grabbing you like that?

> Paige: He wasn't. And that's the scary thing.

> Paige: You should have seen the hate in his eyes, it was scary.

Giorgio: Are you okay?

> Paige: I don't know. I'm pretty shaken up.

> Paige: I'm confused too. Why does he hate me?

> Paige: He cheated. I was a good wife. Yet now I'm the villain.

Giorgio: Guess he's realized what he's lost.

By the sounds of it, he never deserved her in the first place.

> Paige: That's on him. He made those choices.

Giorgio: Maybe he thought he would never get caught.

> Paige: What a dick!

> Paige: Men suck!

Giorgio: Hopefully not all men.

> Paige: Guess there are some okay men out there.

> Paige: Enough about my disastrous life, how about you?

Giorgio: Yours is much more serious than mine. You're sure you're safe staying in New York?

> Paige: Where would I go?

Giorgio: Europe? Italy maybe.

> Paige: My life is here.

I want to say *what life*, but that sounds mean because she does have her family and friends there.

Giorgio: True. What's your next step then?

> Paige: I have no idea. I don't have a job anymore, so I guess I might need to look into that.

Giorgio: You thinking of opening up a new restaurant?

> Paige: I could. This time it could be something I want to do.

Giorgio: And what is that?

> Paige: Italian.

Giorgio: Good choice.

> Paige: Of course, you'd say that.

Giorgio: Because it's the best cuisine in the world.

> Paige: It is.

Giorgio: See you need to come to Italy to get ideas for your restaurant.

> Paige: I thought we were spitballing ideas here.

Giorgio: We are, not my fault mine are awesome.

Paige: LOL

Paige: I have to speak to Lucia's financial advisor. She has left me in charge of all these businesses that she's invested in. Maybe I need to learn about them.

Giorgio: That's a good start. I know a vineyard you can work at.

Paige: Which one?

Paige: Oh. Yes, there is that one.

Stop trying to get her to Italy for your own selfish reasons. I want to catch up with an old friend. Why is that so hard to believe?

Paige: Not sure when I'll get back there. It's too soon.

Giorgio: I get it.

Paige: I should go, but I don't want to have to pack up her things. It doesn't feel right.

Giorgio: There's no right or wrong way. Whatever your comfort level is, is what's best.

Paige: Thanks for understanding.

Paige: She did have other homes that don't have the same memories as the Florence estate, maybe I could check them out.

Giorgio: Any in Rome?

Paige: Funny enough, she has an apartment there. I don't remember where though, I'll have to look it up.

Giorgio: If you need a tour guide…

What are you doing?

> Paige: I'm sure the paparazzi would have a field day over that.

Shit, she's right. They don't even know Giada and I have broken up yet.

Giorgio: You're right, they would.

> Paige: Any news?

Here she is, stepping up and creating a new life for herself, and I am still letting my ex and sister set the rules. I'm a fucking coward.

Giorgio: From their socials, they are having a great time on holidays.

Giorgio: And I guess my hands are tied, I can't out them.

> Paige: True. Can't you do your side of the story without outing them? I'm not sure how all that stuff works.

Giorgio: If only it was that simple, my PR people need to talk to hers and so on.

> Paige: Why the delay?

Giorgio: As modern as Italy is, not all parts are.

> Paige: Oh, I see.

Giorgio: And as much as I love my parents, I'm not sure how they are going to react to my sister's news.

> Paige: Especially with your father's health the way it is.

Giorgio: Exactly. Also, Giada is worried that once she comes out with Allegra that she might lose her job, her contracts, everything.

Giorgio: The paparazzi and gossips are going to have a field day with this once it comes out. Guess it's the calm before the storm, and if I'm being honest, I'd rather the calm.

Paige: I can't imagine what it would be like breaking up publicly. It was hard enough doing it privately.

Giorgio: It's going to suck. I guess that's why I haven't pushed Giada for a joint statement.

Giorgio: Guess I should rip the Band-Aid off soon.

Paige: Only when you're ready. There's no hurry unless you're dating already.

Giorgio: Hell no. I'm not ready for that. Are you?

Paige: Hell no, me either.

Giorgio: We're a great pair, aren't we?

Paige: I'm not looking forward to getting out there again.

Giorgio: Me either. I'm happy as I am.

Paige: Me too. Don't have to answer to anyone. I can sit and read a book all day long if I want to. I can watch whatever show I want.

Giorgio: Guess that's where I'm lucky, I could do that anyway as we didn't live together.

Paige: Makes the breakup easier, you can just ship her things to her.

Giorgio: She never left anything here.

Paige: Nothing?

> Giorgio: No. All her wardrobe was at her place, she popped in and then went home again.

> Paige: Wow. How did you miss those raging red flags? LOL

> Giorgio: I see them now, but I didn't then. I thought I'd hit the jackpot with her wanting to keep our lives so separate.

> Giorgio: We were both so busy I never thought it was wrong.

> Paige: It's not wrong, just different.

> Giorgio: Certainly was. Guess that backfired on me.

> Paige: No, she just wasn't the right woman for you.

She's not wrong there; I was the entirely wrong sex.

> Paige: Shit, I've just seen the time. I better let you go.

> Giorgio: Okay. I like talking to you.

> Paige: Me too. I look forward to our chats.

She does? Why does that make me happy?

> Giorgio: Okay, I'll speak to you tomorrow, stay safe.

> Paige: I will.

And with that, I throw my phone onto the bed and stretch before an idea pops into my head and I pick it back up.

> Giorgio: I'm wanting to announce our breakup.

> Giada. No, why?

Giorgio: Because I'm not sunning myself in Mykonos.

Giada: Fair

Giorgio: I feel like I'm walking on eggshells here in Rome.

Giada: I'm sorry I've left you there to deal with all this. But please, give me a month. I know I don't have the right to ask this favor of you. I have a big deal that I want to close and then I promise we can announce it, together.

I don't want to wait that long.

Giorgio: Fine.

Giada: Thank you.

Giorgio: Why did you not tell me?

Giorgio: Why her?

Giada: I was scared.

Giada: Also confused.

Giada: I've never had feelings for a woman before, not like this.

Giada: I had no idea your sister was into women either.

Giada: Has she been hiding herself from her family?

Giorgio: Yes.

Giorgio: We love her, she knows that doesn't she?

Giada: Yeah. She's worried about your parents.

Giorgio: I understand, but they love her.

> Giada: Give her time.
>
> Giada: I'm sorry, Gio.

Her apology surprises me.

> Giada: Everything we had was real. I need you to know that.

I didn't realize how much I needed to hear that. It's as if the tightness in my chest has been released.

> Giada: I know we didn't love each other, but I had strong feelings of like. Strong feelings.

Guess I did too.

> Giada: Can I be honest?

Giorgio: Sure.

> Giada: It wasn't until things happened between Allegra and I that I realized what love could feel like.

Oh.

> Giada: Too much honesty?

Giorgio: No. It's fine. I wish you had told me sooner.

> Giada: Wish I had too. I was scared. Felt like the train had already left the station.

Giorgio: I would have stopped it.

> Giada: I know you would have.

Giorgio: So you love Allegra?

> Giada: I do.

> Giada: A lot.

Wow.

> Giorgio: Does she know this?

> Giada: Yes.

That's good.

> Giorgio: And your plans are?

> Giada: We don't know.

> Giorgio: May I suggest honesty to the people closest to you as a good start.

> Giada: I'll tell her to talk to her family.

> Giada: You're a good guy, Gio. You deserve happiness and love.

> Giorgio: Can't see that happening anytime soon.

> Giada: Please don't let my baggage mess you up.

> Giorgio: I'm tender, that's all.

> Giada: You're a catch, Gio.

> Giorgio: Look after Allegra. Tell her to call Mamma.

> Giada: Will do.

> Giada: Take care of yourself.

> Giorgio: You too.

> Giada: We'll talk in a month.

> Giorgio: Okay.

15

PAIGE

"Come on, let's go out. I need to leave this apartment. My brother is acting like my jailer," I moan to Callie and Savannah as we sit and watch nothing on TV while sipping our wine.

"He's being protective," Callie states.

I know he is, but it's suffocating. "I get it. He wants to protect me. But does he really think Michael is going to try anything again? It's been a week and nothing."

"Do you have any idea the number of women attacked by their partner or an ex that I deal with on a daily basis? I don't want my sister to be a statistic," Smith snips at me.

I can see the anguish of those cases on his face.

I let out a heavy sigh. "I'm not saying you don't. What I am saying is I'm a grown-ass woman and I am going crazy here. I haven't even had a chance to celebrate my divorce or whatever the hell it is." I stand up and plead my case. "Why am I letting that douchebag dictate my life still? I've had enough."

My brother's face softens. "He's attacked you in broad daylight, Paige, not once, but twice."

"Everything is signed, he got what he wanted. Things have settled down. I'm sure his anger has subsided," I reassure him.

He doesn't look convinced.

"Would it make you feel better if we went to one of my clubs?" Savannah suggests.

Smith raises a brow.

"I've made sure security in all my clubs and bars know he's blacklisted, they have his photo and name, he won't be getting in anywhere," Savannah explains to Smith.

His brows pull together as he contemplates that bit of news. "Would feel safer if you had that protective order on him," he grumbles.

Yes, I know; I'm an idiot for not listening to everyone's advice. And yes, I should have done something about it when he accosted me outside the lawyer's office, but I think he's angry and hurt that I left him. Is that right? Hell no, it isn't, but we were planning on spending the rest of our lives together. I loved him, and, in his own way, he loved me at some point. I honestly wanted the entire mess behind me, and I thought the order would hinder that.

"I'm over worrying about him. It's done. We are finished. He got what he wanted, end of story," I state angrily to my brother.

He huffs unhappily before turning to Savannah. "You really have him blacklisted in all your family's places?"

"Of course, that dick isn't allowed anywhere near Paige," she answers.

Smith nods in understanding.

"Smith, I don't need your permission to leave these four walls. I'm an adult, but I also don't want to worry you," I tell him.

I can see he is grappling with letting me go out, but in the end, he relents, "I'm sorry, Paige. I don't mean to be so protective. It's just …"

"You're not sorry, but that's why I love you," I say, walking over and giving him a hug. "I promise I'll be careful."

He grumbles a little more, but eventually, he lets me go and disappears from the living room to his bedroom to pout.

"Let's get ready to party. I need this so desperately," I tell my girls.

"No getting too drunk, just in case," Callie adds, not one hundred percent on board with the idea.

"Deal, now come on, let's go," I say excitedly.

We all quickly get ready and head on out; it feels good to be outside again. I've donned a little black dress, I have heels on, my makeup is on point, my hair is up in a fierce ponytail, and I'm feeling good.

When we arrive at one of Savannah's bars, we get escorted in and treated like royalty by the staff. We sit and chat for a while, then grab something to eat before moving on to one of her clubs.

We are escorted up to the VIP section upon arrival, bottles with sparklers attached to them continually arrive, the music is pumping, and I'm dancing my ass off and it feels so good. All the tension, stress, and emotions of the past couple of weeks are flowing out of my body. I feel alive. I can't remember the last time I went out and had fun without Michael checking up on me every two seconds. Then when I'd come home, he would accuse me of flirting with other men, all the while he was sleeping with the staff. *He's not your problem anymore.* I can flirt with whoever the hell I want to.

"I need to pee," I tell Callie, who is talking to some guy in a suit.

"I can come," she says.

I wave her away. "The toilets are just there," I say, pointing to them across the room. "You can see me from here, I'm fine," I assure her.

"Fine," she grumbles. She's as bad as my brother, but I still love her.

I head over to the bathrooms, do my business, and when I walk back out, a chill slides down my spine. Unwanted eyes land on me and make me feel icky. I turn around, wondering where the uncomfortableness is coming from, but no one is there. *You're being paranoid, Paige.*

I pull out my phone and decide to FaceTime Giorgio. It rings and rings, but he picks up eventually.

"*Pronto,*" he answers groggily. That's when I realize the man is in bed. He is sitting up, and the sheet has fallen, exposing his bare chest. My eyes zero in on every rippling muscle as I lick my lips hungrily.

Wow. Giorgio has grown since the last time I saw him without his shirt on. His dark hair is all messy from sleep and those chocolate eyes are puddles of cocoa.

"I'm sorry, I didn't check the time." I giggle.

"Paige?" he says, waking up fully.

"I wanted to show you that I'm out and about, getting my single life on, thought it might inspire you," I tell him.

"You're out clubbing?"

I nod while willing the sheet to fall further to reveal if he sleeps naked or not. What am I saying? He's a friend, an old friend, who needs my support, not me leering at him.

"Finally convinced Smith to let me out, look at me go," I tell him as I do a whoop and a shimmy, which makes him laugh.

"How much have you had to drink?"

"Not enough."

"You look like you're having fun though."

"I am. Do you have any idea how hard it is to flirt after being with someone for so long? It's awkward," I tell him.

His brows pull together as he scrubs his face. "You meet anyone nice?"

I shake my head. "I've had a dance with someone, but when he slid his hand over my ass, that was it for me," I confess.

Giorgio's mouth falls open in surprise. I know I told him I wasn't ready for anything with anyone just yet, and I realized that as soon as that guy touched me; it felt wrong.

"I'm not ready for anything like that."

He nods in understanding. "I'm proud of you for getting out and enjoying life."

His compliment warms me. "You should be doing this, too."

Giorgio rolls his eyes and huffs at me. "I know. I know. I'm probably an idiot for agreeing to the month after everything."

"You're a good guy, not an idiot," I say, giving him a wide smile.

"As long as it doesn't bite me in the ass." He groans.

"It won't," I try to reassure him, and that's when I feel a cold shiver down my spine as if eyes are on me again. I freeze.

"Paige?" Giorgio calls out.

"Sorry, just felt like …"

"Is that your new boyfriend?" Michael's breath slithers across my shoulders in the darkness. "Always knew you were a slut. Already found your next victim."

"Paige, fuck, get out of there," Giorgio screams down the phone.

I swallow and slowly turn around, and I'm surprised when I see him; he's dyed his blond hair black, but those blue eyes remain the same. "You shouldn't be here," I tell him as I try to edge away from him slowly.

"Probably not, but I needed to know if you were cheating on me. And you are. Do you have any idea how hard it was for me to watch you on that dance floor with that guy, watch him grope you, touch what is mine. Then watch you continue to flirt with numerous other men all night. And now I find you on the phone with another, sweet-talking him while he's in bed. And you have the audacity to call me a cheater," he sneers.

"Paige, Paige," I hear Giorgio calling out to me on the phone. My hand's dropped beside me and he's probably getting a nice view of the club's floor.

"You need to leave, Michael," I tell him seriously.

"Or what? You're going to get your brother to lock me up. It's not a crime to be here," he jeers at me.

"It is when you are continuously harassing me."

Michael bursts out laughing. "Harassing you? You wish. America is a free country, I can go anywhere I fucking like."

"You shouldn't have been able to get in," I mumble as I continue to try to move away from him.

"Oh, because you tried to ban me. Aw, that's so sweet, but you seem to forget that I know people, too, and some owe me a couple of favors." He chuckles manically.

Fuck.

"If you don't leave in three seconds, I'll scream," I tell him.

Those blue eyes narrow on me and his jaw locks into place before he reaches out and grabs me, placing his hand over my mouth and shoving me against the wall beside the bathrooms. I lose my grip on my phone.

"You listen and listen to me good. I'm never letting you go. You are mine and will always be mine." And seconds later, he is disappearing down a corridor just as Callie and Savannah come rushing over.

"Shit, Paige, are you okay?" Callie asks, seeing me standing there frozen.

"I'll get security onto it," Savannah says, rushing off.

"What did he do?" Callie commands.

Tears start to fall down my cheeks as the shock begins to wear off. "He's never going to let me go, Callie."

Her face falls as she pulls me into a tight hug.

"I'm never going to let that happen."

"He's everywhere. I don't know if you can stop him." I sob.

"I know. I'm sorry, I never thought ..." Callie's voice hitches.

She has nothing to feel sorry about; this is all on him.

Moments later, Savannah comes back to where we are huddled, bringing security with her, and starts to usher us out of the club.

"I can't believe one of my staff let him in. Just know, Paige, I will be dealing with him, swiftly," she says, escorting us into her town car that she organized for us with her personal driver. "I pride myself on my clubs being safe for women, and to have one of my staff let this happen to you is unforgivable. I'm so sorry, Paige."

I shake my head. "It's no one's fault except Michael's, he's gone crazy," I reassure her. She gives me a stern nod before stepping back and closing the door.

Callie and I sit quietly in the car, huddled together as we drive through the Manhattan streets. My stomach turns, knowing how angry my brother is going to be when I get home.

"Shit, my phone. I must have dropped it in the club. Fuck. Giorgio, he's going to be so worried," I curse.

"I'll text Savannah and let her know. Wait, who the hell is Giorgio?" Callie asks as she quickly types out a message to our friend.

Oh. Yeah, that's right, I haven't told her.

"Do you remember that guy I dated growing up in Italy?" I begin.

She nods. "The one who broke your heart and had a cute brother."

Of course, she remembers Luca. One summer, Callie came with me to Italy; we had the greatest time together. "Yeah, that one. He was at Lucia's funeral and gave his condolences."

"Really? Wow, that would have been a blast from the past. Does he look the same?"

I look up at her and grin.

"He looks better?"

I nod.

"And?" She looks at me expectantly.

"I freaked out and ran away from him at the funeral, then I came home and found Michael and somehow we've been chatting ever since," I explain to her.

"You've been chatting?"

"Yeah. We have a lot in common. I didn't know when I messaged him, that he had just found out his fiancée was cheating on him with his sister at his engagement party," I tell her.

"Wait, his sister and his fiancée?"

I nod.

"And you've been talking to him for weeks now?" she questions.

"Every day," I confess.

"Every day?" she says in surprise, her voice going up an octave.

"It's nothing like that," I warn her. "It's nice to talk to someone going through the same thing at the same time."

She shakes her head in bewilderment. "Wow, I had no idea."

"It's nothing, just you know, chatting. No flirting or anything."

"Right." She grins.

I shake my head.

"I thought you hated him?" Callie asks.

"I did. But that was a long time ago."

"True. Still, he broke your heart that summer." Her eyes narrow on me.

"We were kids," I say, but she's right; he devastated me.

"It took you a long time to date after him."

It was a dark time.

"I was on the phone with him when Michael attacked me, he's probably worried," I tell her.

"You think he recorded it? That would be great to show the judge for the restraining order," Callie adds, getting lost in her lawyer brain.

"I don't know, but do you think you could message him and let him know I'm okay?"

"Sure," she says, opening her phone, and I tell her his social media handle.

"Are you fricken serious, Paige? That's him?" She looks up at me. I nod. "Dammit, why can't any of the guys I dated as a teen look like a demigod?" She smiles as she opens the DMs and types out a message to him, letting him know that I'm safe and well, that I've lost my phone, and will be in touch when I find it or get a new one. "Wonder what his brother looks like." Callie grins as she scrolls down his feed until she finds him and clicks on his profile. "Oh man, he's hot, too. Oh, but he's married, and they are having a baby. Aw, that's nice. Wonder if they have any hot single Italian friends to set me up with," she muses before bursting out laughing. This is what I need to put the terror of the evening behind me, so we launch into a full-scale social media audit to see if either man has any hot friends.

"Thank fuck you're okay, Paige," my brother says as we walk into his apartment, and he hugs me tightly. "What the hell happened tonight? You girls were supposed to be looking after her," he yells at Callie.

She's about to yell back, except I push myself out of his arms. "How dare you."

He looks surprised at my venom.

"This is no one's fault but his. The man dyed his hair. He looked completely different. How would we have known he would be there? How did he know we were there?"

My brother rolls his eyes. "Because you girls posted it everywhere, all over your fucking social media," he replies angrily.

"We didn't tag the places," Callie adds.

"You don't think her ex-husband wouldn't know where you all hang out? He knows it's probably at one of Savannah's places. He's been to them all, he could have worked it out from the background," he explains.

Oh.

"I didn't think of that," I say quietly.

"No shit," he states.

"Would you back off? She didn't know this would happen. We are all in shock that he did this in such a public place. You think me or Savannah don't feel bad, but she was going to the toilet, she was just there," Callie explains.

"And yet he still was able to grab her," Smith bites.

"Enough. I will not have you blaming my friends," I say, pointing at him.

"You all promised me," he argues.

"I know, Smith," I yell at him as I start to cry again. "Never in my life did I think the man I thought I would spend the rest of my life with could harm me in any way." My brother starts to speak, but I shut it down quickly. "No, I do not want to hear your statistics about that right now. I want a shower. I need to wipe his touch from my skin. And then when I come back, we're going to have a stiff drink and work out what to do next with that psycho."

16

GIORGIO

> Callie: Paige lost her phone. She wanted you to know she's okay.
>
> Callie: If you need her, contact me.
>
> Giorgio: Thank you for letting me know.
>
> Giorgio: If she needs anything, please don't hesitate to contact me.

"What do you mean, you're leaving for New York?" Natalia asks.

"I have a work thing," I tell her as I shove my necessities into a bag. I'm not lying as I do have some meetings. They were going to be via Zoom, but now they can be in person.

"Are you seeing that girl?" she asks.

"What girl?" I answer. *Liar.* It's the entire reason I am furiously packing my bag. As soon as Paige's call went dead after I had to listen to her being attacked by her ex-husband, I called my pilot and told him I needed to be in New York as soon as possible.

"Your new friend. Is this a booty call?" my sister continues to question me.

"No. Are you absurd? I thought you, of all people, would understand the need to get out of my life for a moment." The line falls silent as she contemplates what I've said. I feel bad for twisting her words to use against her, but I need to get to New York to check on Paige. I can't get past her scream and the fear on her face when she saw him. I can't sit here and do nothing. I just need to see that she is okay with my own eyes, and maybe pay this ex-husband a visit; someone needs to put that little weasel in his place.

"Fine. Do you need a wing woman?" she asks.

"No." My answer comes out with more bite than I wanted it to.

"Wow, okay was just asking," she moans.

"I appreciate your support, but I have work; it's going to be heaps of meetings. It will be boring for you," I tell her.

"It's fricken New York, Gio, it won't be boring," she adds.

Urgh. I shouldn't have told her. Natalia loves New York, especially the parties and shopping; she's not going to take no for an answer.

"Fine. If you want, you can come, but you need to be ready in an hour, or I will leave without you," I tell her firmly.

"You're the best, Gio. I promise I'll be ready to go. Meet you at the airport?" she asks.

"Yes, I'll see you there." I sigh before hanging up. This is going to be a disaster. I'm hoping she'll be too distracted by New York to worry about what I'm doing there. I hope Paige is going to be okay with me turning up; *that's not weird, is it?* I'll only bother her for five minutes and then I'll be gone; I just need to know she's okay. I can't stop seeing the venom in that man's eyes when he looked at her. He's the cheater, he made her leave. None of this is her fault.

Yet his eyes said otherwise.

"You made it on time." I grin as my sister strides onto the jet.

Her dark eyes narrow on me. "Told you so," she states, taking a seat beside me. The hostess brings over my whisky and a glass of champagne to my sister. "Cheers, brother, to having fun in New York," she says, clinking our glasses together.

"This is a work trip, Nat," I remind her.

She shoos my concern away. "I know, but not every single day."

I let out a sigh. "No, you're right, not every day."

This makes her happy. "Good, this can be like a brother-sister bonding trip. I can't remember the last time the two of us went away with each other. It was always you and Luca."

My brows pull together; I'm sure we've traveled together before, haven't we?

"See, you can't even remember when."

"I swear we have," I tell her.

She shakes her head. "Nope, never. I know this because Allegra never invited me on any of her trips, so I always had to go with friends."

Now I feel bad.

"You were busy, I get it, but thanks for letting me tag along, even though I know you didn't want me to," she adds.

Aw, come on, now I feel like a real ass.

"You're right. We haven't had a Gio and Nat trip before, so I promise I'll make time for you."

Her face lights up with a big smile and my cold heart flickers to life and starts to thud in my chest.

My phone buzzes in my pocket, and I quickly pull it out and stare down at the screen.

> Callie: What are your intentions with my friend?

What does that mean? I don't have any intentions toward Paige other than being a friend. *Liar.* What? No, I'm not. We are old friends getting reacquainted. Before we were lovers, we were friends, and that is all we are now, nothing more. *Liar.* Just because I think she's beautiful doesn't mean I want anything with her; the poor woman is being stalked by her ex-husband, she does not need her childhood ex-boyfriend sniffing around. What she needs is an old friend for support. *Liar. Most friends don't hop on a plane and fly halfway across the world.* A good one does.

I think I'm going insane because I'm now arguing with myself. Shaking off my thoughts, I type out a message back to Callie.

> Giorgio: I have no intentions with Paige other than being friends.
>
> Giorgio: My life is complicated. I'm a workaholic, and my engagement has imploded.
>
> Giorgio: No one knows it's over, so I'm keeping this huge secret from everyone except my family. While my ex-fiancée is sunbathing her way through Europe with my sister.
>
> Giorgio: It's been nice talking to someone who doesn't want anything from me other than my ears.
>
> Callie: Well, I'm glad we've cleared that up.

Her friend thinks I'm insane.

> Callie: You broke her heart last time, just didn't want you to do it again.
>
> Giorgio: We were kids, and I was a fool. She had her life ahead of her, all her hopes and dreams, I never wanted to get in the way of that.
>
> Callie: Admirable, but maybe you could have told her that instead of fucking her enemy.

She's right. I should have been a man about how I felt, which was that I could see myself spending the rest of my life with her, but we were so young. And I knew she would have put everything aside for me. I didn't want that for her. I didn't think I deserved that sacrifice.

> Giorgio: Think it was inevitable that I was going to break her heart, but like I said, I was a fool and thought I was doing the right thing.
>
> Callie: So, you're saying that you dated her nemesis so she would move on from you?
>
> Giorgio: In my eighteen-year-old mind, it made sense.
>
> Callie: Did you ever tell her that?
>
> Giorgio: No, I thought that would hurt more.
>
> Callie: You're probably right.
>
> Callie: She's asleep now, the night catching up with her. I'll keep you updated if you'd like.
>
> Giorgio: I'd like that, thanks.

Callie asked some tough questions. I'm no saint. Did I think Paige deserved to live her life without being attached to me and the scrutiny it brought? Yes. But I was always swayed by boobs and blow jobs, I'm no hero.

We've landed and are heading to my apartment in Tribeca, which has great views of the Hudson and the city. It's been a while since I've been back in the city, but I've always enjoyed it.

> Giorgio: Hey, I'm in New York, had a last-minute meeting. Was wanting to see her or is that too much?
>
> Callie: You're in New York?

Oh shit. I fucked up, didn't I? Now I'm being the stalker.

> Giorgio: I'm here with my sister for work, thought I'd say hi. But totally understand if you don't want me to see her.

Callie goes radio silent for a little while before getting back to me.

> Callie: I think it might be what she needs to take her mind off things. You want to come over to her brothers for dinner, say about seven? Bring your sister if you want.

Dinner? I wasn't expecting that.

> Giorgio: Okay, that sounds great. Let me know what to bring.

> Callie: Yourself, wine, and maybe flowers. I'll send the address.

> Giorgio: Okay, I'll see you then.

"I'm catching up with friends for dinner at their place if you're interested," I ask my sister.

"Aw, thanks, but I'm catching up with my own friends. There's a new hot club they want me to try," she tells me excitedly.

I'm relieved that she doesn't want to go, but also, I wouldn't mind the support. I'm nervous about seeing Paige again; I know we caught up at the funeral, but she wasn't in a good way to fully catch up then. *She's not in a good way at the moment, either.* I really need to work on my timing.

My driver drops me off in front of Smith's apartment uptown in Chelsea. I grab my flowers and wine, get out of the car, and head toward his apartment. I message Callie like she asked me to when I arrive. She instructs me to stand in front of the door and when I'm in place, she presses the buzzer, which lets me in. Not sure why there's all this cloak and dagger, maybe it has to do with her ex watching, or she's just fucking with me. When I reach their floor and step out of the elevator, a beautiful blonde is standing outside waiting for me.

"You must be Giorgio," she asks.

"And you must be Callie," I say, greeting her warmly with a kiss on each cheek. She then inspects my flowers and wine and says, "Nice choice," then proceeds to open the door to the apartment and asks me to follow. We step right in, and I realize it is quite a bit smaller than my apartment. We round the corner and I see Paige sitting with another beautiful blonde and her brother, Smith. They all stop and turn toward us, and I see Paige's eyes grow wide.

"Thought I would introduce our special guest tonight, all the way from Italy, Giorgio Fiorenzo," Callie states to the shocked room.

"Gio?" Smith says as he gets up to greet me. "What the hell are you doing here?"

"This is for you," I answer, handing him the bottle of wine.

"Thanks, man. Wow. How the … what …?" he splutters, trying to work out how an old friend he hasn't seen in fifteen years is suddenly in his apartment on the other side of the world.

"I'm here for work but thought I would come by and say hi," I explain to him.

"This is fantastic. I missed seeing you at Lucia's, thank you for showing up with your family. We really needed to stay in touch."

"Yeah, we do. Need to get you back to Italy again," I say.

"I'd love to. Work has been keeping me busy."

"Saving the world," Callie adds, rolling her eyes as she walks past the two of us and takes a seat beside a still-shocked Paige.

"Paige, these are for you," I say, walking over to where she is seated.

"Oh," she says, getting up reluctantly.

This was a mistake. I'm not sure if she is happy to see me. What the hell was I thinking?

"I wanted to see if you were okay," I mumble.

Her brows rise at my confession as she reaches out and takes the flowers from me, our fingers touching and the old spark we once had igniting again as electricity rushes up my arms; she must feel it, too, as she jerks her hands away from me.

"They are beautiful, Paige," the other blonde states, giving her friend a not-too-discreet elbow.

"Oh yes, they are stunning, and my favorite, pink peonies. Thank you so much," Paige says, shaking her head as if to clear the last bit of the surprise.

"How about I put them in some water? Savannah, wanna help me?" Callie asks the other girl.

"Sure. Hey, Smith, do you have any vases in this place?" Savannah turns and asks him.

"I don't know." He shrugs.

"Do you mind helping us then?" Callie grumbles.

Smith looks between the girls and Paige and me and then back to them. "I need another beer anyway. Hey, Gio, want a beer?" he asks.

"Yeah, sounds good." I nod in agreement as the three of them disappear from the living room into the kitchen.

"You're here?" Paige says, looking at me.

"I am."

"How?" Those chocolate eyes widen with disbelief.

"By plane."

She chuckles, realizing her question. "I'm shocked to see you."

"Surprise," I say, giving her jazz hands. What the hell? I've never done such a ridiculous thing in my life, but at least it makes her laugh.

"I can't believe you are here."

"You can touch me, I'm real." As soon as the words come out of my mouth, I realize how dirty they sound and embarrassment spreads like wildfire all over my body. The next thing I know, she is stepping toward me and hugging me.

"I'm so sorry you had to hear that last night." She buries her face into my chest. My arms wrap around her tightly and a sense of calm and relief fills me.

"I was so worried, Paige," I confess to her.

She looks up at me with glassy eyes. "I know. I lost my phone, and I couldn't message you. And I was so worried that you thought something happened to me and there was no way of contacting you and …"

Leaning forward, I press a kiss to the top of her head. "You're safe now."

She nods, and then we hear a throat clear which makes us jump away.

"Here's your beer, man," Smith says as his eyes narrow on me before looking at his sister. I take it from him and take a large drink from it to calm myself down. "Have you two been talking since the funeral?" he asks.

I look over at Paige; I'm not sure what story she wants to tell.

Callie hands Paige her drink as I watch her try to spin a story to her overprotective brother.

"Gio called Paige last night to let her know he was coming to New York when Michael attacked her. She lost her phone and had no way of contacting him back, so I did to let him know that she was okay. Because he witnessed the whole thing," she explains.

"You did?" Smith turns and asks me.

I nod my head.

"I invited him to dinner tonight, thought the surprise would cheer her up," Callie adds.

"It certainly was a surprise," Smith adds.

"A good one," the other girl adds. "Sorry, I'm Savannah," she says with a strange accent, Australian, I think.

"Nice to meet you," I say, shaking her hand.

"Now the introductions are out of the way, I'm starving. Where the hell is that delivery guy?" Callie says.

As if he was summoned, the buzzer goes off.

"Perfect timing," Callie says with a grin.

"I'll get it." Smith sighs, placing his beer on the table.

"I'll help," Savannah adds as she follows him out the door.

"I'm going to grab the cutlery and stuff," Callie says, leaving us alone again.

"We seem to keep clearing the room," I joke.

"I love my friends, but they are weird." She smiles.

"Are you okay?" I ask her in all seriousness.

She nods. "I will be. I've taken a protective order out against him. Smith helped with an emergency one. I'm hoping that will be enough for him to stop."

"And if he doesn't?" Because the face I saw last night didn't indicate that he gave a fuck.

"I don't know," she says quietly.

Silence falls between us, neither one of us knowing what to say.

17

PAIGE

"Thank you all for such a great night," Giorgio says. "It's been great catching up. Don't be a stranger," Smith adds.

It took Smith a little while to warm up to him as he didn't trust his intentions, but once Giorgio told him about his own breakup and what happened, and I explained that we had reached out to each other during a really hard time and have been chatting about what we were both going through, Smith dialed down his overprotectiveness which led to us all having a great night.

"Paige will walk you down," Callie says, urging me forward.

Giorgio smiles as I follow him out the door. "Thanks for such a great night. It's been a long time since I've had laughs like that." He chuckles as we walk toward the elevator.

"They are a great bunch, crazy, but they're mine."

"I'm sorry for surprising you like I did. I needed to know if you were okay," he confesses.

"I'm fine, see," I say, doing a twirl for him.

"I see," he says, his voice dropping an octave, which gives me goosebumps.

No.

This isn't happening. No old feelings resurfacing, get back down into that box that is buried in the depths of my soul.

He rubs the back of his neck, which turns my attention to the thick, tensing muscles. They are nice biceps, really nice, thick biceps. And he smelled so good all night; I couldn't stop sniffing him. He was dressed casually, yet elegant at the same time, with his designer jeans and navy polo shirt. He had a little bit of a five o'clock shadow across his square jaw and his dark hair was messily tamed.

"I was surprised to see you again," I tell him.

He nods in understanding. "I hesitated about coming tonight. Didn't know if it was better if I stayed in the phone or not," he says.

Oh.

When he was an ocean away it was easier, but having dinner with him tonight, with everyone else around was nice. I think it would have been different, if it was just the two of us.

The elevator dings, the doors open, and we step inside. The room suddenly feels small with his looming presence.

"Honestly, I didn't think we would ever see each other again." I vowed to myself that we never would when I was younger, but now that I'm older and a little wiser, I don't know. "You have a life in Italy, and I have mine here. Never thought the two would meet."

He nods in understanding and looks like he might be sad about my comments and that isn't at all how I want him to feel, especially because he's flown halfway across the world to check in on me. Not just me, he has work too, but still he took the time out to have dinner with us all. I reach out and touch his arm; his dark eyes narrow on where I'm touching him. His skin is hot and soft, and with every second my hand stays against his, my heart beats faster, my skin tingles, and my cheeks feel like they are warming up.

"I'm so happy you are here," I say as he looks up from my hand, and those deep, chocolatey eyes begin to swallow me up. The elevator shrinks even more, every movement and breath is amplified. He then reaches out and cups my face; his thumb slides down my flushed cheek and my body shivers, taking me back to a time in my life when he used to touch me like that, with my body now reacting the same way it used to all those years ago.

"I'm so happy to see you, too."

Is he going to kiss me? *Feels like it.* No. Do I want him to? *Um, yes, no, maybe.* We're friends, old acquaintances even. He's Italian; they talk with their hands. He's just talking with his hands, nothing more. *You're reading too much into this, Paige.*

The elevator stops and the doors open. His hand falls from my face and I feel its loss instantly, and I don't know how I feel about that. I told myself when I was younger that I never wanted to see him again and yet here he is. It's confusing, especially the way my body is reacting to him. *It's the wine.* I follow him silently into the foyer, where we stop again. Why is this awkward? It doesn't have to be. I'm getting inside my own head. We are adults.

"Would you like to catch up again?" I ask him. That wasn't supposed to come out of my mouth. He seems surprised by my request as his eyes widen, and his brows shoot high up on his face. I swallow hard, feeling like an idiot for saying it. What the hell was I thinking?

"I'd like that," he answers.

He would?

"Only problem is …"

He wants to but he can't, I get it. It's the polite rejection.

"… we have to catch up at my apartment."

Oh.

"The media don't know Giada and I have split, so seeing me at dinner with a beautiful woman would start rumors," he explains.

Oh.

Wait. Did he just call me beautiful?

"Would that be, okay? I understand if you don't want to come to my apartment, if you want to meet somewhere public—"

"No, that's fine." I shake my head. "Might be safer," I add.

His mouth falls open, and he realizes I'm talking about Michael and his demeanor changes. He tenses as anger rolls through him.

"Hey," I say, reaching out again to reassure him. "I'm going to be okay. He won't get to me again, I promise."

His hand closes over mine and it's nice, familiar even. "I'll make sure he never touches you again."

He almost growls the sentiment, and I shouldn't feel hot and flustered by his comment, but I do. I need to start using my vibrator again, but it's a long time since I've used it. It's hard as my brother and I have been living in such close quarters, and he's a noisy bitch, but I need to do something because my body is on fire, and I need to control it if we are going to catch up again. I nod, not sure what more I can say to that declaration.

"My driver is here. Thanks again for a great night," he says, reaching out and hugging me good night. I suck in a deep breath of his aftershave and let my fingers absorb his taunt body before letting go. I give him a wave and watch him walk out of the building. I head back up to Smith's apartment and I know it's going to be a game of twenty questions where I'm in the hot seat.

As soon as I open the door, it starts.

"Did he kiss you?" Savannah asks.

"What? No," I answer, flustered.

"Did you want him to kiss you?" she presses.

"No," I answer as I frantically look between everyone.

"Bullshit." She chuckles.

"Is there something going on between the two of you?" Smith questions me.

"Oh my gosh, guys, just because he's here, and we dated a million years ago, doesn't mean I'm going back there," I tell them, taking a seat back at the dining table and grabbing my glass of wine. I take a large gulp, needing it to get through their interrogation.

"I think he came here just for you," Callie adds.

My head turns quickly toward her. "He's here for business, with his sister."

Callie lifts her glass and takes a sip. "I said what I said."

"Wait, you dated?" Smith asks.

The room falls quiet.

Um. Yeah. That's right. My brother didn't know about that; he thought it was some Italian douchebag that broke my heart.

"For how long? Was he the guy that broke your heart? Fuck, Paige. Why didn't you tell me? I wouldn't have been so chummy with him," my brother protests.

"I never told you because back then you would have ruined it. We are friends now. Oh, and I'm an adult," I remind him.

He huffs. "Still would have liked to have known. I can't believe you kept that from me all these years."

His pouting makes me laugh. "Once I got over him, I wanted to forget it ever happened."

"That's why he stopped talking to me. Because you two broke up," Smith says, slapping his hand on the table in revelation. "What happened?"

I roll my eyes. "I came back in the summer, and he was dating Bella Gallo."

Smith's eyes widen. "Oh, you hated her." He chuckles.

No shit, brother, hence why I never wanted to see him.

"He did say that he did that because he thought he would mess up your life," Callie adds.

Huh. What did she say? As I glare at my friend.

"I may have asked him what his intentions were toward you. Wanted to make sure you were protected," she confesses.

"You did what? Does he think I have feelings for him? I'm so embarrassed. How could you do that?" I ask her.

"He broke your heart, and I wanted to make sure he wasn't coming back into your life to do it again," she defends her actions.

I frown at her. She didn't have the right to do that.

"Anyway, he got into what happened all those years ago. He said that you had dreams and being with someone like him and everything that comes with his family would squash those dreams, and he didn't want that for you. He thought you were both too young and that if he didn't put distance between you that you wouldn't have been able to thrive," Callie adds.

"That's so sweet. He loved you enough to let you go," Savannah coos.

It kind of makes me angry that he never spoke to me about it.

"He said he was eighteen and didn't want to do something stupid if you continued dating. He knows he would have messed up," Callie explains.

"This man better have brothers because he's so sweet," Savannah adds.

"His brother is married, and his wife is pregnant," I add.

"Dammit. Hope he has hot friends then?" She smirks.

"Why would he do that, though? He really hurt me," I ask them all.

"Boys are stupid at that age, Paige. In his logic it made sense and I kind of agree with him," Smith says, defending him.

"But my life didn't turn out the way I dreamed." I groan.

"And you two could have married and ended up getting a divorce," Callie adds.

"The universe has its reasons," Savannah adds.

"You're not considering dating him?" my brother asks.

"No. He was a shoulder to cry on. I'm not interested in dating anyone," I tell him.

My brother shrugs his shoulders in response. "Well, ladies, I'm going to leave you to it, good night, I have work in the morning," he says, leaving us.

"Now he's gone. Did he kiss you?" Savannah asks.

"No, he didn't. It wasn't anything like that," I tell her.

"Really? Because the chemistry is still there between the two of you and he's fuckin' hot."

"Would you stop putting ideas into her head," Callie warns her.

This has her bursting out laughing. "You thought about kissing him, but he didn't make a move," Savannah states.

I don't answer.

"Busted," she says.

"Fine. I did. You saw him, the man looks like a damn supermodel off the pages of Italian *Vogue*." They both nod in agreement. "I did ask him if he wanted to catch up again." They both squeal with delight. "He said yes, but I'm not ready for anything, guys. Please don't hype me up about Giorgio. I truly want his friendship, nothing more. I'm too scared."

"I promise to keep my enthusiasm down." Savannah smiles.

"Smith seemed to take the news about Giorgio and me okay, but I don't know if he would like the idea of me having dinner at his apartment by myself."

"Say no more. You're having dinner with me and Savannah, whatever night, and you're sleeping over at my house," Callie adds.

"I won't be sleeping over at his place," I warn her.

"I know, but you will need to debrief afterward, and we will be waiting with the wine for it," Callie states.

Giorgio: Thanks again for a great night.

Paige: Thanks for coming, it was nice catching up.

Giorgio: It was like old times.

Paige: Yeah, it felt like you had always been in my life.

Giorgio: Same.

Giorgio: Is Tuesday night, seven, okay for dinner?

Paige: Sounds great. What do you need me to bring?

Giorgio: Nothing but yourself.

Paige: That I can do. See you then.

> Giorgio: Night, P.

Oh, he hasn't used my old nickname in such a long time.

> Paige: Night, Gio.

"You like that don't you, P?" he says. Wrapping my hair around his hand, he twists and pulls me up from all fours as he continues to rut into me. "Strangling my cock with your tight cunt, like my dirty girl."

"Yes," I moan as his cock fills me to the hilt, going deeper than before with the new position, my tits bouncing in time with his thrusts.

"You're mine, Paige. You were my first and you will be my last, do you hear me?" Gio tells me and his thrusts quicken as he starts to chase his impending orgasm. "Say it, Paige."

"I'm yours." I moan as he hits the hidden sensitive nerve deep inside me that makes my toes curl.

"Say my name, the world needs to know who is owning you." He growls.

"Gio ... Gio owns me," I scream as my walls tighten around him, his thrusts pushing me over the edge.

"I own you, you're my good girl." He groans as he fills me up.

"Fuck," I curse as I bolt upright, my body on fire, every nerve ending tingling, and a bead of sweat crosses my brow. "What the hell was that?" I pant, then panic laces my body as I nervously look around the room as if people would know what I was dreaming about. I still, making sure my brother didn't hear me orgasm in my sleep.

What is wrong with me?

18

PAIGE

I upped my gym routine today, hoping to get rid of this sexual energy around me. I can't keep having sex dreams about Giorgio, it's embarrassing. We're having dinner tomorrow night, and I don't want to walk into his place like a horny teen. I'm heading home for a shower and probably a service with my vibrator while my brother is at work. It might be time to invest in an industrial-strength one instead because an hour and a half at the gym hasn't cooled me down. I'm lost in my own world and don't notice Michael standing out the front of Smith's apartment until I'm closer than I'd like. I duck down an alley and suck in a couple of deep breaths; this can't be happening. The protective order is in place. Why is he at the apartment? I pull out my phone and call Smith, but he doesn't pick up. No. Panicked tears well in my eyes as I look around the corner again; he's still there. What the hell am I going to do? The next thing I know, I'm dialing Giorgio.

"This is a pleasant surprise," he says, greeting me warmly.

That's when I lose the ability to speak, my throat becoming dry as if I've swallowed the Sahara, and nothing but a squeak comes out of my mouth.

"Fuck, Paige, are you okay?" he asks.

"No."

"Where are you? Send me a pin."

With shaky hands, I send him my location.

"Are you safe?" he asks as I hear crashing and cursing.

"Yes, I'm in an alley."

"Shit, traffic is bad going uptown, fuck," he yells away from the phone. "Is it safe for you to get into a cab or an Uber?"

I suck in a deep breath and have a look around the corner. Michael is staring at his phone and looking around, but not in this direction.

"Yes," I whisper. If I turn left and go around the next corner, I'll be out of his line of sight.

"Good, I'm sending you my address. I'll wait downstairs for you," he tells me.

"Okay," I squeak, trying to stave off the panic.

"Paige, I've got you, okay? I promise I will not let him hurt you," he tells me earnestly.

"I know."

"Good, now go when it's safe. I'll be waiting."

And with that, I end the call and take another look around the corner. He's still standing there looking frustrated. *You've got this. Just walk out as if you are a normal person, there are hundreds of people on the street, he won't notice it is you.* I take the first step from my hiding area and my legs almost give way, but I push on and knock into a couple of people before righting myself. *Shit.* Head forward and keep moving, which I do, and turn the corner, my heart racing and sweat beading all over my skin. Someone is looking out for me as I see a cab and rush toward it. I open the door and the driver nods. I give him the address and within seconds, we are taking off into the traffic and heading away from Michael. I can breathe now, and I sink back into the seat. I quickly message Giorgio that I'm in a cab. He tells me he is waiting for me.

It feels like an eternity as we head downtown, but eventually, we make it to Tribeca, and I see Giorgio standing out the front of his apartment waiting for me. Relief fills me, seeing him standing there with a deep scowl on his face, but it disappears as he realizes it's my cab that is pulling up in front of him.

He opens the cab door and leans in. "How much?" he asks. The driver tells him, and he gives him the cash before shutting the door again. He then opens my door and holds out a hand for me. I graciously take it, and the next thing I know, he is pulling me into his arms and mumbling things to me in Italian. That he was praying that I would make it to him in time. I stare up at him and in that moment, the entire sidewalk disappears, and all I see is this man looking down at me with the deepest worry across his face, as he continues to mutter about my safety and all the things he wants to do to my ex. The next thing I know, I'm grabbing his face and kissing him.

I'm blaming it on the adrenaline.

He stills in my arms before he quickly removes my lips from his.

Oh.

Shit.

What the hell was I thinking?

"Get inside," he growls as he takes my hand and ushers me past the doorman and down the corridor toward the elevator. He slams his hand against the metal buttons with such force it makes me jump; the elevator door opens, and we get in. He's angry. I shouldn't have kissed him. I've ruined things. He's done this to help me, and I've been a complete and utter creeper and launched myself at him. *He was just being kind, Paige.* He lets go of my hand in the elevator and runs his hand through his hair, cursing in Italian as he puts distance between us. I've really messed up, he's not happy.

The doors open directly into his apartment—I hadn't noticed he pressed the penthouse—and he strides ahead of me, still cursing.

"Gio, I'm sorry. I wasn't thinking. I was panicked and the adrenaline ... I shouldn't have kissed you." My apologies stop him, and then he strides toward me, my feet moving me backward quickly until my back hits the wall.

"You think I'm upset that you kissed me?" he growls at me angrily.

I nod quickly in reply.

"Fuck, Paige," he says, nearly pulling his hair from its roots. "Do you have any idea how long I have waited to have your lips on mine again?"

Wait, what?

I shake my head no, unable to speak.

"The reason I pulled away wasn't because I didn't want to kiss you," he says, reaching out and caressing my face.

It wasn't?

"I panicked because I didn't want someone to photograph us together. Those assholes could be anywhere."

Oh.

So, it was because he was worried about the paparazzi.

Shit.

No one knows he's single.

"Do you have any idea what they would do to you if someone caught that? They would crucify you," he explains, his face softening. "Giada is Italy's sweetheart. They think she can do no wrong. You would forever be known in Italy as the other woman."

Okay. That seems logical.

"I'm sorry," I whisper.

"Never apologize for putting your lips on mine." He grins as his thumb wipes an errant tear from my cheek.

"You saved me and I ..." My breath hitches as I try to explain the panic that Michael had filled me with.

"You're safe now," he says, reassuring me.

"I always felt safe with you," I confess, looking up into those dark cocoa pools. Silence falls between us as tension swirls around. My breath is shaky with need as I lick my lips, those dark pools following the path of my tongue. Then he's leaning closer to me. He's going to kiss me. This is it, what I've been dreaming about these past couple of nights.

The sound of the elevator doors opening breaks the moment, followed by a female voice calling, "Hey, Gio, you home?"

We both jump back from each other and turn to look at who has arrived. The most beautiful woman I've ever seen appears; she looks vaguely familiar, probably a supermodel.

Oh no. Did I crash a date?

She stops in her tracks as she sees Giorgio and I standing there, dark-brown eyes widening as she looks between the two of us.

"Did I interrupt something?" she asks, arching a brow at him.

Giorgio sighs and turns to me. "This is my sister, Natalia," he says, explaining who the woman is.

Natalia.

His sister.

Shit, the last time I saw her she was tiny. Oh, my goodness, she is gorgeous.

"Nat, this is my friend Paige."

His sister's head swings to him, then back to me.

"As in, Paige, your first love who you caught up with at a funeral?" she questions him.

He groans at the description. "Yes, that Paige."

Her eyes widen and a huge smile falls across her face. The next thing I know, she is rushing toward me and pulling me into a hug.

"Nat," Gio calls out in warning.

"I'm so happy to finally meet you," she says almost giddily.

This is unexpected. "It's nice to meet you, but we've met before when you were very young," I say.

She shakes her head. "Of course." She giggles.

"You never told me she was this stunning, Gio," she teases her brother.

He shakes his head and mouths "sorry" toward me over her head.

"Please, I'm all gross from the gym," I say, leaving out the part about running into my stalker ex.

"And yet you look amazing."

She could get a job as a hype girl. I need her to walk around with me all day giving me compliments.

"Why didn't you tell me you were having company over? I would have made myself scarce," she says in Italian.

"Wasn't planned. My ex-husband breached the protective order I have against him. I called Gio for help and here I am," I explain to her.

"She speaks Italian," Gio adds unnecessarily.

"I get that now," she says, rolling her eyes at him. "And are you okay?" she asks before turning to her brother and glaring at him. "Has he offered you a drink? Do you need water, wine, tequila?"

"Not yet," I answer with a smile.

"You're the worst host, Gio," she reprimands him. "I think what we need is a bottle of tequila and some shot glasses."

"I'll get them." He groans as he disappears into the kitchen.

"Come sit," she says, ushering me over to the sofa.

I didn't get far into Giorgio's apartment, so I've only noticed now the incredible views. "Oh wow," I gasp, looking at the floor-to-ceiling windows that show off the Hudson River, over to Long Island, and the Empire State Building.

"It's a great view. I'm here so much that I forget what it's like to see it for the first time," she says, following me over to the window.

"I can only imagine how amazing it would be at night with all the lights."

"Don't worry, I'm sure you'll get a chance to see it at night." She chuckles beside me.

"Your brother and I are old friends," I tell her.

She shrugs. "I know." But the smile she gives me tells me she doesn't believe it at all.

"Drinks, ladies. You're going to need this," he says, handing me a shot. I take it and throw it back.

"Hell yeah, that's the spirit, raw dog that shot," Natalia calls out.

Giorgio chokes on his shot. "What the hell, Nat?"

"Get your mind out of the gutter, she did the shot without salt and lime. I can tell we are going to get on well. She's already better than ninety percent of all your girlfriends."

"She's not my girlfriend."

"I'm not his girlfriend." We both reiterate to his sister.

She waves her hands, ignoring our words. "Paige, do you like shopping?" she questions me.

"I never had money to shop before, but I guess now I do. I'm apparently a countess. I have no idea about designer clothes or anything like that," I explain to her, the tequila loosening my lips more than they normally would.

"Oh no," Giorgio groans.

Oh no, what? What does that mean?

Natalia's eyes widen and a huge smile falls across her face. "Are you asking for a makeover?"

No, I don't think I was asking for a makeover. Those words never left my lips.

"Here, you're going to need this," Giorgio says, handing me another shot of tequila. "Just go with it." He grins as I take the shot from him. I throw back the tequila and do as he says and go with it. This is the kind of distraction I need after today. I'm suddenly agreeing to go out tomorrow with Natalia, where she is going to turn me into a modern-day Italian countess.

"I did the same with Luca's girlfriend, Lilly," she tells me.

"I'm not his girlfriend."

"She's not my girlfriend," Gio and I repeat to her, which she conveniently ignores.

Suddenly, my phone starts ringing; saved by the bell. I grab it out of my bag and see that it's Smith. "Excuse me for a moment," I say, getting up off the sofa and moving away from them.

"Hey, sorry I missed your call, I was on a stakeout. Everything okay?" my brother asks.

"Oh yeah, everything's fine," I tell him.

"Are you drunk?"

"Maybe."

"Are you with Callie and Sav?" he asks.

"Nope, I'm with Gio and Natalia, his sister. Boy, has she grown up, she's so beautiful you have to catch up. On second thoughts, no you can't meet her, you and your womanizing ways are not welcome near her."

"Hey, I'm offended. How come you're over there?" he questions me.

"Gio saved me from Michael," I blurt out.

"He did fucking what? What do you mean he saved you from Michael?" my brother screams down the phone. I turn around and look over at Gio in a panic. He rushes over and takes the phone from me.

"Smith, hey, it's Gio," he says.

"Yeah, she's safe .... He didn't see her. She was able to get into a cab .... I don't know why he was there .... Yeah, I know .... She's fine here, my driver can take her home when she's ready ... I'd do anything for her."

I bite my bottom lip hearing Giorgio say that he would do anything for me.

"My brother's a good guy, you know," Natalia adds, distracting me from the boys' conversation. "Not sure what happened between the two of you all those years ago, but I remember him moping around the house for what felt like forever." She groans while rolling her eyes.

See, I assumed he moved on and that was it.

"He never wanted to settle down after that," she adds.

"He had a fiancée?" I add.

Natalia shakes her head. "Who ran off with his sister." She smirks. "I think it was the pressure from our parents that pushed him to it. They were not a great match."

"They looked good together," I add.

She raises her brows at me. "You looked him up?"

"After running into him at the funeral. It had been fifteen years since I last saw him."

"Long time."

I nod my head.

"Long time to still be curious, too." She winks.

"Would you stop thinking whatever it is you think is going on between us? Nothing will ever happen between us again."

She doesn't look convinced.

19

GIORGIO

I don't know what is happening, but my sister and Paige are currently dancing on the coffee table to the Spice Girls. I think it might be time to cut them off from the tequila. My phone buzzes in my pocket, and I see it's Smith, again.

"Hello," I say, answering the phone.

"Are you having a party?" Smith asks.

"Hold on," I tell him as I flick the phone to video and show him what is currently happening in my living room.

"What the hell are they doing?"

"Letting go, I think the words were," I explain to him, getting up off the sofa and moving away from the chaos.

"They sure are doing that." He chuckles. "Is Paige okay?"

"Somehow, I think this little venture with tequila and the Spice Girls might be helping."

"Guess she needed to let loose in a safe place. It's been a long time since I've seen her laugh like that, she looks happy," he confesses to me.

I look over at the two of them and he's right; the dark cloud around her seems to have shifted.

"Any news on that asshole ex?" I ask him.

He lets out a sigh. "He must know where the security cameras are near my place because he avoided them all. It's her word against his. I sent one of my boys down to the restaurant to investigate, and he had an alibi, a staff member said she was with him."

What a fucker.

"I'm assuming it's the same staff member Paige caught him fucking."

"Yeah, probably, but without evidence there is nothing I can do to put him behind bars," he explains before giving a frustrated huff.

"What do you need from me? I can go down and rough him up. I have a diplomatic passport so—"

Smith bursts out laughing. "You didn't just say that to an NYPD detective."

"No, I said it to the older brother of Paige Johnson."

Smith's eyes widen, and then a full-blown smile falls across his face. "You never heard this from me …"

"Enough said," I tell him.

He gives me a knowing nod.

"I'll bring her back to your place once she's finished," I tell him.

"If she's not in a good way, is it okay if she can crash? She's a lightweight," he explains.

"Of course, I have a spare bedroom already set up. And she can borrow some of Nat's clothes."

"Thanks, Gio. I appreciate that you've been a great friend to her through all this," he says, giving me praise.

"She's done the same to me too. Thankfully, my ex is too busy taking selfies to be stalking me."

Smith nods in acknowledgment. "How are you doing, really?"

"Just waiting for the public announcement, it feels like once that is out there, I'm free. At the moment I'm still in limbo."

"Guess a couple more weeks in the grand scheme isn't that long," he adds with a shrug.

It's true. *It could be worse, much worse*, I think as I look over at Paige.

"I'll let you go. The girls seem to have gotten louder, I didn't think that was possible, so good luck with all that," Smith jokes, then hangs up the phone.

I turn around and see the two of them having the time of their lives together. Seeing my sister laughing with Paige, both relaxed, thaws my stone-cold heart. Giada, even though she had much more in common with Natalia than Paige does, I don't think I could ever see her getting drunk and dancing on coffee tables, not unless it was for social media. The most relaxed I've seen Giada is, funnily enough, with Allegra in Greece.

"Gio, join us," Natalia says, calling me over. My first thought is to wave her off like I normally would, not wanting to be seen being silly, but something in me decides to let loose instead. So, I do. I grab the bottle of tequila, swing a shot back, and join the girls dancing to something absurd on the stereo and let myself go.

"As fun as this party is, I've got to go," Natalia says.

Huh, go? Where? Why?

"You two have been so much fun, but I have this opening I'm supposed to be at," she explains as she rushes up and kisses me on the cheek. "Loved your moves, brother. Who knew you had it in you?" Then she moves over to Paige and gives her a tight hug. "Love you, girl, tomorrow don't forget, you and me, shopping up a storm."

Paige groans but gives my sister a smile. "I'm in your capable hands," she tells her.

"I won't let you down, I promise," Natalia states as she steps away from her. "Hey, you're welcome to grab a change of clothes from my room," she says before turning and heading out of the living room.

Paige and I look at each other and burst out laughing. I turn the stereo down to a normal level and collapse on the sofa. Paige does the same beside me.

"Thanks for hanging out with her," I turn and tell Paige.

"I love her, she's great." She grins.

"Yeah, she is," I say, beaming with pride. "We need to get food into us, otherwise this tequila is going to be the death of us."

"Yes, please, I'm starved." Paige groans as she curls herself up into a ball.

"What do you want?" I ask, pulling out my phone.

"Pizza, hot, greasy, slice of pie."

I still; she can't be serious. New York pizza is not pizza.

She bursts out laughing. "Don't get all Italian on me. After a big night of drinking, there is nothing better than New York-style pizza."

"If that's what you want ..."

"It's what I want. Pepperoni please." She grins.

With a huff and a pout, I reluctantly ordered New York pizza. "They will revoke my Italian citizenship if they ever find out."

Paige rolls her eyes. "You're so dramatic." She chuckles as she slaps my arm playfully. "Gee, your arms are so ..." she mumbles as she starts squeezing my bicep, before quickly pulling her hand away. "I didn't say that in my head, did I?"

I shake my head, indicating no, and watch as her face turns bright red.

"Okay, you two, I'm off, don't do anything I wouldn't do," Natalia states, coming back looking like a different person. How did she get ready so quickly?

"I made him order pizza," Paige calls out to her.

Natalia stills and looks over at me. I nod, and she bursts out laughing. "I knew I liked you, Paige." And with that, she disappears into the evening.

At some point, the sun had set and now there's nothing but the twinkling lights of the Manhattan skyline before us.

"Oh wow," Paige says, noticing at the same time I do, and she gets up off the sofa and rushes over to the window. "It's beautiful," she gasps, staring at the view.

"It is," I agree, except I'm not looking at the lights, my focus is completely on her. She turns slowly when the silence between us gets too much and realizes I'm looking at her, not the view.

"Why did you have to break my heart, Gio?"

Her question catches me off-guard, and I take a couple of moments to work out how to answer that. "Because you deserved to have a life, not live in a fishbowl."

"But we would have lived there together."

Does she not think I thought of all that? "We were young, love wouldn't have been enough." I knew that I would have fucked up, no matter how much I loved her. I wasn't the man I am today.

Her brows pull together. "You broke me that day you chose her," she tells me as tears well in her eyes. "You broke me," she repeats.

Fuck.

She wipes her tears away. "Don't think my heart was ever the same since," she confesses.

Those chocolate eyes look up and into my soul, a soul that only she's been able to touch.

It's always been her.

Every woman I've ever been with, I've compared to her.

"Mine either," I whisper in agreement as a memory filters through.

"Giorgio, what a surprise," Lucia says, answering the door.

"Is Paige here?" I ask, my heart thundering in my chest. It has been a month since that day. I've realized I made a mistake, and not because I found Bella with one of my friends while away, but because being with her I realized she's not Paige, she will never be her, and I've been too stubborn to swallow my pride and tell Paige that.

"I'm sorry, she's not here."

"When will she be back?"

"She won't be back. I'm afraid she's headed back to America," Lucia tells me.

No. No. No.

"You broke her heart, my boy, what did you expect?" the older woman tells me. My eyes widen, not realizing that she knew about the two of us. I should have known she knew everything because of how close she and Paige are.

"I just need to speak to her," I plead.

She shakes her head. "She's gone."

Fuck.

"I still love her," I confess to Lucia.

"I know, I can see it, but unfortunately you made your choice, and she made hers," she says, giving me a small smile.

"What if she never talks to me ever again?" I ask her.

"I'm sure she will, give her time," she tells me.

Fifteen years later, and I guess we are having that discussion now.

"I can't turn back time, Paige. I wish I could. I would have changed so many things," I tell her.

"You would have?" she asks, raising a brow, surprised at my admission.

"Of course, don't you know I have regretted that decision all my life? I came back for you, but you had gone. I called. I emailed. I messaged. I even sent letters. You erased me from your life."

"You erased me from your heart," she bites back.

"I've never erased you from there," I confess.

Paige shrinks back at my words, and she starts shaking her head. "Don't say that," she tells me.

"It's the truth. You were my first love," I tell her honestly.

"Don't," she warns me.

"You don't want to hear what I wished I had said to you fifteen years ago?" I question as she tries to move away from me.

"No, I don't," she argues back.

"You scared to hear it?" I push.

"I've got to go. I've had enough of walking down memory lane," she tells me as she steps around me and walks over to where her bag is.

Fuck, I pushed too far.

"Paige, I'm sorry, okay," I say, reaching out to stop her; she pulls her arm from my reach, and it feels like a slap to the face.

"Look at us now, all these years on, we're supposedly older and wiser," she says, grabbing her bag from beside the sofa. "I can't do this," she says, waving her hand around the room.

Do what?

"You were right all those years ago, Gio. I don't belong in your fishbowl," she says, picking up her bag and slinging it over her shoulder.

What does that mean?

"Thank you for helping me today, I appreciate it, but I've got to get home," she tells me and starts making her way to the door.

"What about the pizza?"

"Enjoy it," she says, ignoring me.

"Paige, wait, please, don't leave like this."

She stops and whirls around to look at me. "I have to go," she tells me, those dark eyes wide and glistening with emotion.

"I don't want you to," I tell her.

"And that's the reason why I have to," she says, shaking her head. "Our lives have imploded, Gio. Whatever this is"—she circles her hands between us—"is ... two old friends catching up, nothing more."

"You and I both know that's not true," I tell her honestly.

She gasps as her mouth falls open.

"I can't erase the feeling of your lips on mine. Now that I've had a taste, I want more."

"No," she whispers.

"Yes," I nod, slowly walking toward her. "Fifteen years I've been waiting for them to be on mine again."

"Gio," she says, standing her ground.

"What? Do you want me to lie, Paige?" I question her.

She bites her bottom lip as she continues to stare at me, the little crease between her brows etching deep. "I can't," she whispers.

"Can't what?"

"Give you more," she explains, and a single tear falls down her cheek.

I'm an asshole.

What the hell, have you forgotten why she is here today?

"I'm sorry, Paige, I ... I wasn't thinking."

She sniffles.

"Please don't cry, baby girl," I say, reaching out to her; she eyes my outstretched arm suspiciously. I wiggle my fingers and she drops her bag and rushes into them. She wraps her arms tightly around me, a feeling I'll never stop loving.

"I'm sorry," she mumbles against my chest.

Leaning back, I make her look up at me. "You never have to apologize to me."

"I kissed you on the street. I brought up the past."

"It's what friends do," I say, giving her a wide smile, which makes her chuckle. "Plus, tequila likes to help blur things too."

"Damn tequila." She grins.

I reach out and push back a lock of her hair, and I get a whiff of her coconut perfume and a sense of déjà vu hits me, bringing me back to a moment just like this one.

"I think you're the prettiest girl here."

"You do?"

"I do."

"You're just trying to be kind, Gio, I appreciate it. But don't you have to get back to Chiara? She's been eyeballing you all night."

"And yet here I am with you."

"Because you're a good friend."

"Should a friend think about what it would be like to kiss another friend?" I confess to her.

"Gio."

It's a smell I can still remember now. It lingers in the air in my memory as if I can smell it here and now. My legs were shaking with nervousness, and I could feel my dick twitching to life, wanting to harden thanks to my uncontrollable hormones at the time, and I remember trying to tell myself to calm the hell down, to not embarrass myself with a hard-on as I kissed the girl. After what felt like an eternity, our lips met, and a gasp fell from hers at the connection, and I shoved my tongue in there thinking that is what you were supposed to do. Then our teeth gnashed together, saliva swapped, and tongues dueled; it was not the greatest of first kisses, but I remember as the summer continued, we got better at it.

"Are you okay?" she asks.

I shake my head, forcing the memory back. "Just remembered something."

"What?" she asks.

"Nothing." It's the last thing I want to tell her, especially after the moment we just had.

"Come on, tell me," she pushes, stepping out of my embrace. *No, that's not what I wanted. I like having her in my arms.*

Do I tell her?

"Was it bad?"

"No, just an old memory," I tell her.

"Which one?" she questions.

"Your perfume, it reminded me of our first kiss."

"Oh," she answers, surprised.

"See, that's why I didn't want to say anything, now it's awkward," I tell her.

"Well, especially after I nearly ran out the door because we were talking about stuff from the past." She chuckles.

"There's that," I agree.

"Wasn't the greatest first kiss, was it?" She grins.

"Hey, you were as bad as I was," I tease.

This makes her giggle, and the sound is one of the best sounds in the world.

"True, but I remember we got better as the summer progressed," she says.

"We did."

We both stare at each other, remembering our old make-out sessions, and all I want to do is show her how much I've improved, but thankfully, I'm saved from my inner thoughts by the house phone. I walk over to it in the foyer and pick it up.

"Mr. Fiorenzo, we have a pizza down here for you," the bellman tells me.

"Thanks, send them up," I say, hanging up. "Pizza's here."

Paige chews on her lip as she weighs up her decision.

"You said it was good pizza, and I can't send you home with an empty stomach, my nonna would haunt me if I did."

Paige laughs and shakes her head. "Fine, I'll stay for pizza, but only because I want to see your face when you realize I'm right about New York pizza."

I roll my eyes at her. "That will never happen."

20

GIORGIO

"What?" I ask, entering the kitchen and seeing my sister giving me a look.

"What do you mean, what?" She glares at me as I continue over to the coffee machine and make myself a cappuccino, ignoring her question. "Did you have a guest stay over?"

"No."

Natalia huffs. "Why not?"

"Paige has her own bed," I snip as I continue to make my coffee.

"Like that's stopped you before." She groans.

Turning around to my sister, I narrow my eyes at her. "Paige is not like any of the other women that I've had over before. You will treat her with some respect."

Natalia sits up, clearly shocked by my words. "Guess I hit a nerve there."

I scrub my face. I shouldn't take my turbulent emotions out on her. "What happened last night?"

I turn back to my coffee machine to distract myself. "Nothing, we talked, ate pizza, and then I escorted her home."

"Thanks for everything today, Gio, you were a lifesaver." Paige smiles as my driver stops in front of her brother's apartment.

"Anytime."

An awkward silence falls between us as we both try to work out how to say goodbye to each other.

"And I'm sorry about all the other stuff," she adds.

"Nothing to apologize for."

"Yeah, there was, but thank you for being gentlemanly enough to pretend nothing happened," she says with a smirk.

"I can assure you, there is nothing gentlemanly about me, Paige."

Her eyes dip to my lips ever so quickly before returning to my eyes; she swallows hard and a pink flush rises across her cheeks. She stares at me for a couple more moments; I can see a war raging behind those chocolate eyes.

"Fuck it," she curses, and the next thing I know, she launches herself at me, again. Thankfully, this time we are hidden from prying eyes, except for my driver, who quickly assesses the situation and steps from the car, giving us privacy.

Her lips still taste of pizza sauce as they crash against mine. Her fingers run through my hair, sending a shiver down my spine. Reaching out, I grab her, positioning her against me, thanking the lord that she is still in her thin activewear as my fingers sink into her ass and pull her hard against me. My dick rises to the occasion, but he needs to know nothing is happening to him tonight other than my hand wrapping around it when I get home. She continues to grind herself against me, feeling every inch of my hardness against her heat, and I'm grateful for the tinted windows; otherwise, the good people of Chelsea would be getting a free show.

"Fuck, I hate that you feel so good," she curses as she continues to devour me.

"I fucking love that you do," I curse back. She gives me a huff as she continues to rock against me. And before I get a chance to offer my fingers for service, she pulls away from me. No, don't do that, it was getting good.

She stares down at me with puffy lips and the faintest beard rash.

"I needed to know," she explains.

"Needed to know what?" I ask as I pull her tighter against me, making her shiver.

"Nothing," she states as the realization of where she is seated—right against my dick—sinks in. She quickly slides off me and straightens herself out, her eyes dipping to where my dick is, hard and encased, wanting nothing more than to sink inside that tight pussy; the same one he used to be inside every night in the summer.

"Well, thanks again," she says, reaching for the door handle and pushing it open. My driver grabs the door for her, opening it the rest of the way, and the busy sounds of the Manhattan streets break into our bubble.

"Hey, Paige," I call out as she slides out of her seat and steps onto the sidewalk. She turns back and peers into the car. "You're still going to catch up with Natalia tomorrow, aren't you?"

"If she wants to, of course," she says, giving me a warm smile.

"Thank you, I know it would make her happy. She's harmless, just excitable," I warn her.

"I had fun with her tonight, it will be a welcome distraction from my life. Plus, I need all the help I can get in the clothing department," she says.

"You look great to me," I say, looking her over hungrily.

Her cheeks turn red at my compliment. "I better go, Smith will be worried. Again, thanks and I'll see you around," she says, trying to back away from me quickly.

"Tomorrow," I answer.

She frowns. "Tomorrow?"

"We were going to do dinner," I remind her.

"Oh, yeah, that," she answers hesitantly. I don't like the sound of that. "Have a good night, Gio," she says, then walks away from the car.

"Dean, make sure she gets in safe," I yell out to my driver; he nods and closes the car door. I watch as he escorts her to the apartment's front door, she keys in her code and disappears inside. Dean watches until she has gotten into the lift before returning to the car.

I let my head fall back against the seat.
What the hell am I going to do about Paige Johnson?

"You know I'm catching up with her in a couple of hours and I'm going to ask," Natalia cautions me.

I shrug because it's up to Paige to tell her whatever version she wants of what happened last night, and I'll go along with it. I take a sip of my coffee and let the caffeine infuse my body. Ah, that feels good.

"I like her," she blurts out.

"I like her, too," I add as I continue to sip my coffee.

"You *like* like or only like?" she asks.

"Not sure what the difference is, like means like," I reply, eyes focused on my drink.

"Urgh, men," she grumbles. "Do you like her as a friend, or have your old feelings resurfaced, and now you're finding yourself liking her more than a friend?"

She's more observant than I've given her credit for. "Nat, we are friends. We can only be friends. She's going through a traumatic marriage breakup, with an ex-husband who isn't taking it well that they are over. As for me, I am stuck in fucking limbo because my ex-fiancée is living her best life in Greece with my sister, while the world thinks we are this fairy-tale couple, and I can't say shit about it because I agreed to help her career."

That was a lot more than I anticipated saying.

"How long have you been bottling all that in?" Natalia chuckles.

"A long fucking time, it seems." I grimace.

My sister sighs. "You shouldn't have to hide that you and Giada have broken up if you don't want to. It's not fair that she's doing this to you, especially after everything."

She's right. I know she is and now, being around Paige again, my feelings on the whole waiting for a time that suits Giada's career have started to change. She's the one that messed up, yet I have to be accommodating to her needs above my own. *You just want to be able to touch Paige in public.* Maybe. Okay, yes. I don't want to be hanging out with Paige and worry that some paparazzo catches us in a compromising position, labeling her the other woman in the world's eyes, when it was Giada and Allegra who are the villains in my story.

"Speak to Flora about making your own statement. Screw Giada and Allegra," she says angrily.

"I can't out them."

"Then don't. Say that she's on holiday with her best friend, helping her heal from the breakup. I don't care about them, I care about you," Natalia states.

"I'll think about it, okay?"

"Fine," she grumbles.

Ciao, I'm here to meet with Mr. Michael Nelson," I say to one of the employees after knocking on the back door of Paige's old restaurant.

"He's in his office," they say, pointing down a corridor. "I can take you there, follow me," the chef says. We walk through the back of the kitchen, down a corridor, and toward his office.

He gives the door a hard knock twice. "Wait here, he'll be out in a moment," he says gruffly before walking away from me.

Great customer service.

Moments later, the office door opens and out walks a brunette who is fixing up her top; her eyes lock with mine for a moment before she scurries away.

"Who the fuck knocked on my door? I said I was busy," Michael curses from inside his office.

Anger flares beneath my skin; this man is repulsive, taking advantage of his staff like this. Technically, he's single, but I wouldn't be surprised if this is how he's conducted himself during his marriage. I step through the doorway of his office and narrow my eyes on the man dressed in a crumpled white chef's jacket. His blond hair is messily tousled, and he has beady blue eyes and a grating French accent. This man, and I use that term lightly, had Paige's undying love, and he threw it away? This is him? *You messed up like him*, a voice inside me says. I'm nothing like this man. I knew I fucked up when I let Paige walk out of my life; this moron thinks that her being in his life is him doing her the favor.

"Oh, hi, who are you?" he asks, standing up abruptly from the chair he was sitting on.

"I'm here to make you an offer," I tell him.

He raises his brows high. "What kind of offer," he questions me.

Slowly, I walk further into the office, making sure all of my six-foot-three height is displayed as I move toward him. "I'll give you a million dollars to leave your ex alone."

Michael's eyes spring wide at my offer before it settles in and he bursts out laughing. "A million, fuck you, she's worth way more than that. You can tell that bitch I deserve at least ten million."

Something in me snaps when I hear him call Paige a bitch and the next thing I know, my hand is around his throat and I have him pinned up against the wall. He's panicking, trying to get free. He shouldn't be fooled by the ten-thousand-dollar suit because what's underneath it has been carved from hours at the gym and in the boxing ring. I've studied all forms of martial arts and self-defense. Because of who my family is, I never wanted to be caught short. So, he can wriggle and move, but I have him locked down.

"Not so cocky when you have to deal with someone your own size, are you?"

"Fuck you," he spits at me.

"No, fuck you, you piece of shit. I'm going to tell you once and only once. Leave Paige alone or I will make sure your entire world is burned to the ground," I warn him as my hand constricts around his throat. His face pales and then turns red as I start to cut off his circulation before I release him. He slides down the wall and sucks in a couple of deep breaths before he launches himself at me. I see it coming a mile away and greet him with a punch to the stomach, which has him falling to his knees.

"Fucking bastard, I'm calling the police," he screams.

"You think they are going to be able to help you against me?"

Michael coughs and splutters as he continues to hold his stomach. "Fuck you and that dumb bitch. I'm going to make you both pay," he curses at me.

"Try me, motherfucker. I'll guarantee you will regret it."

He spits at my shoes as he hauls himself up. "I'm not afraid of you. I get it, that mouth of hers will make any sane man do crazy things for it." He chuckles before my fist meets his face and splays him backward onto the floor, blood trickling around his mouth. He wipes his mouth and grins. "Get the fuck out of my restaurant. You see, here in America, I have the right to put a bullet in you if I feel like my life is being threatened, and I would say this little meeting shows just cause, don't you think?" He chuckles maniacally.

This man is more fucked up than I realized. Not wanting to push him any further, and with my point made, I leave his office.

21

PAIGE

"Thanks for picking me up," I say, greeting Natalia as I hop into the car. Quickly, I look up to see if it's the same driver we had from last night, because I'm embarrassed at the way I threw myself at an unsuspecting Giorgio. *Not that his dick was complaining.* That was true. I could feel how hard I was making him through my thin activewear; he always was a big boy.

"As if Gio would have it any other way." She grins, looking like a supermodel. Is this how she looks just to go shopping? Because I would have said she was off to the Met Gala, dressed as she is in head-to-toe designer. I look down at what I'm wearing—a blue sundress, tan sandals, my hair pulled up in a messy bun, sunglasses to ward off the hangover, and no makeup. How does she look so bright and awake when she partied as hard as I did and then went out afterward, too?

"Did you drink fewer shots than me last night? Because I don't know how you were able to go out after all that."

"Trained professional." She grins. "Did you have a good night?" Her dark eyes narrow on me. What does she know? Did Gio tell her that I kissed him? No. Maybe, it is his sister. I didn't tell Smith or the girls, not yet. I'm not sure if I ever will. *She might just be making conversation.* This is true; I'm all up in my own head when it could be nothing.

"Watching your brother eat a slice of New York pizza kept me entertained. He grimaced and whined the entire time, but I know he secretly loved it."

"Really? Wish I'd seen that, he's such a food snob. I can't believe you got him to try it. He is one of the most stubborn people I know. He really likes you if you got him to do that." She laughs.

"We're friends, old friends," I reiterate to her.

Natalia rolls her eyes at me. "My brother says the same thing about you."

Not sure if I'm relieved or not.

"But I'll stop prying because we have serious shopping to do, and we need a plan," she says.

Serious shopping?

"Also, I have Gio's credit card, so we can go crazy." She grins.

"I have my own money, I won't need his," I add quickly; I don't want her to think I can't afford this. I also don't need Giorgio's money either.

"Can I ask you something personal?" she asks.

"Depends on what it is," I answer.

She nods. "Who are you now? My brother said something about you inheriting a title and stuff. I'm so much younger, so I don't remember you or your family, sorry."

That is a valid question. I forget that she's younger and wasn't around when Gio and I were seeing each other. So, I start explaining to her all about Lucia and her world that I've only started learning about.

"No way did your great-aunt invest in Yvette Sanchez designs. I love her clothes. Have you been to her atelier in Paris? We should go. And then you can introduce me," she says excitedly.

"Sounds like I need to head to Paris. I have an apartment there, too, apparently, as well as Rome."

"No way, where in Rome?"

I pull out my phone and bring up the email I got from Lucia's business manager, who shared with me all the property and businesses and assets I apparently now own. When I click on the address in maps, I turn it around and show Natalia.

"No fricken way. You're neighbors with Luca and Lilly. They literally live on the other side of the Spanish Steps," she tells me. Wow, that's a small world. "Gio's place is near the Villa Borghese Gardens, not far though." She gives me a smirk.

Good to know, I guess, if I ever need to borrow a cup of sugar or something. We then get talking about the houses and the hotels I now own and where they are located; she knows more about the areas than I do. She then explains to me how my title works in Italy, that it doesn't mean anything to anyone unless you are in that circle already. She continues to say that her parents would know a lot more about what Lucia did in that world than she does and that I should speak to them, especially regarding my great-aunt's charities and what needs to be done with them. All the information she's given me is invaluable, but also overwhelming.

"Here we are at Saks Fifth Avenue. I thought it would be the easiest, I didn't want to overwhelm you." She grins like a Cheshire cat as we get out of the car.

"Miss Fiorenzo and Miss Johnson, welcome to Saks on Fifth Avenue. My name is Nicole, and I will be your personal shopper for today," the beautiful redhead introduces herself to us. The salespeople introducing themselves to you thing is new. I've never seen that before, or is that what the VIP experience is? "Now I've pulled some items for you, Miss Fiorenzo, as per your request, and they're waiting in your personal stylist suite upstairs. I hope they are to your liking," Nicole states, and we follow her into the department store and up to our private suite.

What is this life? Certainly not mine.

Waiting for us in the luxurious suite is a bottle of champagne and rack after rack of clothes, shoes, bags, and accessories. I've died and gone to couture heaven. One of the staff presents Natalia and me with a glass of champagne, and I take a nervous sip; this is not a world I am accustomed to.

"I thought we would be walking around the shops. I had no idea this existed. I told one of my friends that we would catch up with her out there," I say to Natalia in Italian.

"Message her, tell her to come up," Natalia suggests.

I pull out my phone and message Savannah to come up to the private suites instead of schlepping with everyone else. I had invited Callie, but she had to work, damn lawyer stuff. She texts back that she's on her way, which I relay to Nicole. While I wait for Savannah to arrive, I slowly look at all the dresses and outfits they have pulled for me.

"I asked them for a selection of gala, evening, and cocktail," Natalia explains—I didn't realize there was a difference—before continuing. "Business attire for meetings, then casual dresses, smart casual, new lingerie now that you're single as well as accessories. We are turning you from Paige Johnson of New York to Countess Paige from Italia."

"Countess Paige, it will never get old hearing you called that," Savannah says, bursting into the room full of excitement.

Rushing over to her, I greet her with a hug. "Can you believe all this?" I whisper to her.

"Natalia, this is one of my best friends, Savannah. She owns some of the hottest bars and clubs in the city, you're going to like her," I say.

Savannah and Natalia greet each other warmly and quickly chat about where Natalia went last night. When Savannah learned it was one of her places, she was excited, loving it. Sav tells her to let her know next time she's there and she'll look after her, which makes Natalia squeal and hug her again. I think those two are going to get along. A staff member hands Savannah a glass of champagne, which she gladly accepts.

"So, what are we dressing for?" Sav asks.

"Natalia is transforming me from plain Paige to Countess Paige."

Savannah breaks out in a wide smile. "Yes! I'm here for it. Paige is so beautiful, but her ex hated that she was and always made her wear these drab clothes. He never wanted to see her in anything sexy. Under all that, Paige has a banging body. She also needs to get back some of that confidence her ex took from her."

I had no idea Sav felt that way.

"Also, we have to find the sexiest dress possible as she's got a date with your brother tonight," Savannah adds.

"Wait, what?" Natalia squeals and looks over at me, upset that I never told her that.

I glare at Savannah for dropping that tidbit. "It's not a date. And after last night, I don't think we need to catch up, we did that last night."

"She's embarrassed because she threw herself at your brother in public and he knocked back her advances," Sav adds.

I groan and scrub my face, lamenting my best friend's loose lips.

"Wait, you did what?"

"It was nothing. Wow, look at this dress, it's stunning," I say, changing the subject.

"Paige?" Natalia questions me.

I huff and throw back the rest of my champagne. "Thanks, Sav," I grumble. "Look, it wasn't anything. He rescued me from a dangerous situation with my ex. I was so relieved when I saw him that I stupidly kissed him on the sidewalk in the middle of the street," I explain before switching to Italian. *"And I know that was incredibly stupid as I could have created a scandal for him if anyone had seen."*

"No fair, I don't speak Italian, come on." Savannah pouts.

"I wish you had because those bitches don't deserve my brother protecting them," Natalia states angrily, which surprises me.

"It was stupid. We're friends. He's been a fantastic strength for me since my breakup. I'm not ready for anything with anyone."

"I'm just going to look at these clothes. Let me know when I can come back into the conversation," Savannah adds as she walks over to one of the racks.

"He's lighter around you. I saw it last night. Gio can be uptight. He

has a lot on his shoulders with the family business, plus pressures from my parents, who want grandchildren, and with my father's health not the best, he doesn't want to let them down. That's why he decided to marry her, like I said last night, not because he loved her. She didn't want anything from him, especially not his heart, so that made it easy for him."

"He wouldn't have asked her to marry him if he didn't love her a little," I say.

Natalia shakes her head. *"I was there when he told her he never loved her."*

My mouth falls open in surprise.

"They were only together for three months when he proposed."

Three months?

"Papà had another turn, and his wish in the hospital was to see Gio married, so he could pass on the business to him. He's old school, like that," she says, rolling her eyes. *"Our sister really pushed for her, for them, and he liked that being with her his life didn't change. That she looked good on his arm for events, that she knew how to work the room. That woman loved the spotlight more than him."*

He wanted someone to be his arm candy. *That could never be me.* I saw her picture; she is stunning and as I look up into the suite's mirror and see myself, I deflate. Why would someone like Giorgio want me? It's because we have history. If he met me in the street as is, there would never be a chance.

"See anything you like?" Savannah asks, noticing my sudden mood change.

"I don't know. I'm not sure any of this is me. I can't wear designer, look at me," I say to the girls. "I need a moment." I make my way to the door.

"The restrooms are on your right," Nicole advises before I slip out of the room and head in that direction.

This life isn't me.

What the hell was Lucia thinking, making me a countess, giving me a life I neither earned nor deserved? *I'm no one special*, I tell myself as I push the door to the restroom open, and enter the closest stall, then pull the seat down. I need a couple of moments, it's all too much. I can never fit into this world; no matter what designer I have on my back, they will always know I'm an imposter.

"Paige, are you okay?" Savannah asks, walking into the restroom.

I push the door to my cubicle open and she walks in.

"What happened? What did she say to you in Italian that changed your mood?" she asks.

"This isn't me, Sav. This world. I'm not rich. I don't know what fork to use or which glass I should sip from. The life I thought I was heading toward now doesn't exist. I don't know who I am. I have an ex-husband who's more invested in me after we've broken up than when we were together. I have my first love come back into my life and he looks so fucking good."

"He really does," Sav agrees.

"And now he's saying and doing things and looking at me how I always wished my husband would. But he lives in Italy and is a fucking prince, who lives in a fishbowl and is a fricken billionaire and likes to date supermodels. And yet kisses me like I'm the only woman in the world for him."

Savannah stares at me in surprise. "Something did happen last night?"

I nod.

"We kissed in the car before he dropped me home. It was amazing," I confess to her.

She tries to contain her excitement but stamps up and down instead. "Why don't you want to see him tonight, then?"

"Because look at my life, Sav, it's a shit show. Michael is stalking me. I'm a prisoner in my brother's home. I have no job. No direction. Like, what the hell am I doing with my life?"

"Whatever the hell you want, babe," Sav says.

"I don't know what that is, but I sure as hell know it can't be with Gio. That man will only break my heart again. I can feel it, Sav, and I don't know if I will recover if he does."

"I had no idea you were battling all this. Why didn't you tell me or Callie?"

"You both have so much on your own plates. You don't need my crap, too," I tell her.

"That's what friends are for."

I let out a heavy sigh.

"Why are you putting so much pressure on your flirtation with the Italian stallion? Don't forget he's gotten out of a relationship, too. I can't imagine he's looking for his next happily ever after," Savannah states.

She's right; even if it wasn't traditional, he was serious enough to marry her and his sister did betray him. Am I being selfish to think that he's looking for anything more than a rebound?

"Why can't the two of you catch up for old-time's sake and have a little fun? It doesn't have to be anymore. There's no need to overthink it all," Sav says.

Maybe she's right; I'm overthinking it all.

"There's too much history there for a bit of fun. We didn't know each other well back then, but he broke me, I'd say permanently, Sav. I don't think my heart has ever recovered, and I'm too fragile to put myself in that kind of situation again."

Savannah reaches out and places a reassuring hand on my shoulder. "Well, come on then, let's work out who the hell you want to be, back inside with all those delicious clothes." She opens the stall door and we both step out to see Natalia standing there. As soon as she sees me, she rushes over and hugs me. I'm taken aback by her gesture.

"I promise I won't push you and my brother together again," she whispers to me in Italian.

"Come, ladies, let's shop," Savannah states as she ushers us out of the bathroom.

And boy, do we shop.

22

PAIGE

Paige: Hey, I'm sorry, can we raincheck tonight? I wanted to take Natalia out for dinner to say thank you for today.

Giorgio: That's fine. I have some work to catch up on. Have fun.

"Thanks for today, I had so much fun. I'll see you tonight," I tell Natalia as I step out of the car, Ray, the driver, helping me with my bags. I took a few things, including my outfit for dinner tonight, and the rest are being delivered tomorrow.

"Okay. See you later." She waves excitedly as Ray walks me to the door.

I punch in my code and push through the glass doors, thanking him for his help. He heads back to the car, and I walk toward the elevator, stopping to check the mail first. I put my hand into my handbag to grab the key and realize my phone's missing. It must have fallen out in the car. It is still outside, so I drop my shopping bags and rush out the door to stop the car, but they pull into traffic before I have a chance to get to them.

"Fucking look at you, you're pathetic, trying to be someone you're not." That voice, the one that used to light my body on fire, now turns it to ice. Turning around, I see a pissed-off ex-husband glaring at me. My eyes narrow as I notice the black eye he's supporting. "Oh, you noticed that bruising. You can thank your boyfriend for that. Trying to pay me off to stay away from you."

I shake my head; has he lost his mind? "I don't know what you're talking about." And how the hell did he know that I was here? Is he tracking me? Has he been waiting all day?

His eyes widen, his face turning red. "You're fucking Italian asshole. Who came into our restaurant, assaulted, then threatened me."

Gio?

No. Why would he do that?

"I don't have a boyfriend," I yell at him.

"You're just a slut fucking him then," he spits, wagging his finger in my face.

I shake my head again. "No, he's a friend," I try to placate him as he's scaring me.

"Bullshit."

"Please, Michael, you shouldn't be here," I whisper.

"I have every right to demand to know who my wife is fucking, don't you think?"

Michael's become unhinged; I see it now. Has he always been like this? Or has the breakup triggered something?

"I'm not your wife," I remind him.

He grabs me. "You will always be my fucking wife." He grunts as his fingers dig into my arm.

"You're hurting me," I say, trying to wrestle away from him.

"I don't fucking care, you're hurting me with these lies. Why do you need to be protected from me? I'm your fucking husband."

Is he serious right now? Look what he is doing to me.

"Open the fucking door, Paige," he says, violently pushing me up against the glass door to my brother's apartment complex.

"No," I tell him, my heart pounding loudly in my chest.

"You never do as you are told," he spits before his hand connects with my face in a hard slap.

I'm stunned silent.

"Now open the fucking door," he yells at me.

"No," I reiterate, standing my ground.

His eyes narrow, and I brace for another slap, but as I watch, his hand moves in slow motion, and that's when something clicks inside of me. My knee comes up, hitting him in the balls just as his hand connects with me again, but this time, he hits my jaw instead of my cheek, rattling my teeth. I shake it off as Michael drops to the floor like a sack of potatoes and then I run. On wobbly legs, I rush down the street through the bustling traffic and away from my insane ex-husband. I need help. I need to find the closest police station and get them to call Smith. I look around to see if he's following me, but as I do, I trip over the gutter and end up splayed out against the concrete. The hard surface slices up my bare legs underneath my sundress, my hands sliding across the rough surface.

It hurts.

Everything hurts.

A crowd starts to gather around me, helping me up. "Please, can someone call nine-one-one? My ex just attacked me," I scream at the people looking at me with concern. Over their shoulders, I see Michael getting up and staring at me; he hesitates a couple of moments before he decides to get out of there, running in the opposite direction.

"Paige, Paige," a familiar voice calls out, and I see Natalia heading toward me. I push the bystanders aside and rush toward her. "Oh my god, Paige, look at you," she states, concern lacing her face.

"Michael," is all I pant.

Her dark eyes widen, and she wraps her arms around me and rushes me back to the apartment. "Ray, call Gio," she yells at her driver, who nods. With shaky hands, I type in the passcode, and we step into the foyer, where I collapse, knowing I'm safe. I absently notice all my bags are still where I left them. "Are you okay?"

I shake my head. "No." My body begins to shake, the shock catching up with me.

Her driver knocks on the glass door, and Natalia lets him in. "He's on his way. I'll wait for him outside, miss," he tells her before handing her something and disappearing outside again.

"Okay, let's get you cleaned up," she says, helping me to get up off the floor, and I hobble toward the elevator as she grabs the bags.

"My phone, I need to call my brother," I say as panic rushes through my veins.

"I have it. Let's get you upstairs."

Giorgio is the first to arrive as Smith is on the other side of town. Callie is in a meeting and Savannah was at the hairdresser when Natalia called them to let them know what happened.

"Where is she?" I hear Giorgio's panicked voice as he enters the apartment. A slew of Italian curse words fall from his mouth as he drops to his knees in front of me, his hand running over my bloodied knees, raising goosebumps over my skin. "Did he do this to you?" he asks darkly, his chocolatey eyes almost molten as he looks up at me.

"That was me trying to get away, but this—" I hold my hand up against my face where he hit me, "—was him, and these—" I turn my arm and show him the bruises, "—was him too." More Italian curse words. I reach out and interrupt his threats of violence. "Please, leave him alone, he's dangerous."

His face falls as he takes in my plea. "He has no idea how dangerous I can be, *Amore mio*."

I don't want to start a war between them. "Let the police deal with him, please, Gio." I let the tears fall.

His face softens. "Okay." He leans forward and kisses my hands.

It's not long until Smith arrives, bursting through his front door as if he's on a raid. He clocks me on his sofa, curled up next to Gio, and rushes over. I get up and wrap myself around him as I break down again.

"He's going to jail, Paige. I promise you, this man is done," he tries to reassure me.

"Why is he doing this to me?" I question my brother.

"Ego or he's insane, I'm not sure yet," he says softly. Noticing the bruises on my face, his hand touches them gently. Moments later, Callie and Savannah rush through the door and head toward me with a million and one questions. It takes a while to untangle myself and head back to the sofa. Giorgio has moved to stand with his sister away from us, speaking in hushed Italian.

"I don't think New York is safe for you anymore, Paige. Maybe you should go up to the place in the Hamptons," Smith suggests.

"You don't think he can track her there," Callie adds.

"Not when he's in jail."

Callie huffs. "You know this world, Smith, the good guys don't always win." My brother's eyes narrow on Callie, but he nods in agreement.

"Why doesn't Paige go overseas? Can't you track Michael via his passport? So, if he does somehow not end up in jail, he's easier to track," Savannah suggests.

"She's not wrong," Smith agrees.

"Paige can come back with us. We have our own jet, he would never know she's left," Natalia pipes in.

"True, harder to track someone on a private jet," Smith adds.

The group continues to talk as if I'm not there, reorganizing my life until I'm unable to take it any longer and get up, storming out of the living room and into my bedroom and slamming the door. I let out a scream of frustration. How the hell has my life turned to this?

"Paige." Smith knocks on my door.

"Go away, I need a moment," I yell back.

I melt down in my room until I'm too exhausted to continue and collapse onto my bed. Obviously, I've been quiet for too long because Smith opens my bedroom door.

"Are you okay?" he asks, peeking around the door.

"No," I answer, my lip wobbling as I sit up in bed.

He comes over and takes a seat beside me. "I'm sure today was scary for you," he says, talking calmly.

"I would never have thought the man I saw today was the man I was supposed to spend the rest of my life with."

Smith nods. "Because he's not the same man, that man's gone."

"Did I do that to him? Did I make him into this monster?"

"None of this is your fault, but I do think he's dangerous, Paige," he says, concern etched on his face.

"I think so, too."

"As much as I don't like it, I do think if you head to Europe for a bit, it might be good for you. Plus, Gio has the contacts to keep you safe," Smith suggests.

"By myself?" I pout.

"Savannah has indicated that she could come over for a bit. Callie and I can put in for vacation time and spend it with you when it's approved," he explains.

"How long would I need to be gone for?"

My brother shrugs. "I don't know, long enough for Michael to be put in jail or he moves on."

"You really think I should go?"

"As much as I have loved us living together, you're cramping my style," he jokes.

I throw a pillow at him. "You wanna get laid."

"I do. I haven't been able to since you moved in, and my hand is getting sore."

Ew. I scrunch up my face over my brother's TMI.

"Honestly, you need to get out of New York. Lucia has homes all around the world. Take a vacation if you need one, or go check out some of the businesses you inherited, see if any of them need anything, and start enjoying this new life she's given you. You have a second chance at being whoever you want to be," he suggests.

"You think that's Countess Paige?" I joke.

"Who the fuck knows, but anything is better than living in fear because of some pindicked asshole," he says angrily.

He's right. What happened today was scary, and he's escalating; who knows how far he will go next time, and I don't want to find out.

"Gio is offering you a lift to Italy, and you love it there. Go check out Rome or Florence."

I shake my head. "I can't go back to Lucia's, not yet," I say, my lip quivering with emotion.

Smith reaches out and places his hand over mine. "That's fine. Go to her hotels in Greece, she has that villa in Sardinia, the world is literally your oyster."

"Have I turned into a poor little rich girl, not knowing which house to go to?" I say, bursting out laughing, my brother joining in with me. The tension from earlier slowly releases from my muscles with each chuckle.

"It's kind of what it's sounding like."

I let out a heavy sigh. "Where do you think I should go?"

He shrugs his shoulders. "The plane is going to Rome, so why not start there and then see where it takes you?"

"Guess I'm going to Rome, then."

23

PAIGE

"I can't believe we are going to Rome in a private jet," Savannah squeals as we board Gio's plane.

"You made it," Natalia says the second she sees us board, and she gets up to give us both a hug. "We are going to have so much fun."

Gio is sitting at the back of the plane on his phone, staring at his laptop. He looks busy, but he glances up at us and nods before going back to his work.

"Would you ladies like champagne?" the flight attendant asks as we take our seats, placing a glass of champagne next to each of us.

"I want to raise a glass to you both, to thank you for welcoming me into your lives and I can't wait to show you both my world," Natalia exclaims as she raises her glass and we all cheers.

"As long as you introduce me to some Italian stallions, then I'm all for it," Savannah adds.

"Don't you worry, when the Italian men see you, they will fall to their knees and offer you anything you want." Natalia grins.

"I'm liking the sound of Italy more and more." Savannah chuckles as we sit back and fall into a natural rhythm of chatting. Smith messaged me this morning to let me know that Michael had been asked to present himself at the closest police station in violation of the protection order and that he would keep me in the loop regarding it. Honestly, I'm so happy that I'll be gone for all of that.

After flying for a couple of hours, we've been fed and drunk copious amounts of champagne, and Natalia and Savannah have both fallen asleep. I can't sleep on planes, even private ones, so I get up and head to the back where Giorgio is, and I take a seat beside him.

"You seem to be having fun," Giorgio says, looking up from his computer.

"Those two together are trouble, I already know it." I chuckle.

"I can see it. Thanks again for being so nice to Natalia, it's hard for her to make female friends without them wanting something from her or her family," he explains.

That sucks for her. Natalia is awesome. Even if I've only known her a little while, I know she's such a nice, caring person, someone I would love to be friends with, plus neither Sav nor I want anything from her other than her friendship.

"We both love her. She's going to be a great tour guide around Rome."

He raises a brow. "That should be interesting." He smirks.

I'm sure it will include stops at designer stores and bars, which is fine by me.

"How are you?" he asks, his eyes falling onto the bruise on my cheek.

"Okay, as I can be."

He nods in understanding.

"Did you pay Michael a visit the other day?" I question him. It was surprising hearing Michael tell me that Gio paid him a visit and gave him a black eye; I would never have thought he was capable of doing that.

"Yes, I offered him a million dollars to leave you alone."

A gasp falls from my lips. He did what? A million dollars, who has that kind of money to offer someone?

"He wasn't interested in the money. He was hell-bent on revenge."

That's when I knew he was insane, a normal person wouldn't turn down that kind of money, no matter what," Gio adds.

"What would have happened if he had accepted? You would have been out a lot of money," I question him.

"If it meant you were safe, it was worth it," he tells me seriously.

My broken, cracked little heart gently thuds in my chest. "You hardly know me."

"Hardly know you?" Gio huffs at my comment as his eyes narrow on me, then leans forward. "I know everything I need to know about you, Paige. The way your lips taste of strawberries when I kiss them."

I bite my bottom lip, remembering what it felt like the other night to have his lips on mine.

"And the fact that after all these years, you still smell like coconuts. I can't look at one without remembering what it felt like to bury my face into the crook of your neck and inhale your scent while my cock drove into you."

Oh.

My throat becomes dry; is it getting hot in here? "Gio ..." I say his name, more as a whisper than a warning.

"Just like that, you used to whimper my name as your fingers tangled in my hair and my tongue licked up every last drop of your sweetness."

Fuck.

Heat flushes my face and along my chest; this was not at all what I was expecting when I came over to chat. Goosebumps prickle against my skin and my knees pull together, trying to stave off this throbbing need that he seems to awaken in me. Abruptly, I stand and head to the bathroom, needing a chance to get myself back under control. As I slam the door shut, something stops it. When I look up, Gio is holding it open.

"What are you doing?" I hiss as I rattle the door.

His hand grips the top of the bathroom archway, his muscles straining against his polo shirt. "You don't need to run away from me, P," he says, using my childhood nickname.

"I think I do, Gio."

"Why? Do my filthy words have you so hot and bothered that you need to rub one out while remembering all the things I used to do to you? I can assure you I've refined my skills."

What the hell has gotten into this man? Has the altitude gone to his head?

"If it has, that's none of your business," I bite back.

His eyes darken with heat, and I get lost in those molten pools. "I can help."

"That's nice, but I'm learning how to be an independent woman. It's the journey I must take."

He growls at my rebuff.

"Your fingers wouldn't be able to get you off like mine can," he adds, leaning in as his eyes dip to my mouth.

I'm sure he's right, but that's not the point. I'm way over my head with this man; he's not the inexperienced young boy he used to be.

He steps away from me, letting me close the bathroom door.

"Shit. Shit. Shit," I curse as I stare at my flushed face in the toilet mirror. *He was offering to help. To what, join the mile-high club? It's been too long since you've been laid, you should have taken him up on it.* My friends are just there. *So?* I huff, frustrated with myself for letting him get me worked up so much. What the hell was he thinking, saying those things to me?

Storming out of the bathroom annoyed and still sexually frustrated, I walk over and take a seat beside him again. He raises a brow, noticing the mood I'm in.

Leaning forward in the chair, I say, "You can't say those things to me ever again. Do you hear me?" I point my finger in his face for good measure.

"I was stating facts," he says, shrugging his shoulders.

Urgh, this man is frustrating. "I don't care if you're Casanova himself, we are just friends."

His jaw tightens, and I can imagine him grinding his teeth. "Noted, Paige," he answers gruffly.

"Good, I'm glad we're on the same page," I say, getting up and making my way over to my seat. I set my boundaries with him because if I don't, I know I am going to jump that man. My life is chaos right now and I'm not in the right frame of mind to be dealing with a man like him.

Eventually, we land and two sets of cars are waiting for us on the tarmac. Gio storms off the plane and toward his car.

"What's with him?" Savannah asks.

I shrug and pretend it doesn't have anything to do with me.

"Ignore him, he's in a mood, probably hating the fact he is back to reality," Natalia states.

I frown, but it quickly vanishes when Natalia hugs me tightly.

"I'm so happy to have met you both. Let's catch up tomorrow for drinks and shopping," she suggests.

"Sounds great," Savannah answers for me as we wave her goodbye. The staff have loaded our bags into the back of the car, and we jump in.

"I'm nervous," I tell Sav.

"Why?"

"I'm about to visit the home that I own in fricken Rome." I chuckle at the absurdity of it all.

It takes us about an hour to get from the airport to my new home, but we make it. The bellman sees us pull up and greets us warmly. I explain who I am, and he quickly gets to helping our driver get our luggage out of the car.

"You're VIP now," Savannah says, elbowing me in the ribs as we are escorted inside. The bellman—or concierge, as I've been advised—hands over an envelope with the apartment's keys. He explains that someone is here twenty-four-seven and will look after all deliveries for me. He also adds how sorry he is for my loss and that Lucia was a wonderful lady and would always take the time to chat with him. That was nice to hear, but it still feels like a gut punch knowing she's not here and I am.

"We're not getting in that are we?" Savannah asks, spying the old lift waiting for us.

"You'll be fine, everywhere has lifts like this," I reassure her as we enter the death trap. Its cogs squeak and creak as we ascend to the top level.

"I'll take the stairs next time. I'll have the tightest ass by the time I leave." Sav shivers as we get out of the lift. Grabbing the keys out of the envelope, I open the door and step inside my great-aunt's apartment, one I haven't been to in years. We enter through the grand foyer, with its Italian marble floor, and into the living room. Lucia's antiques fill the spaces as sunlight beams in from the large windows that lead out to a terrace.

"Are you fricking kidding? Paige, look at the view," Savannah says excitedly as she opens the glass doors and steps out onto the terrace. "Nothing but miles of Roman rooftops and ancient ruins, this is spectacular. I'm never leaving. I've already fallen in love with Italy," she declares, shouting from the terrace and making me laugh. "I can see now why you come here."

"There's something magical about Italy," I agree.

"Nat needs to find me a hot Italian stallion and then I can live happily ever after with you here."

"Sounds like a solid plan," I tease.

I show Sav her room and the concierge helps her with her bags while I head toward the main bedroom, Lucia's, and step across the threshold, waiting to hear her laugh and smell a cloud of Chanel No. 5 in the air, but there's nothing as I look around the empty room.

I miss you, I think, trying to contain my tears as I take a seat on the bed. *I need you. I don't know what to do anymore. You always knew what to do. I can't do this alone. Why did you have to leave me? I wasn't ready.*

24

GIORGIO

I will not check social media again!
But I click on Paige's profile to see what she is doing for the hundred and sixth time. Photos of her and her friend doing all the touristy things: Colosseum, Sistine Chapel, throwing a coin into the Trevi Fountain, so many photos of food, and of her enjoying said food. I overstepped the line on the plane, especially after everything that had happened the day before. Could I be any more self-absorbed? What kind of man tries to flirt with their ex after her ex-husband assaults her? *Me.* This dickhead. And then to be completely shut down and told that you're just friends, well, I'm not going to lie, that hurt my ego. I thought things were happening. Like we had slowly slipped back into how we used to be.

"Gio, you're back," Lilly says, walking through the door of my parents' home for Sunday lunch, and I greet her with a hug.

"Hey, man, how was New York?" Luca asks, walking in after her.

"New York was good."

My brother's eyes narrow on me. "What kind of business were you doing there?"

"Was to do with the wine, finding new distributors and stuff," I lie.

"Anyway," Lilly says, playfully hitting my brother in the chest, "I got to hang out with Paige and her friend Savannah yesterday with Nat," she says.

I should be surprised but I'm not, because I've been obsessively watching her socials. I nod but decide to remain close-lipped.

"They were so much fun. I love them. She's really nice and speaks highly of you," she adds.

She does?

"She told us what you did for her regarding her ex. What a horrible guy. I can't believe someone as nice as her is dealing with a monster like him. I'm glad you whisked her away from all that," Lilly explains.

"I happened to have a space on the jet." I shrug.

"Still, it was nice. And she's a countess, like how cool is that? I mean, you guys don't know what it's like to be normal, but to one day inherit like she did a life she knew nothing about is mind-blowing," Lilly continues, singing Paige's praises.

"Lilly, you made it. How is my grandbaby growing? Come, let me see, you must be hungry," my mother calls out across the room. Lilly gives me a smile, walks over to my mother, and disappears into the kitchen with her.

"She's always hungry." Luca chuckles. "Anyway, Lilly can't stop talking about how much she likes Paige. They had a great day out together, I mean, even Nat loves her. I'm curious as to how you feel seeing her after all these years," Luca asks.

"It's been nice catching up."

He frowns. "That's it. It's been nice catching up," he says, mocking me. "That's the kind of line you tell our parents. What the fuck is really going on?"

I scrub my face and sigh. "I like her. Is that what you want to hear?"

"Yeah, pretty much." He grins.

I shake my head, annoyed.

"What are you going to do about it?" he asks.

"Nothing. Technically, the world still thinks Giada and I are together. She has an asshole ex and is dealing with that. I'm not adding to her full plate because I can't control the way I feel," I explain to him.

"But you would if you could?" he presses.

"What do you want me to say, Luca?" I ask angrily.

"I don't know, Gio," he argues back.

My brother is only trying to help me, but I don't need him butting in; I have everything under control.

"What do you want to happen?" he questions me.

"Nothing, okay, can we leave it and enjoy today's lunch?"

Luca glares at me, but I try to ignore him. Thankfully, my parents come back out of the kitchen.

"Where's your sister?" Mamma asks.

"Which one?" Luca asks.

"I know where Allegra is," Mamma answers, her eyes drifting over to me. "I'm talking about Natalia."

"She's always running late." My brother chuckles as the staff starts to bring things to the table.

"I'm here," Natalia declares, walking through the door.

"Oh shit," is all I hear from my brother.

"Paige, Savannah," Lilly exclaims as she rushes to greet the two women.

"Guess you're not going to be able to hide from her now." Luca chuckles before he walks over to say hi.

"Paige, welcome to our home. We are so happy you could make it," my mother says as she greets the women.

"Thank you for having us. Your home is so beautiful," Paige says, hugging my mother.

"You didn't tell me you were bringing guests," I tell my sister.

"Didn't think I needed your permission." She shrugs before giving me a look.

"You don't, I just didn't realize they were coming."

"Why would it matter? Do you have a problem with them?" she asks.

I shake my head. "No, of course not."

"Good, then it's going to be a great lunch with friends," she says excitedly before joining everyone else.

Get it together, Gio, they are your family's guests. Except I hate how my eyes track her every movement. That the sound of her laughter soothes me, that the damn coconut scent she's wearing evokes memories of things I shouldn't be thinking about. What I also notice is that she looks refreshed. A week in Rome and color seems to have seeped back into her skin, the dark circles vanishing from under her eyes. There's a lightness to her that wasn't there in New York. She turns and sees me, her eyes light up and a smile falls across her face; she seems happy to see me. But I thought … thought that I had messed things up on the plane.

"Gio, hey," she says, walking over and kissing my cheeks.

"This is a wonderful surprise," I say, looking down into her dark eyes, hating how the tiny fragments of my heart throb against my chest and something else throbs against my pants. Her cocoa hair is pulled up in a ponytail, and she's dressed in a figure-hugging white summer dress. I can tell it's designer by the way it falls over her body perfectly. She looks like an angel sent down to torment the devil in me. "You're looking refreshed," I tell her.

"I do?"

I nod. "Rome agrees with you."

"It's been a whirlwind of a week, but it's nice not having to look over my shoulder, even though I do, out of habit."

My hand curls tightly beside me, thinking of everything her ex has been putting her through. I think I'm going to make some calls next week to see what I can do to make his life a little harder than it needs to be.

"You two look like you've been having a great time."

"You've been watching?" she asks as her tongue slides along her glossy lips, my eyes tracking the movement.

"I have." I'm not going to deny it because she can see that I have.

"Good to know you're still keeping an eye on me. I thought you had forgotten about me." She smirks.

"I could never forget about you, Paige."

Her breath hitches at my admission and before she gets a chance to say anything, we are called for lunch. I escort her toward the table, and she takes a seat beside me, which makes me happier than it probably should.

Lunch continues as it normally does, with everyone talking over the top of each other. It's loud and chaotic, but it's my family.

"Ladies, will you be here for the Summer Ball?" my mother asks.

"When is it?" Paige asks.

"Next month," Natalia answers.

"I'll be back in New York then. I'm sorry that sounds like it would be awesome," Savannah adds.

"You never know, your date today could change that." Natalia winks.

"So true," Savannah answers excitedly.

Date? Does that mean Paige has a date, too?

As if reading my mind, Lilly asks that exact question to her.

"Oh no, that's all her." Paige laughs.

Thank fuck.

"I'm steering clear of men for the foreseeable future," she adds.

Oh.

Lilly looks over at me. "That's understandable."

"Didn't take long for you to jump on me after breaking up with your fiancé," Luca says, nudging his wife.

"Luca," she gasps, looking over at where my parents are seated.

"Luca was the runaway groom," Natalia explains to our guests.

Paige's mouth falls open in surprise.

"Because I found her sleeping with my best friend right before the wedding," Luca adds.

"And then you hightailed it to the middle of nowhere in Scotland. Where no one could find you for ages," I remind him; it was a stressful time.

"Exactly, that was the point," Luca states.

"Then how did the two of you meet?" Paige asks.

"He rented my cottage from my sister, who was on her way to Africa, where I was working as a doctor to surprise me for Christmas. Little did she know that I was on my way back, sick of dealing with my fiancé sleeping with all the nurses behind my back," Lilly explains.

"There was a blizzard outside, it was the middle of nowhere, and this angel walked into the cabin and I thought I had died and gone to heaven," my brother states as he leans over and kisses Lilly.

"Something like that, except he left out the part where I walked in on him naked," Lilly adds.

The girls burst out laughing and the conversation continues to a different topic.

"We should go to Paris to get you your dress," Natalia says to Paige as we are sitting outside in the courtyard with our drinks. "You said your great-aunt invested in Yvette Sanchez, the designer, we should go to her shop and find you something to wear. You can also check out your investment too. Hey, Gio, do you mind if we borrow the jet to take it to Paris," Natalia calls out to me.

I look over at where Luca and Lilly are seated. "Why don't we all go? Lilly needs a dress, too," Luca states.

"Doubt she's going to have anything maternity-esque for me, but I'll never say no to a trip to Paris," she says, rubbing her ever-expanding stomach.

"You might as well come too, Gio, seeing as we are all tagging along," Luca tells me.

"I'll have to check my schedule," I reply gruffly. I don't think Paige wants me there.

"You never come on these trips. New York was the first time you spontaneously jumped on the jet," Natalia adds.

Paige turns to look at me, her brows pinching together.

"He had a last-minute work meeting," Luca explains.

"There was no meeting in New York," my father says, inserting himself into a conversation that doesn't concern him.

"I don't tell you everything that is going on with me," I tell them.

"Clearly, as we didn't know there was a problem with Giada," Mother chimes in.

Wow, low blow, Mamma.

"Now it's my fault that I didn't know my fiancée was having an affair. Thanks, family, you're a great support," I say, standing up, annoyed by this conversation. "Take the jet, get the dresses. I've got to go, I have a ton of work I have to get done before Monday," I tell the room.

"You can't leave yet, you said you were dropping Paige home," Natalia calls out.

I did too.

Fuck.

So much for my dramatic storm out.

"I'm ready to go now. I have to call my brother. He'll send out a search party if I don't," Paige says, rolling her eyes as she stands up and starts thanking everyone for a lovely day.

She follows me outside, the entire family on our heels as they all stand on the stairs and watch us get into my car. I open the car door for Paige, and she gives the crowd a wave before getting in. I shut the door, then walk around and get into the driver's side. I start the car and click the button for the gate to open and head off. We sit in silence for a bit until Paige can't take it anymore.

"I don't think it was your fault for not seeing what was happening between your sister and fiancée. It was a harsh thing for your mother to say, but I'm assuming she doesn't understand the 'who' of the matter."

My hands grip the steering wheel tightly as her coconut scent swirls around me. I'm going to be smelling her in this car for days; it's going to drive me crazy.

"No, she doesn't," I answer as I continue to drive.

Silence falls between us again.

"Are we okay?" she asks, turning toward me as we stop at a red light.

"Yes, of course."

"Then why haven't you messaged me?"

"Why haven't you messaged me?" I reply.

She remains silent and so do I; we don't talk again until I pull up out the front of her apartment.

"Thanks for the lift," she says, but doesn't move to get out. She shifts in her seat and turns to me. "I miss your messages. They have been the highlight of my days after Michael. I hate that I miss you, too. Somehow you have crept back into my life and now I don't know what it's like without you in it."

"Get out of the car," I tell her.

Shock resonates on her face, her lip quivering at my harsh words. She reaches for the car door at the same time I do mine. I slam my door with such force it shakes the car, and she does the same. Getting angrier and angrier with every step, I follow her in silence.

"You don't need to walk me to my door, I'm fine," she snips as we both storm past the concierge.

"I promised Smith I would."

She lets out a huff but doesn't fight me on it. It's not a lie, but it's also not the truth; it's an assumption that he would want me to protect her and so I should. We step into the small antique elevator, and she angrily presses the button to the top floor. As soon as the doors slam shut, confining us into the cramped space, I move toward her, placing my hands on either side of her, my fingers wrapping around the iron. A gasp falls from her lips at my sudden proximity.

"Gio," she says, as much a warning as it is a plea.

"Do you have any idea how much it's killing me to watch your stories of flirting and dancing with other men?"

"Oh," she answers, her mouth falling open.

"I don't have the right to demand the same treatment for me, but I want to."

"Um," she says, then bites her lip, her chest shaking with an unsteady breath. I'm probably making her uncomfortable, especially after what happened in New York. I don't want her to think I'm a monster like her ex. I step away and rake my hands through my hair in frustration. I want her. So damn much that my entire body gets strung so tightly every time I'm around her. My mind ponders over the what-ifs and the thoughts of a different life if I had the balls to go for it. She could have been mine, forever and always.

"I'm sorry, Paige, I .... Being near you ... it ... it brings up things and I don't know how to push them back down so I can be around you like a normal fucking man."

Her brows pull together, but her words are cut short as the elevator stops and the buzzer cuts through the tension swirling between us. On unsteady legs, she turns and pushes open the door, but I don't move. She stops when she realizes I'm not following.

"I can't come into your home, Paige," I say through gritted teeth.

"Why not?"

"Because if I step over that threshold I don't know if I'm going to be able to keep my hands off you."

Her lips form a perfect O in response before she nibbles her bottom lip again, then turns around and walks toward her door. "Are you coming then?" she calls out to me.

25

PAIGE

Seeing Gio wrestling with his needs is the biggest turn-on. I've never had someone literally vibrating with so much lust that they need to hold themselves back from me.

It's hot.

He gave me an option. The ball is in my court, and honestly, maybe it was the wine I had with lunch or the dolce vita-ness of being in Italy, but I thought, fuck it. When do I get to do something for myself? I haven't stopped thinking about what it would be like to be with Giorgio again since the moment he stepped back into my life. Every single time I thought about going further, something made me hesitate and maybe that was New York and all the links I had back there, pulling me away from this. I just want a moment for myself to feel beautiful, desired, and wanted. To feel like a woman again after everything Michael put me through, and Giorgio Fiorenzo is the man to help make this happen.

Letting go of the elevator door, I walk the couple of steps toward my apartment before turning. Gio is standing in the elevator, holding the door open, his dark brows pulling together. Perhaps wondering about my angle, hoping I might finally give in to this undercurrent of familiar flirtation that has been swirling between us for weeks.

"Are you coming then?" I ask, then slide the key into the lock and open the door.

His eyes widen, his brows shooting up high on his face before he steps toward me, his palms hitting either side of my head against the doorframe and making me take a step back. The heat smoldering from his dark chocolate eyes is intense and hot, forcing a shiver to run down my spine.

"Paige," he hisses, and I watch his veins strain against his biceps, his fingers digging into the doorway.

I bite my bottom lip and stare at this beautiful man. "I know," I answer him.

"Fifteen years I've waited to taste you again," he confesses.

Shit.

As I swallow down my nervousness, I say, "And you don't think I've wondered the same thing?"

He shakes his head. "I wouldn't know, you blocked me."

"Of course, I did. You broke me," I bite back, the swirling heat inside of me quickly turning into a raging inferno of anger as I remember seeing the two of them together.

"Paige, get inside," he commands, which has me standing up taller. Where the hell does he get off talking to me like that? The sudden change in tactic has given me whiplash. "If you don't turn around and shut this front door, then I'm going to fuck you in this doorway and fill the corridor with your screams."

Oh.

I quickly move inside, putting my bag on the side table before moving further into the apartment. Is it wrong to have sex with my childhood ex here? Am I desecrating the apartment somehow?

"Get out of your head, Paige," he tells me as he closes the door, then pulls his wallet out of his pocket along with his phone and places them on the side table next to my bag.

How does he know I'm in my head? I could be thinking about anything right now. The moon, the stars, and eggplants suddenly come to mind.

"You're doing it again," he says, stalking slowly back toward me.

He's right. And I hate that he is because he's giving me this cocky look that says, *It may be fifteen years, but I still know you*, and it's true, but I don't need him to know it's true.

"Get on your knees, P," he demands.

Get on my … what? I've never had a man talk to me like that before, but somehow, I feel compelled to do as he asks. It's the accent, the voice, any woman would do what he asked, listening to that deep-timbered voice. My legs buckle and I slide to the floor.

He reaches out and cups my chin, turning it up toward him as he looms over me. "Such a good girl." He grins, which starts my nerves firing on all cylinders. I've seen this happen in porn, but it's never happened in real life. Is that why Michael cheated? Because I wouldn't get on my knees for him? He never asked, never wanted to do anything adventurous. Like fucking me over the restaurant's kitchen bench—guess he only saves that for his mistresses. "Paige," Gio's voice thunders around me, making me straighten. "Unzip and take me out, you need something to concentrate on, so you will get out of your fucking head."

I hate how he can read me so easily. I'd thought after all these years the connection we had wouldn't still be there. That being around him would feel different, but it doesn't; it's as if he's always been there.

"Paige," he growls again, knowing I've let my mind wander. My hands quickly unzip his jeans; he's thickening right before me as my hand slides over the taut material, pulling a hiss from his lips. I like that sound. So, I do it again, running my nails along his material-covered cock. I watch as his body tenses underneath my touch. *I can't believe I'm doing this.*

This is the new you, Paige—bold, empowered, sexy. Yes!

With that new mindset, I set about having the best fun I can have as my hand slides down his underwear and pulls him out.

Oh.

Hello there, big boy.

"Paige, eyes on me," Gio commands, and honestly, the words *yes,*

Daddy are on the tip of my tongue. Who the hell am I? "I want to see your eyes widen as I slide my cock all the way to the back of your throat, ready?"

Am I? *Yes!*

"Wait," I say, which makes him still. I don't want to ruin this moment, but I think we need to set some boundaries first. "We need rules."

"Rules?" he repeats, arching his brow at me.

"This," I say, waving my hand between us, which is a little hard on my knees, but he should get the point. "I can only offer you my body, nothing more."

His body tenses at my request. "Why?"

"Honestly? Because you terrify me."

"We don't have to do anything," he says, reassuring me.

"Oh no, I want to, it's just ... my heart can't take anymore. She's locked up safe until she's ready. I'm not ready," I tell him honestly.

"I get it. I just want to make you feel good, Paige."

I can do that.

I want to do that.

Okay, let's do that.

Opening my mouth wide to let him know I've made my choice, he gives me the barest of nods as I stare up into those dark pools of cocoa. His cock slides between my lips and all the way to the back of my throat. I've always been good at taking dick—next to no gag reflexes. *Yay, go me!* Haven't had a chance to use it in a long time though. My hands rest on his hard thighs for stability. I love the way his brow pulls together the further he pushes down my throat, the way they then arch up in surprise at me being a good girl and taking all of him.

"You're so fucking perfect," he growls as my mouth wraps around him. I adjust a little before tightening everything around him. "Fuck," he groans, throwing his head back, then ever so slowly, slides his dick out of my mouth until the tip is on my tongue. I reach out, wrap my hand around his shaft, and start to move it up and down. "Yes," he croons as the tip slides in and out of my mouth while I push back the skin and suck on his sensitive tip. "Fuck, Paige. Do you have any idea how I've dreamed about this?" he confesses.

Nope, had no clue until right now.

"Every fucking night I've dreamed it was your mouth sliding along my cock instead of my hand. Taking me all the way down just like this." His hand cups my face as I continue to work him over. "It's even more perfect than I could ever have imagined."

Tingles hit the spot right between my thighs, and I almost buckle, but I don't because I want to do a good job. I want to show him how good I can be, but I'm also hot as hell kneeling here, and with every groan, moan, and grunt that falls from his lips, the hotter I get. Thank goodness I'm wearing a dress as one of my hands slides up and under my hem and I find my underwear soaked. Pushing the material to the side, I slide my fingers into myself and moan against his dick.

"Paige, are you touching yourself?"

I nod, as I can't quite answer that question verbally.

"Does sucking my cock make you so wet that you have to touch yourself?"

Again, I nod around his cock.

"Fuck," he curses, his dark eyes shimmering with heat. "Take off your dress," he commands.

His cock falls from my mouth, but I'm not sure about that. I don't feel my best. This man sleeps with supermodels; he's used to seeing naked perfection right in front of him. Last time he saw me naked, I was young, and time hadn't ravaged my body or the copious amounts of coffee, champagne, and croissants I've eaten over the years.

"Paige," he says softly, cupping my face. "I think you are the most beautiful woman in the world."

In the world? Oh, come on, maybe this room, as it's only me.

"Just your fucking lips have me wanting to come all over them. Seeing you naked in front of me will probably have me exploding in five seconds flat."

He's just saying that. But when I look into his eyes, I don't think he's lying.

"You really have no idea what you do to me, do you?" he states.

Not really.

"You trust me, don't you?" he asks.

"Of course, I do."

"Then trust me when I say I want you, Paige. I will always want you. Even if it's for just a night, I'll take whatever you want to give me."

I bite my bottom lip as my heart thunders against the little box I've put it in to protect it. My hand reaches up behind me and I unzip the dress. I just had his cock in my mouth, I shouldn't stop there. He helps me slide the dress up and over my head before throwing it to the floor. Thank goodness I went with nice underwear today, a pair of basic white bottoms and a bra.

"Fucking perfection." He sighs as those dark eyes roam over every inch of my body, lighting a trail over my skin as they go. Might as well keep going. I unhook my bra and let the girls go free. I've been blessed with great boobs, so I'm confident in them, at least. He reaches out and plucks a nipple as soon as they're free, sending goosebumps over my body. Then my hands move slowly toward my underwear. *Just keep going, Paige.* I hook my fingers, pull them down, and awkwardly get them over my knees and throw them to the side. Gio licks his lips as he takes in all of me and for the first time in my life, I feel worthy. How does he do that? One look and he makes me feel secure, safe, and desired.

"Fuck, Paige, all the things I want to do to you." He groans.

Yes. Do them. Do whatever the hell you want to me if you keep looking at me the way you do as if you've won the fucking lottery.

"Slip those fingers back between those folds," he commands and without hesitation, I do.

He grins at me. "Good girl, now, keep touching yourself while sucking me, but … do not come, do you hear me?" he warns.

What does he mean, not come? That's not fair.

"Stop that," he hisses, noticing my inner monologue getting a workout. "When you come, I want it to be either on my face, my fingers, or my fucking cock. Do you hear me?"

Oh, my eyes widen in surprise.

I hear you loud and clear and I'm all for those suggestions.

"Good, I'm glad we cleared that up." He grins and slides his cock back into my mouth.

26

PAIGE

We continue along a knife's edge, getting close to going over and then moving away again. It's hot, and it's making me wetter as it feels like I've created a puddle on the ground. I'm getting close and he must sense it as he reaches out and tugs my arm, the one currently between my legs.

"Stop."

And I do, letting my hand fall. Without missing a beat, he grabs my hand. He leans over and slides my fingers into his mouth, moaning around them. My eyes widen and my legs wobble as I watch with fascination as he licks every inch of my skin clean, which thickens his cock with every lick of my fingers. The sounds falling from his lips could have me going off without the aid of my fingers.

"Fucking perfect, just as I remember." He moans.

My cheeks burn brightly with embarrassment, heat, and need.

So hot.

"Stand up," he says, and I quickly get up off my knees. "Take off my shirt," he commands. And my shaky fingers start to unbutton his dress shirt before removing it and throwing it to the side. He is magnificent, every inch of him is pure muscle. My hands run along the ridges of his six-pack. Gosh, that is hot.

"Now put these fingers back into your cunt," he commands.

Oh.

This feels more intimate face-to-face instead of me on my knees.

"Go on, don't get shy on me now." He grins.

Gio, as a boy, was hard to resist. Gio, as a man, is downright dangerous. I do as I'm told and slide my fingers between my ever-increasingly wet folds, his eyes watching with heated desire. Knowing that his tongue has just slid along the same skin that is inside me, makes me wetter; it's as if he's fucking me with his fingers instead of my own. Gio's hand slides down over mine and I still; my heart thunders in my chest and my breath hitches. What is he going to do now?

He puts a small amount of pressure on my hand pushing my fingers further inside me, making my eyes roll back as he helps me find the sensitive nerves deep inside me and a moan falls from my lips.

"Fuck, that's it." He groans. "Keep going. I want you to hit that deep spot, the one that makes you see stars."

Yes.

I want that. I nod and bite my lip, following his commands. I don't want him to stop. I know that as much as I declared we can't do this again, I'm going to. We're going to fall back into bed together, just like we always did while growing up. This all feels so good, so familiar, and so right, and that scares me. *Concentrate on what's happening now, Paige. Forget about tomorrow, you can't deal with it now, enjoy today for what it is.* So, I do.

Gio leans in, and I feel his heat all around me as he runs his nose along the sensitive part of my neck, his lips barely touching my skin, but it sends waves of heat flooding my body.

"There's not a day that goes by that I haven't thought about you, Paige. Every night when I closed my eyes for years, your tear-soaked face haunted me. The only woman I've ever loved, and I broke her. If I could have ripped out my own heart and offered it to the gods to get you back, I would have. You are the single biggest regret of my life," he confesses.

"Gio," I moan as he continues to help drive me higher and higher.

"I know I'll never be the man I once was for you," he confesses, and I want to tell him he's wrong, he still is, that I don't think he has ever not been, but I'm too scared to say those things out aloud.

Instead, tears well in my eyes as I try to suppress the emotions he's pulling from me; it's a weird situation to be in—he's pushing me physically to the brink, but in the same breath, he's doing it emotionally, too.

"If all I can ever be to you is a friend, then I'll take it. I can't spend another fifteen years apart from you, Paige, not now that I've found you again."

Tears slip down my cheeks as he continues to furiously work me over.

"I will happily stand on the sidelines and watch you fall in love with another man because I lost that right all those years ago, and that's my penance to bear. All I want in this world is to see you happy."

Fuck.

"Gio." His name comes out as a strangled moan before his lips capture mine in a searing kiss.

"It will always be you, Paige," he confesses, pushing me over the edge and kissing me again, swallowing my moans as he makes me come all over my fingers. He gives me a couple of seconds to compose myself before letting go of me and walking away, cursing to himself as he runs his fingers through his dark hair.

He can't say those things when I am standing in front of him physically naked and now emotionally naked, too. How dare he make me come and then walk away. Moving toward him, I grab his arm, pull him back, and push him against the hallway wall.

"What the fuck, Paige?" he curses as he hits the wall.

"How fucking dare you," I yell in his face.

His eyes widen as he stares into my angry face.

"You can't say those words to me, then walk away as if they were nothing," I tell him.

"I shouldn't have said them."

His visible regret at saying those beautiful things is like a sucker punch to my stomach.

"How fucking dare you regret those words," I yell at him as I slap his bare chest.

"Paige, ouch, what the hell?" he hisses as he grabs my arms and holds them beside me, so that I won't slap him again.

"You can't say all those things to me and walk away," I tell him again.

"There's nothing else left to say. I fucked up. I shouldn't have crossed the line between us. I shouldn't have pushed to remind myself what it feels like to have those lips wrapped around my cock." His eyes dip to said lips. "I shouldn't have allowed myself to taste you, now it's seared in my soul. It is going to torture me until the end of time. I should never have reminded myself what it was like to watch you come because that sound will haunt my ears. Having you back in my life has brought the sunshine back into my world that I never knew was missing. I can't step further into that sunshine, Paige. And I'm sorry that I can't be what you need. What more is there to say?" He lets my hands go.

Fuck him for saying those things and making my heart beat for him again.

"Nothing more to say? For you there isn't, but for me there is," I say, poking his hard chest. His eyes widen at my anger. "I loved you with all my heart, Gio, all of it. So much so that I don't think anyone else ever stood a chance because that day you walked away from me, you took it with you. I hate that you broke us that day. I hate that you ripped our future away from us. We could have been happily married all these years. We could have had kids. We could have built a fucking life together, but instead, now I'm stuck with an ex-husband who abused me, cheated on me, and whittled me down into a person I don't know anymore. Then you turn up like a white knight riding in to save the day. But instead of getting the best version of me that you had all those years ago, you're now seeing the broken and messed-up version. You made me fall in love with someone I shouldn't have because you felt like you needed to save me. From fucking what, Gio? Because guess what? Now I'm here in your world. I'm about to join your fishbowl and I'm having to do it alone."

Gio stares at me for a long moment, the deafening beating of my heart sounds like it's in stereo through the apartment. The next thing I know, Gio is launching himself at me, kissing me. It's an angry kiss between us, a kiss built up with tension, need, lust, forgiveness, and everything we didn't have the nerve to say to each other.

He pulls away and looks almost feral with desire as he turns me around in his arms and pushes me up against the wall. He kicks my feet apart and a hand comes and slaps my bare ass, which makes me moan. I can feel my liquid heat sliding down my legs.

His lips move to the juncture of my neck. "You've always owned me, P, and you always fucking will," he curses against my skin as I feel him nudge at my entrance. "No woman has ever or will ever own me like you do," he declares, pushing himself into me, pulling hisses and moans from each of us as he stretches me around him.

I feel so full.

He then wraps his hand around my ponytail and pulls me back flush with him, which pushes him even deeper.

"I still fucking fit perfectly. Your cunt was always made for me, Paige. Nothing feels better than this feeling right now."

I bite my bottom lip as he starts moving. My body feels like it's on fire as he slides between my folds, pushing every single button inside me.

"You feel like home," he whispers against my skin.

He's right, and I hate that he is.

This wasn't supposed to happen. I wasn't supposed to fall for someone so soon after everything. *Gio isn't a stranger, he was the love of your life.*

That's what scares me. I don't want him to break me again.

"You're so tight, Paige, fuck."

As he continues to work me over, the little bite of pain of his hand wrapped around my hair, the furious thrusting dragging my nipples across the wall sending sensations across my skin, lights every inch of me on fire.

His other hand slides away from my hip and down between my legs; I arch my back, pushing myself harder against him to accommodate his fingers.

"Yes," I hiss at the contact when his thumb slides over my sensitive clit. He continues to rub, making me wetter with each circle. He then slides a finger inside of me while he continues to thrust into me. I feel full, oh so full, it's too much yet not enough. When he finds his rhythm with all the moving parts, I start to see stars, and my body flushes as the blood pumps all around me, but I don't want him to stop.

Never ever.

"I'm close," I pant.

"I know, baby," he coos, and his fingers work some magic voodoo on my pussy, and the next thing I know, she hurtles her way to the edge and jumps straight off over it, sending me into a spasming heap as I close my eyes and see the universe in all its glory, feeling like I've been transported to another dimension. "Fuck, Paige, you're so tight when you come. That's it, baby, squeeze it, use me to drain every last drop of your pleasure from me."

Gio's dirty talk has improved one hundred percent in the last fifteen years, and I am here for it. Usually, I don't enjoy it, but when it's coming from his mouth, it seems that I do. He continues to fuck me until his groans and moans start to get louder and his perfect rhythm begins to falter.

"Turn around," he grits out as he pulls himself out of me.

I hate that my body instantly mourns the loss of his dick as I quickly turn around.

"Fuck, Paige," he curses, then bites his bottom lip hard. I watch him holding his hard dick as white ribbons of release land all over my chest, painting me. I've never been one for the *pearl necklace* as such, but watching his eyes flare with heat as each stream hits my boobs, nipples, and stomach makes me want to jump him again. "You look fucking perfect," he says, admiring his artwork. I run my fingers through the wetness on my nipple and suck it from my fingers. "Fuck, Paige," he groans before he reaches out and wraps his hand around my throat, pulling me to him and kissing me hard. So hot and a little taboo as he tastes himself on my tongue. "Perfection." He grins as his hand moves down and starts to rub himself all over my breasts. His fingers pluck my nipples, and his palm glides over my sticky skin, rubbing himself further across my body. I would never have let anyone do this to me, but seeing how much this is turning Gio on, turns me on. "Mine," he says, moving from one breast to the other, marking me. My head falls back and my eyes close as I try to control my hormones that keep firing on all systems.

Suddenly, Gio is pulling away from me, making me open my eyes, and I watch as he falls to his knees this time. He grabs my leg and pulls it over his shoulder.

"You need another, P, I can see it." He grins before his tongue slides along my wet folds. *Just go with it, Paige.* He begins lapping at my wet folds, then starts to tease me; one minute, he's sucking on my clit, pushing me higher and higher, and the next, he is tasting my lips. Then he's back again, working over my sensitive bud until my legs start to shake and then he moves away again. He keeps building me up higher and higher until he inserts two thick fingers and curls them inside me, sucking hard on my clit. The next thing I know, I'm screaming and thrashing against the wall as I flood his face with my wetness, something I've never done before and I'm too limp to even have the energy to be embarrassed over it. I'm a limp noodle as I start to slide down the wall. Thankfully, he is there to catch me.

27

GIORGIO

I've fucked Paige into oblivion, and that makes me feel on top of the world. Picking her up, I walk through the apartment in search of a shower. After a couple of attempts, I find her room and the en suite bathroom. She groans when I put her down to turn the shower on; she's all sleepy and grumpy and it's adorable.

Adorable? You're losing it. I don't care if I am. All I know is the moment my dick sank inside her, I was home. *Game over.* There will never be anyone else for me but her. I must be patient as she's not quite there yet.

She gasps when the water hits her, but as soon as my fingers start massaging her shoulders, she relaxes, pressing her tight little ass against my dick.

"This feels so good." She moans as I lather up the soap and start washing myself off her skin. Watching myself come all over her tits was the hottest thing in my life and something I want to do over and over again. Will she let me? It looked like she enjoyed it, especially when she licked it off her finger. Hottest thing ever. Porn dream come true. She's fucking perfect. We're perfect together.

I continue to rub my hands over her soft skin. My dick is rising to the occasion again, which is not surprising, but I'm not sure she's quite ready for it yet.

When I finish making sure she is clean, I look up and find her chocolate eyes assessing me. I know what's going on inside her, probably listing off all the ways she can kick me out of her apartment and pretend what happened didn't.

"Hey, what happened?" she asks, frowning at me.

"What?" I answer, confused by her question.

"Your face went sad. One minute I thought you were seconds away from pushing me up against the shower wall and having your way with me, and then suddenly, your face dropped."

Oh.

Usually, I can hide what's going on in my head, but I guess I let my façade slip for the moment.

"That's exactly what I was thinking," I answer honestly.

She reaches out and cups my face. "What made you sad?"

"The fear that you were going to kick me out before I had a chance to fuck you again."

"Oh," she says, her hand dropping from my face.

Shit. I messed up. Again. I shouldn't have told her what I was truly thinking. She probably thinks I'm crazy or, even worse, a stalker like her ex.

"You want to keep fucking me?" she questions.

Now it's my turn to reach out and cup her face. "Yes. I never want to stop."

She bites her bottom lip as she mulls over my confession. "Maybe we should try a second time, you know, just in case the first was a fluke and—"

I don't let her finish the sentence before my lips are on hers, pushing her up against the shower wall. She lets out a small squeak before she wraps her arms around my neck and pulls me to her.

Yes.

I pick her up and make her wrap her legs around my waist, not breaking our kiss as I turn off the shower. We stay conjoined as I carefully step out of the shower.

"Be careful," she squeals when I wobble a little.

"Always," I tell her before kissing her again. But for safety reasons, I pull myself from her lips as we exit the bathroom and enter her bedroom, grabbing a towel on the way past and throwing it down on the bed. I straighten it out, then lay her down on it. "Stay there," I tell her before running back into the bathroom and grabbing another fluffy white towel. I quickly dry myself off and then bring the towel to her; she's sitting up on her elbows watching my every move. I throw the towel at her, making her scream before I wrap it around her. She's like a little white cocoon pinned to the bed as I lean in and kiss her again. Moans fall from her lips as the kiss heats up. She then nips my lip, surprising me. I stare down at her and she laughs. A laugh that is so carefree it fills my soul with joy.

"Let me go." She giggles, trying to buck against the towel.

"Never." I smirk.

She stills, understanding the double meaning behind that answer and stops fighting me. I sit up and release her and she leans forward to wrap her arms around my neck and the next thing I know, she's pulling me onto the bed and straddling me. She looks down at me and smiles.

"Maybe never is okay," she says.

Hope blooms in my chest. Is she saying that maybe we have a chance?

Before I can say anything, she's lined herself up against my cock and is sinking down on it.

"Fuck," I hiss as her heat envelops me. My hands come out and grab her hips.

"I don't know what's going to happen, Gio, but what I do know is, I like fucking you," she tells me honestly.

"I like fucking you."

"Good to know." She grins. "Give me time, though, for whatever this is, okay?" she asks.

"I'll wait for you, Paige," I say, reaching up and caressing her face. I need her to know I'm all in, whenever she's ready.

"I know you would," she says, then starts slowly moving up and down my cock. I let her take the lead this time, letting her set the pace. She stares down at me as my hands cup her breasts and my fingers pluck her nipples. This is the most beautiful view in the world, watching her take what she needs from me.

"What the hell is going on here?" a female voice shrieks from Paige's doorway.

"Fuck, Sav," Paige answers, sitting up in bed. Her hair is a mess from the multiple times we had sex. After the fourth time, we fell asleep, and I guess that is where we find ourselves now.

"You dirty bird. Gio, here are your jeans, you might need them," she chuckles, throwing them across the room, watching as they land on the edge of the bed before turning around and closing the door.

"Fuck, fuck, fuck," Paige curses as she jumps out of bed and rushes around her bedroom naked, trying to find clothes to change into. I throw back the covers and put on my underwear and jeans, and by the time I'm dressed, so is Paige.

"Are you okay?" I ask her as she rushes out of her closet in a panic.

"I don't know," she answers honestly. "I … it's just … I didn't want anyone to know about us."

Oh.

My chest deflates at her answer.

"Not until I knew what this was," she says, waving her hand between us.

"Come here," I say, reaching out and pulling her to me. She reluctantly comes to me, and I hug her tightly. She wraps herself around me and hugs me back. "There's no label on us, okay, so don't feel like you need to add one."

She looks up at me. "Of course there's no label. As far as the world is concerned, I'm the other woman. You're still engaged to someone else," she says, unwrapping herself from me.

Shit.

I keep forgetting about that. Paige is right; the world still thinks Giada and I are the perfect couple.

Fuck.

Giada and I need to make a statement that we are no longer together and be done with this charade. I owe it to Paige.

"I'll sort that out."

She gives me a small nod before moving away from me and walking out the door. This isn't good. The reality of what we've done is hitting her and I can't be mad. I've chosen to protect Giada instead of Paige. Better face the music. I walk out of the bedroom and down the hall to the living room; the girls stop whispering as I enter.

"I'm just going to grab my things and leave you to it," I say, grabbing my shirt off the ground and my socks and shoes, too. Paige nods and her friend frowns at her but doesn't say anything. I grab my wallet and phone, then walk out the door, choosing to finish getting dressed outside rather than inside. I hope this doesn't change anything between us, not when I was so close to showing her what life could be like if she gave me a second chance.

28

PAIGE

Watching Gio walk out the door with his shoulders slumped made me feel bad. I shouldn't have thrown his engagement in his face. I know there is nothing there; I've seen the pictures of Giada DJ'ing in Mykonos with his sister by her side. Still, hearing all the declarations he'd made toward me in that moment, I felt like the other woman because I had hope. Hope that maybe Gio and I can have a second chance, but we can't because the world thinks he's happily in love with Italy's sweetheart, Giada.

It's a mess.

"Tell me everything, don't leave anything out. I can tell something steamy happened, your clothes were spread out across the apartment like dirty little breadcrumbs," Savannah states.

I let out a frustrated sigh. "We're going to need wine for this story," I tell her.

"On to it. Stay there, you're obviously exhausted from riding dick all afternoon." She jumps up off the sofa and heads into the kitchen. I shake my head at my no-filter friend. She brings back a bottle of red and proceeds to uncork it and pour us both a glass. "Now go," she says, handing me my glass.

"I don't know how to explain what happened," I tell her, then take my first sip of wine.

"Um, how did you go from family lunch to dick riding?" Savannah asks.

Okay, I guess that is a big leap. "We talked, we argued, he said nice things, then said dirty things and next thing I know we are doing it," I say, giving her the CliffsNotes version.

"And was it good?"

I nod as I take another sip of wine, my cheeks flushing from the memories of what that man did to me more so than the wine. "We did it four times."

Savannah squeals and I do too, then we burst out laughing.

"Totally knew it. The quiet ones are always the freakiest," Savannah states.

"That is so true."

Sav's eyes widen. "Did you two do freaky shit?"

Is him blowing his load on me and rubbing it all over my body each time we had sex freaky? Then yeah. He loved marking me.

"I can see it on your face, you did. Oh my god, how the hell am I ever going to be able to look at him again?" She chuckles, taking a sip from her glass.

"I don't know if I'm going to see him again," I tell her.

"What? No. Good dick is hard to find," she explains.

This is true.

"He's technically still engaged. How would it even work?"

"Do you want something to work, or do you just want sex?" she questions me.

"The thing is, he wants something to work between us and he said he's willing to wait until I'm ready. What happens if I'm never ready?" I ask her.

"You won't know unless you try. You can go around in circles thinking about what if. It's up to you if you think he's worth taking a chance. I know he's technically engaged to someone else, but that will end eventually. Until then, you believe what he says."

That is a scary leap though. "He's hurt me before."

Savannah sighs. "I'm sure he did, but honestly, babe, it was fifteen years ago, and you guys were kids. I wouldn't be holding that against him."

She wasn't there; she doesn't know how hard I took us breaking up, but she's right. We were teens, and it's stupid as an adult to keep holding on to something like that; we're not the same people we were then. Maybe she's right and I've been using the past as an excuse to not dream of a future.

"You're so smart, Sav."

"I really am," she says, and we both start laughing again.

"Enough about me, how was your date?"

She rolls her eyes. "Why do you think I'm home early? He was a nice enough guy, but too young for me."

"I'm sorry."

"Oh, I'm not. He made me come, so guess the date wasn't a fail after all." She chuckles.

"Wait, you had sex with him? When? Where?" I ask, shaking my head.

"Downstairs in the garage, in his car. I told him I had fun but wouldn't be going on another date with him unless as friends. He agreed. I made a joke about my vibrator getting a workout as it has been a while. He offered to help me out, and figured when in Rome, do a Roman, so I did. That boy's mouth was sublime, I could sit on his face all day long."

I choke on my wine.

"We're catching up tomorrow, it should be fun. We didn't have plans, did we?"

"No."

"Good, the things I want to do to that boy," she says before taking a sip of her wine.

Oh my gosh, she's insane.

> Paige: Thanks for today.

> Giorgio: Thanks for lunch or the orgasms?

> Paige: Both.

> Giorgio: You're welcome.

Taking a leaf out of Savannah's fuck-it book, I've decided to ask Gio to come over again for some fun. I've never ordered a booty call before.

> Paige: I was wondering if you had any plans tomorrow.

> Giorgio: Just work, why?

Of course, he has work; *it's Monday, Paige, most people start their working week then.*

> Paige: All good.

> Giorgio: Paige.

I can hear his commanding voice through the phone screen.

> Giorgio: Say what you wanted to say.

You can do this. He's already been inside you, just ask him to do it again.

> Paige: Fine. I wanted you to come over and do what we did today, again.

I hit send. Shit. No. That's too much. What the hell was I thinking? It's probably a turnoff—a woman being that forward.

> Giorgio: Look at that, my day has suddenly become free.

I burst out laughing at his comment.

> Giorgio: I'll be over at nine.

> Giorgio: You'll have the house to yourself, won't you?

Paige: Yes, all day.

> Giorgio: Good. See you then. Rest up, you're going to need your strength for tomorrow.

I fall back against the bed and scream into my pillow.

The concierge has just called and let Giorgio up, and now the nerves have kicked in. Savannah told me to wear my silk robe and nothing underneath it because *"you both know why you're there, no need to pretend."* I'm now rethinking her suggestion as my nipples press against the fabric. *It's too late now.* Panic rises in my throat, what do I do? *Act natural, Paige. You're both consenting adults.* It's all fun and games sitting behind a screen and typing out what you want, but standing here now, it's nerve-racking. There's a knock at my door, which makes me jump. I bite my lip and hesitate before I move toward the door. Opening it, I'm greeted by Giorgio looking as handsome as ever in tailored shorts, a polo shirt, and deck shoes. In his hand is a large bouquet of flowers, pink peonies, to be exact. *Oh. That's sweet.* His eyes widen as he notices what I'm wearing, and a smirk falls across his lips.

"Come in," I say, holding the door open for him. He nods and enters the apartment. I close the door behind him and follow. He places the bouquet in a vase on the dining table. Then he is stalking toward me. He grabs my face and gives me a searing kiss.

"I couldn't stop dreaming about you last night," he states.

Oh.

"My dick was hard the entire night. Do you have any idea how hard it is to sleep like that?" He chuckles.

He was hard all night thinking about me. Why is that hot?

"I'm guessing that can't be comfortable."

"It's not," he says as he starts to walk me backward, and the next thing I know, he's lifting me and placing me on the kitchen counter. *Guess he isn't messing around.* "Did you wear this for me?" he asks, grinning as he runs his finger along the silky neckline which has dipped to almost exposing my breasts.

"Maybe," I answer coyly.

"And did you wear no underwear for me, too," he growls as his hands disappear up the split in my robe, finding me bare for him.

I nod.

"I don't know what I did to deserve you, Paige, but I will pray at your altar every damn day giving thanks for you letting me back into your life," he states sincerely before pushing my legs open and sliding his fingers up my inner thighs. I wiggle as the tingles race over my skin until his fingers find my folds. He pushes my legs open even more, giving him better access as I lean back, resting my hands on the cool marble countertop. His thick fingers find my opening and slide in, making me hiss.

"Already so wet for me."

His fingers curl against me, sliding in and out. Yes, this is how I want to start all my mornings.

"That's it, baby, take it like the good girl you are."

Gio's words are always so filthy and I'm into it, so much. Never thought dirty talk or calling me a good girl would turn me on. I mean, I'm not in a porno, and yet here I am, making a mess on the kitchen counter because of those filthy words. His thumb then glides over my sensitive clit, pulling moans from my lips.

"You're so close, baby, grip my fingers, tighter, tighter, yeah that's it, fucking perfect. You're always so fucking perfect, Paige. You were made for me."

"Yes, yes, yes!" I scream as he pushes me over the edge, my head thrown back, my eyes closed as those thick fingers continue to make my body shake with every movement. It takes me a moment to come down, but Gio waits until my eyes are back on him before pulling his fingers from me. He then brings them to his mouth, sucking my wetness from his skin. So fricken hot watching him do that. He makes me feel like the most beautiful woman in the world when he does.

"I'll never get sick of tasting you," he tells me.

I don't think I want him to either.

He then wraps his hands around my waist. "Where do you want me, sweetness?"

Biting my lip, I look around the room and land on the terrace. He turns and follows where I'm looking. I've never done it outside before. The terrace is completely enclosed; no one can see in as there are no towering buildings surrounding it like there would be in New York.

"Your wish is my command." He grins, picking me up. I wrap my legs around his hips as he holds me in his arms to cross the room. He kicks his shoes off on the terrace and sits down on the sun lounge first, my knees settling on either side of him.

"You look absolutely beautiful, Paige," Gio says, stilling. My brown hair is out and cascading around my shoulders, my robe has slid off my shoulder and is exposing my breast, and I'm flushed from my earlier orgasm.

"Because you make me feel beautiful, Gio," I tell him.

"That is my job to tell the woman I'm with how beautiful she is," he declares.

"Not many men are like that."

"I don't care about other men, Paige. I care about whether I make you feel good or not," he declares.

"You always make me feel good," I tell him as I place my hands on either side of his head.

"Every lover should make you feel good."

Sadly, that hasn't been my experience. "Is that what you are to me, my lover?" I question him with a grin as his hands reach out and grip my ass.

"Yes." Those cocoa eyes darken as he stares at me. I think I can handle that title. *Lover.* It sums up what we are doing—messing around without the other bits. It sounds nicer than booty call or friends-with-benefits. He then unties my robe enough that both breasts fall out. He leans forward and captures one in his mouth, his tongue rolling around my nipple and tender bites skimming the peaks, sending goosebumps over my skin. I lean forward to make it easier for him, and I feel like a goddess, having a man like Gio worshiping me as he concentrates on giving each breast the same amount of attention. I can feel the coil inside me begin to tighten. How does this man continuously make me so horny all the time? He's like instant lady Viagra. I continue to hump him as he consumes himself with my breasts. But I need more, so much more, from this man. My hands fumble for the button on his shorts, making him chuckle as I struggle. He lets go of my breasts and helps me. My hands then grab his shirt and peel it off him; I love watching every muscle ripple across his broad chest as he tries to shimmy out of his shirt. I throw his shirt to the side while he kicks off his shorts and underwear. It's so naughty being naked on my terrace in the sunshine while everyone goes about their day.

I shimmy down his legs so I can find my prize, and there it is, standing tall and proud, waiting for me. I love his cock. It's thick and veiny. I run my hands over the velvety skin, loving the feeling it gives me as I slide over it. I've never been enamored with a cock before, but it is beautiful. Cocks can be beautiful, can't they? *You don't see any cock appreciation clubs, do you?*

"Paige," Gio says my name in warning, and I realize I've been sliding my hands up and down for a while now, lost in my thoughts. "Get out of that head and put my dick in your mouth," he commands.

Yes, sir, you don't have to tell me twice. I slide the skin down and wrap my mouth around the sensitive tip. He wraps his fingers in my hair, controlling how he wants me to suck him off. I give him a couple of deep throats as I hum around him, making him hiss. I read that in *Cosmo* once and it really works. *Focus, Paige.* I continue to work him over, alternating between licking and sucking, which pulls deep guttural moans from his lips that send shockwaves to my center.

"Fuck, Paige, I don't want to come in your mouth, but it feels so good." He moans as he continues to fuck my face, his hips straining as he tries not to push himself too far down my throat. I look up at him and when he notices, blinding heat swirls behind those dark eyes. "You want me to come down your throat, baby girl. Those eyes are telling me to fill your mouth up, is that right?"

That sounds hot. Yes, please. I hum my answer around his cock.

"Fuck, Paige," he curses as determination fills his face. "Get ready for me, baby. I want you to swallow everything I give you, every last drop, you hear me?"

Yes, loud and clear. I relax my throat and take him further.

"Fuck," he curses. His fingers tighten in my hair and his hips fall out of rhythm as he starts to lose control. That's it, Gio, you can lose control with me. Give me everything you have, I'm yours. And with that blinding realization—that I'm his, that I have always been his—I take every bit of him down my throat as he roars his release.

"Such a good fucking girl, Paige," he coos as I lick my lips and grin up at him. He then pulls me up his body and kisses me, not minding that he can taste himself on my tongue. "I never want to let you go," he says, pushing the hair from my face.

"I don't think I want you to, either."

He stills beneath me, his mouth falling open in surprise at my comment. "What do you mean?"

"I don't know yet," I tell him honestly.

His fingers run through my hair, then he holds me in place so I can look at him. "I don't want to share you, Paige. I know I said I'd stand on the sidelines and watch you be happy with someone else. *I lied.* I can't stand the thought of you being happy with another man."

Oh, wow, that's a big declaration. "I don't want to see you with another woman, either."

Relief falls across his face. "Never. I would never do that to you ever again," he declares, pulling my lips to his and kissing me. He then presses his forehead against mine. "I'm yours, forever and always."

And that's the thing; I know I feel the same too.

29

GIORGIO

"What's going on between you and Paige?" Luca asks. We are currently on our way to Paris looking for dresses for the girls for the Summer Ball that is happening in a couple of weeks.

"Nothing," I answer. I'm not purposefully lying to my brother, but Paige and I had agreed that we wouldn't tell anyone about the two of us. We wanted to stay in this bubble by ourselves for a little longer. The only person who does know is Savannah, and only because she busted us that first time, but she had to head back to New York early to deal with a problem at work.

Luca's eyes narrow on me. "I call bullshit."

"We're friends."

"Still call bullshit. You can't stop looking at her."

"She's a beautiful woman."

"Something's happened between the two of you. I can sense it. Maybe I'll ask Paige and she can tell me," he says as he stands up.

"No, you won't," I hiss, grabbing him and pulling him back into his seat.

Luca's eyes widen, and a smirk falls across his face. "Knew it."

I roll my eyes at my annoying brother. "Fine. Do not fucking say anything. I mean it. I promised Paige no one would know," I say, leaning in.

"I wouldn't say anything," Luca reassures me.

"You can't tell Lilly."

"Oh, come on. That's not fair." My eyes narrow on him. "Fine," he grumbles.

"We've been seeing each other for weeks and I'm happy. So fucking happy," I tell him.

Luca looks at me with his mouth open, surprised by my comments. "That's amazing. She's great. I'm happy for you." Then he frowns. "What about Giada?" he asks.

"I've sent her message after message about it, but she's not replying. I've even texted Allegra, nothing. I don't know what to do."

"Release the statement. Fuck her," Luca says angrily.

"I can't do that right before the Summer Ball, it would overshadow it, especially outing Allegra and Giada."

Luca rolls his eyes. "Mamma and Papà would understand about the ball. They want to see you happy. They are worried about you."

"I know they are, but we raise so much money for the charity that night, I can't mess that up. People count on those donations."

"Your broken engagement won't stop people from donating, Gio. Wouldn't it be nice if you and Paige could walk into that event arm in arm, especially as her great-aunt co-chaired with Mamma for so long? It's a great way to honor her memory."

Shit. I forgot that Lucia was involved with this ball. Does Paige know? I don't think she does. Luca is right, it would be wonderful walking into that ball with her on my arm.

"Even if I announce the breakup today, I won't be able to be seen with Paige, otherwise they are going to think I've been having an affair."

"True. This is a huge mess, Gio. You should have announced your separation ages ago." Luca sighs, looking over at me.

"Yes, I get that, but I wasn't expecting to fall in love with someone so soon," I argue. Then I shut my mouth, quickly realizing what I've just said.

"You love her?" Luca asks, a wide smile on his face.

"You don't have to be a dick about it. I haven't even told her that. She knows my feelings for her are strong, but not this strong."

"I can see it on your face, man, she really makes you happy."

"She does," I agree, looking over to where Paige is sitting with my sister and my sister-in-law, laughing and joking as if she is already part of the family.

And I can't wait until she is.

"It's so hard to be this close and not touch you," I say as Paige takes a seat beside me on the jet.

"Won't be long until we are by ourselves, and you can touch me as much as you want." She smirks.

That wicked woman, making me hard when I can't do anything about it. "We could join the mile-high club, if you want," I say, flicking my head to the bathroom behind us.

Her eyes widen as her cheeks flush. "One day, when there aren't so many people on the plane."

I raise a brow at her. "Noted, Miss Johnson, I'll kick them off the return leg, they can find their own way back to Rome," I tease.

She shakes her head at me.

"Actually, I wanted to talk to you about something, but haven't had a chance because my mouth seems to be preoccupied by your pussy."

Paige gasps at my words and then playfully nudges me, which has me laughing out loud, getting a few looks from my family, not used to hearing the sound of my laughter.

"Not sure if anyone has told you this yet, but my family's Summer Ball, your great-aunt was on the board for it."

Paige's eyes widen at my revelation. Judging by her reaction, she didn't know.

"What does that mean? Am I supposed to be helping? I had no idea. Why did no one tell me?" she asks, shooting a million questions at me.

"Probably because it's been a long time since Lucia had been well enough to help physically. She would call my mother and talk about it and she would help choose the charities for that year. Lucia also liked to do things under the radar, as much of a diva that she was, she was also humble."

"I had no idea," Paige says, shaking her head.

"The ball is doing a tribute to Lucia at this year's event, I thought you should know."

Tears well in her eyes. "Thank you," she says, reaching and squeezing my arm.

"She helped raise a lot of money for wonderful charities, we wanted to thank her for all that she did." More tears flow freely from her now as I lean over and wipe the tears from her eyes. "Don't cry, babe. It breaks my heart seeing you upset."

She shakes herself. "They are happy tears. I assure you. I hate that she kept so much from me about her life. I would have loved to know about this ball she was involved with. Why did we never go? Was she ashamed of us?"

"Lucia didn't like the fanfare when it came to helping people. She helped so many people anonymously and I guess she just didn't think about telling you because to her it wasn't a big deal." I explain what I understand from what my mother has told me.

"Every time I think I know her, I learn something new about her," Paige says with a somber shrug.

"You're going to do her proud, Paige. Once you get a handle on everything she's left you, you're going to do amazing things."

She looks up at me slowly. "You really think I can?"

I nod my head. I believe in her.

Paige then gives me a blinding, bright smile. "I think I can, too," she confesses. And seeing that spark of confidence in herself has my heart warming.

I don't know myself anymore.

PAIGE

"Welcome to Yvette Sanchez Boutique, I'm Yvette." A beautiful brunette comes up and welcomes us warmly.

"It's an honor to be here with you. I'm a huge fan," Natalia says, trying to contain her excitement.

"That makes me so happy. I've been following you for years now and I think you are one of the most stylish young women in Rome. We should do something together," she says, giving Natalia a huge compliment.

"Yes. I would love that," Natalia squeals.

A dark-haired woman comes around and hands us champagne and sparkling apple juice for the pregnant ladies in our party. Lilly invited two of her friends, Mackenzie, who's also a doctor, and Zoe, who runs her own charity in Spain; they are sisters. Zoe is currently pregnant, too; she is about the same as Lilly.

"Sorry, Yvette, let me introduce you to Paige Johnson. She is Lucia's great-niece," Natalia explains to the designer.

Her dark eyes widen, and a smile falls across her red lips. "I have heard so much about you," she says, greeting me warmly. "I owe so much to your great-aunt. Her company that helps launch designers is the reason I am here today. I couldn't have expanded and grown without her investment."

Antony explained that one of her investments was a company that helped fund artists; the company would give a business loan to them to help them reach the next level in their careers. They have the option of paying back in full the entire loan or leaving it as an investment and becoming partners with the company. It's not easy to get funding, there's a board of professionals in the field, and you must supply business plans and a heap of paperwork to show you're serious.

"It's so lovely to meet you, too. I had no idea Lucia did all this, so I'm sorry I never met you sooner. But I only realize now that I have some of your dresses Lucia has bought me over the years. Wow."

Yvette waves my apology away. "Amazing. Your great-aunt was one of the most amazing people I've ever met. I love that she gave no fucks about what anyone thought about her. She wore diamonds and drove an old vintage Mercedes when she was in Paris. Honestly, she was, and still is, an icon to me," Yvette says, squeezing my arm tenderly. Tears well in my eyes at her beautiful compliments. "Can I show you something I've been working on since she's passed? I hope you don't mind."

I nod and Yvette ushers us upstairs from the boutique to where her offices are. "Here," she says, opening a door to a room that is covered in sketches. "My next collection is a homage to your great-aunt; it's called the Countess Collection," she explains.

I stare in bewilderment at the drawings that are pinned to the wall, each with a modern twist on something Lucia would have worn. Tears begin to slide down my cheeks as I take in each one. "She would have loved this."

Yvette comes to stand beside me and wraps an arm around my shoulders. "Yes, she would have. And you know she would have stolen the show on the runway." This makes me chuckle because she would have.

"Thank you," I say with a sniffle.

"It's my pleasure, as I said, I owe her my career. Would you …"

Yvette hesitates, and I encourage her to continue with what she was going to ask. "Would you like to consult on this collection?" she asks.

Me?

"I know nothing about fashion."

Yvette chuckles. "But you know Lucia."

That I do. I nod, trying to stave away the tears that keep wanting to fall. "I'd love to," I say, hugging the incredibly nice fashion designer.

"I didn't order a side of tears with my couture today," Lilly says which makes us chuckle.

"Come on, let's find you the perfect dress," she says.

"Thank you so much for an amazing day." I hug Yvette goodbye. Giorgio and Luca have arrived to pick us up from the boutique. Zoe and Mackenzie left earlier in the day.

"Did you have fun ladies?" Luca asks.

"We certainly did." Lilly grins as she kisses her husband.

Giorgio looks over at me and I can see the longing in his eyes to be able to do the same thing to me.

"My feet ache. Can we head straight back to the hotel?" Lilly groans.

"Of course, my love," Luca says, staring down adoringly at his wife.

"I have to catch up with friends, so I'll grab an Uber," Natalia says, waving us goodbye as she disappears up the street.

"You guys take the car, I'll take Paige to her apartment. I'm sure she wouldn't mind freshening up before dinner tonight," Giorgio says.

Luca and Lilly look over at us. "You think walking around Paris is a good idea?" Luca asks.

Giorgio's face falls. I'm guessing it's not. The driver opens the door for us. "The hotel is around the corner; the driver can drop us off first and then he can take Paige to her apartment," Luca suggests and Giorgio huffs as we get into the car. It's not far to the hotel, and Lilly and Luca get out of the car just as Giorgio's phone rings.

"I've got to take this," he says, holding up his phone. "Meet you in the lobby at seven for dinner," he tells his brother, who frowns at him before ushering his tired pregnant wife away.

"Thanks for that," he says, grinning at me as he hangs up my phone. "Didn't think I was going to be able to get rid of them," he says as we settle back into the car as it takes off into traffic again. Lucia's Paris apartment isn't far from the hotel they are all staying at. I've stayed there a couple of times when I've visited Lucia. Girls' trips to Paris were always one of my favorite things.

"It's killing me not being able to touch you in public," he whispers to me.

"Me too."

We sit in silence until the driver pulls up out the front of the apartment.

"We're going to have to be quick, in case," he warns me.

I nod, I will not mess this up. I step out of the car confidently as if I have always done this and head toward the foyer where a handsome young man greets me.

"Welcome, Countess Johnson, it is a privilege to be of assistance to you," he says.

It's still a trip being called *Countess*. "Thank you," I say as I follow him through the ornate antique marble foyer. He stops and grabs an envelope from the wooden reception desk and hands it to me.

"Here are the keys to your apartment. Your bags are already waiting for you there. Allow me to get the elevator for you," he says as I take the envelope from him. He presses the button to my floor and then closes the brass antique elevator doors behind us.

"This is surreal, I'm heading to my apartment in Paris," I tell Gio as a giggle falls from my lips.

"This is your life now, you better get used to it." He grins.

"Is this how you've always lived?" I question him.

He shrugs his shoulders. I take that as a yes. The elevator stops and Gio opens the door for me as I pull out the keys and open the door with them. I throw the keys on the side table and rush toward the glass windows, knowing exactly what I'm going to see when I open them and step out onto the balcony. My hand twists the ancient knob as I pull open the large glass doors that lead out to the balcony and there it is in all its glory, the Eiffel Tower. That sight will always give me goosebumps. I loved this apartment for that view and Lucia loved it because right underneath us were the designer boutiques.

Giorgio hovers behind me, not daring to step out onto the balcony which overlooks the street. That's right, he's not meant to be seen with another woman. Letting out a sigh, I step back into the apartment and close the glass door.

"Come here," Gio says as I step toward him. He reaches out and cups my face, bringing our lips together in a slow, languishing kiss that sends shivers all the way to the tips of my toes. "I've wanted to do that all day." He grins.

"Is that all you've wanted to do?" I tease.

"Hell no, let me show you all the dirty thoughts that have been running through my mind." He smirks before launching himself at me.

31

GIORGIO

We've arranged for dinner on top of the Eiffel Tower. Lilly and Luca's friends are in town, so they are joining us for dinner tonight, too.

"Not sure if you realize, but Zoe is married to Matteo and Tomas," I whisper to Paige as we walk through the VIP entrance to the restaurant.

"She said something today at the boutique, but I thought I heard it wrong. And they have a child together and she's pregnant again?"

I nod my head.

"I mean, look at those two men. I understand why she'd be pregnant all the time." She giggles.

My body tenses at hearing Paige notice how good-looking Matteo and Tomas are. I place my hand at the small of her back and lean in as we walk. "Are you saying one of me isn't enough?"

Her cheeks flush at my comment; she turns and looks up at me. "You're enough for me, Gio."

And in that moment, under the Eiffel Tower surrounded by people, all I want to do is kiss the ever-loving hell out of her, but I can't. Because she's not mine yet, not publicly anyway.

"All I want to do right now is kiss you, and I fucking can't," I curse.

She links our pinky fingers together as we walk. "One day," she says, giving me a wide smile. I don't deserve this woman at all.

We are escorted up to the restaurant and shown to our private room. It has the most magnificent view over all of Paris.

"This is beautiful," Paige declares as she stares out the window. She's dressed in a gorgeous emerald-green cocktail dress, her brunette hair cascading around her shoulders in waves. Natalia has loaned her some jewels to wear with the dress. Which I make a note of, I need to get her some. She looks regal even, every inch the countess that she has now become. Every day since leaving New York, I can see she is becoming more at ease in her new skin, her new life.

"Wipe your mouth, you're drooling," my brother whispers, elbowing me as he walks past.

Reluctantly, I pull my eyes from where Paige is standing admiring the Parisian skyline and engage in a conversation with our friends.

"Where's your lovely fiancée? Thought she would be here tonight or is she back filming again?" Matteo asks as I choke on my whisky. He's a famous Spanish actor back in Barcelona and knows Giada through the business.

I stiffen at Matteo's question, and I don't quite know how to answer it. I look over at where Paige is talking to Lilly and Zoe.

"Um …"

"She's too busy fucking our sister to be here tonight," Natalia says as she interrupts our conversation. Matteo and Tomas choke on their drinks as the room falls silent. My heart is thundering in my chest as panic sets in.

"What the hell, Natalia?" Luca says, breaking the awkward silence.

"I'm sick of it. It's not fair, Giada can spend the summer in bed with Allegra while Gio does what? Just puts up with it? She messed up, not him," Natalia explains to the group.

"Natalia, enough," Luca warns her.

I reach out and pull my passionate sister to my side and place a tender kiss on her forehead. "I appreciate you sticking up for me, but it is not our place to out them," I whisper against her ear.

"I want you to be happy, Gio," she says, looking up and giving me a pout.

"But I am," I tell her as my eyes trail over to where Paige is sipping on champagne. Her brows are pulled together, watching the room intensely.

"Wait, Giada and Allegra are together?" Matteo asks.

"Matteo," Tomas warns, glaring at his partner.

"Natalia offered up the information," he says, rolling his eyes.

"I think it might be a family matter, Matteo, we should leave it," Mackenzie adds. She's Zoe's older sister and one of Lilly's best friends. She's become very close with Lilly, working on charity projects together. Luca gave Lilly her own charity as a wedding present called Lilly's Place, a refuge for humans who have been trafficked throughout Europe. A place they can go before moving back into society. Mackenzie's family rescues women from dangerous situations and brings them back to civilization. They were the ones who found Lilly when she was kidnapped and brought her home safely. Ever since then, Mackenzie and Lilly have been tight. Now that Lilly's pregnant, Mackenzie has offered to come on board to help at the charity, moving from Spain to Italy. She's the only one Lilly would trust to run the charity while she's on maternity leave. Luca may have offered her a lot of money to take the job so that Lilly wouldn't have to work through the pregnancy so much.

There's a tap of a glass that silences the room. Lilly moves to the front of the room so everyone can see her. "Thank you everyone for coming to Paris this weekend, it's been too long since catching up." Everyone nods in agreement. "You're some of my closest friends, and it means the world to me that you are all here. I wanted to say a huge thank you to Mackenzie for taking over my position at Lilly's Place, and I'm sorry, Zoe, for stealing your sister." Zoe wags her finger at Lilly while laughing. "I wanted to let everyone know that Lilly's Place will be one of the charities that the Summer Ball is raising money for." The room erupts in applause. "Just wanted to say it wasn't because I'm sleeping with one of the board members." She smirks, looking at my brother.

"This year we hired an independent board to choose the worthiest charities to make sure it was fair," Luca adds as he looks proudly at Lilly.

"I'm excited that we can bring Lilly's Place and the girls' plight to the most influential people in Europe at this ball, but my dear brother-in-law is worried his messy situation—as my passionate sister-in-law so eloquently explained earlier—would cause the focus to not be on the wonderful charities, but I don't believe that to be so," Lilly states as she glares at me.

Is this her giving me her blessing to announce Giada and my break up?

"I trust the people in this room with my life, some of you have literally saved it. So, I'm asking that what is discussed in this room tonight doesn't leave these walls," she states firmly, looking between all her friends.

"In the vault, Lilly," Mackenzie states.

"Yes, of course, we would never say anything," Zoe adds as both Matteo and Tomas nod in agreement.

"Thank you. Gio, would you like to continue?" Lilly suggests.

Me? Right. Yes. I guess I should explain. Especially as the four of them were there the night of my engagement party. My hands clam up, my throat dries out as all the eyes in the room are on me.

"Gio walked in on Giada and Allegra doing it at their engagement party," Natalia explains, point blank for me.

There's an audible gasp as the boys' mouths fall open at that bit of information. "So, your father wasn't sick?" Matteo asks.

"He wasn't well upon hearing the news that the engagement was off due to Giada cheating, but not with whom," Lilly adds.

"My sister is scared of revealing her true identity to our parents," I explain.

"I understand that feeling," Tomas adds. His father is the head of a conservative political party back in Spain. His having a son who is bisexual hadn't gone down too well.

"And Giada is worried she will lose her career," I add.

"It's a possibility, but I don't think that will happen. Look at me, my female fan base tripled when they found out about Tomas and me," Matteo declares.

"That's because most of them wouldn't mind being in the middle of the two of you." Zoe grins at her two men.

"They could only dream of how hot it is being in the middle of the two of us." Matteo smirks as he leans over and kisses his wife's cheek. Zoe flushes at his declaration as she playfully pushes him away. "Two beautiful women, men would go crazy for them. Tell her to give me a call, I can help her navigate her new life if she wants. And if they do give her a hard time in Italy, I know a Spanish TV show that would love to have her on it," Matteo states as he sends a wink my way.

Wow. Okay.

Then he turns to his partners. "See, I told you I saw them hooking up in Ibiza. And you and Zoe told me I imagined it. I was right," he says, looking between them both.

"Don't think now is the time to gloat about that," Tomas says, nudging his partner.

"Oh, sorry, Gio, that was insensitive of me." Matteo cringes.

I'm not surprised by his admission. "It's okay. Giada and I should never have gotten engaged. I thought I was doing the right thing for my parents, but in the end, it's created a huge mess."

"None of it is your fault. You may not have been in love, but you were committed to her. And after all this time, you're still covering for them while sacrificing your own happiness," Natalia adds.

How can I not love my sister for her staunch loyalty?

"Gio is worried that if he says anything about the broken engagement, he will overshadow the ball," Lilly adds.

The group erupts with encouraging words as they all try to reassure me that my statement about the broken engagement won't affect the ball or the monies raised.

"Giada and Allegra's story isn't for me to tell the world," I say.

"Then don't. I'm sure you can announce your separation without a reason. Who cares if the media speculates as to why? They will, even if you tell them the truth," Tomas states.

He's right. I hadn't thought about it like that. I look around the table at all the encouraging support from them, and maybe, just maybe, this nightmare can be over without too much fuss. My eyes land on Paige and she gives me a reassuring smile.

"You're right. Hopefully, in a couple of weeks another scandal will replace mine." I chuckle.

"That's the spirit. Now what we need to do is find Gio a good woman because he deserves it," Zoe says, raising her glass.

"I know so many women that would love to date you, Gio. Let me know when you're ready and I'll hook you up," Tomas suggests.

"Don't think he's interested in actresses anymore," Matteo jokes which makes me laugh.

I look over at Paige to reassure her, but she's not there anymore.

"Can you excuse me for a moment? I need the bathroom," I say, excusing myself from the conversation to work out where Paige is. Walking out of the private room, I scan the restaurant and find the bathrooms; she must be there. As I head in that direction, I see her step out of the bathroom and take a deep breath. When she looks up, her eyes widen as she sees me. I storm toward her and when I meet her, I grab her face and kiss the ever-loving hell out of her.

"Gio," she gasps as our lips duel.

I press our foreheads together. "Please don't ever leave like that again."

"I couldn't listen to your friends trying to set you up," she confesses.

"I know, I'm sorry about that. I will walk right back into that room and declare that I'm in love with you if you want me to," I tell her.

She takes a step back from me. "What did you say?"

Fuck.

This wasn't how I wanted to tell her. "I'm in love with you," I say quietly.

Her eyes widen as they glisten with emotion. "You are?"

I nod. "I am."

"Why?" she questions me.

"Why?" I repeat. She nods her head. "Because when I'm with you, the world ceases to exist. Because I look forward to being with you. You make me smile every day and make my heart beat uncontrollably in my chest. I wake up looking forward to the day, knowing I'll get to see you. I'm a better man with you."

Paige's bottom lip quivers. "Gio."

I shake my head. "You don't have to say a thing. I've tried to hide how I feel about you, Paige. *But I can't.* I need you to know I'm all in. Whenever you feel the time is right. I want a second chance with you. I want to give you the future you deserved, that we always planned on having."

She wraps her arms around my neck and kisses me. "I think I want all of that, too," she declares.

Yes! "Do we walk back into that room and tell everyone?" I ask her.

She bites her bottom lip. "Do you think it will stay a secret if we do?"

"I trust all those people in there."

"What if your family doesn't like me? Or thinks I'm a gold digger or something?

Her concern makes me chuckle. "Paige, you're rich in your own right."

"Oh, yeah," she says as her cheeks turn pink with embarrassment.

"My family already adores you," I reassure her.

"Oh."

"You ready for this?" I ask her.

She links her hand with mine. "Are you?" she says, raising a brow.

"If it means I can sit at that dinner table and touch you, then fuck yes."

Paige giggles. "Okay then, let's drop the bombshell."

I couldn't be any happier than I am right now as I pull Paige back through the restaurant and into the private room. Everyone standing stops what they are doing as we walk into the room. Their eyes bounce between Paige and me, then to where our hands are linked. I bring our hands to my mouth and kiss her hand.

"Oh, this just got interesting." Matteo chuckles.

Might as well drop another bombshell tonight.

"Paige and I are together. We have been for a while now, but we've kept it a secret due to my situation. I'm in love with this woman, always have been, since I was sixteen. We would appreciate it if you kept this a secret until I can publicly uncouple myself from the mess I'm currently in. The media will have a field day if they find out, and I can't do that to her. I promised her all those years ago I wouldn't let it happen and I'm not breaking that promise now," I declare to a shocked room.

"I knew it," Natalia declares as she rushes over to us. "Oh my god, I'm so happy. This is perfect, so fricken perfect. I love you two together," she says excitedly.

"Welcome to the family." Lilly grins as she hugs Paige.

"I'm happy for you," Luca says, shaking my hand.

"My mind keeps getting blown tonight," Matteo says as he gives me a hug.

"Not the only thing that will be," Zoe quips as she walks past to talk with Paige, and Matteo playfully slaps her ass.

"I know this seems strange, but you understand why I've had to keep everything under wraps," I say to the boys.

Tomas clutches my shoulder and gives it a squeeze. "You owe us no explanation. As long as you are happy, that's all that matters."

"I am, for the second time in my life. The first was when I fell in love with her as a boy."

"Aw, never thought I would see Gio get mushy. I like it. It looks good on you," Matteo says, wiggling his brows.

"This is your second chance, then?" Tomas states.

"It is, and I'm determined not to fuck it up."

"Good, now let's eat, I'm starving. Unless there are any other bombshells you want to drop tonight," Matteo asks.

"Nope, that's it."

32

GIORGIO

We're back from Paris and I've left Paige in bed, exhausted, as I grab my phone. I press the number and it rings.

"Gio?" Allegra picks up.

"Hey, long time no speak."

She lets out a heavy sigh. "I know it's been a while, just … I didn't know what to say to you."

"You look like you're having a great time in Mykonos."

The line falls silent for a couple of moments. "It's nice here, I can be myself."

That's good.

"Are you and Giada happy?" I ask her.

"Would it be horrible of me to say deliriously?"

This makes me laugh. "No, it wouldn't. I want you to be happy, Allegra."

"But my happiness is at your expense, though."

"Actually, it was a blessing in disguise what happened that night." She gasps down the phone at my admission. "If you hadn't done what you had, I would never have gotten the love of my life back."

The line falls silent again.

"What did you say?" she questions me.

"What I said was I'm finally happy."

"You are?" Her voice cracks with emotion.

"I am. Not saying what you did was right, but I'm so fucking happy you did it."

"Fuck, I wasn't expecting that," she says.

"I wasn't either. A lot has happened since you've been away."

"Sounds like it has."

"I think you should come back and tell our parents you're gay."

Silence fills the void again.

"What happens if they don't want me anymore? What if they cut me off?" She sniffles down the phone.

"I'll be here for you, same with Luca and Natalia."

She scoffs at that. "They hate me."

Hate's a strong word.

"Maybe you can make it right with them. Have you ever apologized to Luca and Lilly for the stunt you pulled in Edinburgh?"

"No," she answers weakly.

"That might be a good start, don't you think? You're about to become an aunty soon, don't you want a relationship with your nephew?"

"I do."

"Then tell them that, be honest with them. Apologize for being such a bitch all these years."

"Tell me what you really think." She scoffs.

"You know you have been, don't act surprised."

She laughs at that. "And what about Nat? She's never liked me."

"It's not that she doesn't like you, it's the total opposite, she wants you to include her in things. Luca and I did everything together, you did your own thing, and that left Natalia by herself. She just wants to be included, by you, by all of us," I explain.

"Really?" she asks, sounding shocked.

"Yeah. Our trip to New York was the first time I've ever traveled with her, just the two of us. I felt bad about that."

"You went to New York?"

"Long story. But I want you to try to be a part of this family. We love you, Allegra, but you have to start trying," I warn her.

"I'm so scared," Allegra says, bursting into tears.

"We are your family, and we love you."

"I've let everyone down," she cries.

"Who? Who have you let down?" I ask her.

"Mamma and Papà. They want me to marry a good man and have grandbabies."

"Do you not want a family?" I ask her.

I can hear her sniffling on the other end of the phone. "I do, one day."

"Do you think Mamma cares where that baby comes from as long as her house is filled with them?" I tell her, which pulls a chuckle from her lips.

"You're making this sound so easy." She moans, hiccupping through her tears.

"It is when it comes to family."

"Do you think Papà can handle my news?" she asks.

"Yes."

She lets out a shaky breath. "Okay, I'll come home and tell them."

Relief fills my body. "Are you sure? I don't want to pressure you into it."

"I'm sick of living with this secret," she confesses.

"Do you want the entire family there or just me?"

"All of you. I might need Lilly to resuscitate Papà." She chuckles.

"I can arrange that," I tell her.

"Gio, I don't deserve you as a brother. After everything I've done to you, here you are still trying to protect me. I'm so sorry. I never meant for any of this to happen." She cries down the phone. I can hear how sorry she is for making the choices that she has.

"I forgive you. It's water under the bridge for me. What I do want is for the world to know that Giada and I are not together anymore. Not the why or who, I just want that noose cut from around my neck."

"I can do that, Gio," Giada says down the line, surprising me. I had no idea she was there. "Consider it done."

"Just like that?" I ask, trying not to be skeptical.

"Yeah, just like that. I'm sick of hiding who I am and who I love. It's exhausting, I'm done living in the shadows. I'm sorry for putting you through this, Gio. I don't deserve your compassion, but I'll never forget it," she says.

Wow. That's unexpected.

"It's going to be okay, Gia, this isn't going to ruin your career. Matteo said to give him a call if things don't work out here, he'd love you to be on his show."

Giada squeals on the other end of the phone. "No way. He said that?"

"Yeah, he did. I was just with him on the weekend in Paris."

"Wait, so he knows about Allegra and me?"

"Natalia was very forthcoming with the information," I tell her.

"She never did like me." Giada chuckles. No, she didn't, but I don't need to say anything more when it comes to that. "We don't have anything in the next couple of days, maybe we should come back and face the music," Giada states.

"You willing to come back to that media scrutiny?"

"I was thinking about accidentally dropping some nudes online after releasing our statement, that might take some of the pressure off you." Giada laughs.

"Don't think we need to go that far, but I appreciate the sentiment."

"I'll keep them in my back pocket, just in case," she jokes.

"We'll see you in a couple of days. Do you mind organizing it with Mamma and Papà?" Allegra asks.

"Consider it done."

"Thanks, Gio," Allegra says before hanging up.

That went better than expected. Fingers crossed they keep their word and this entire mess will be over soon.

"Your phone won't stop beeping," Paige says, nudging me awake.

Huh. What? I roll over and grab my phone, and sure enough, the thing is lit up like a Christmas tree.

"Fuck." I sit up in bed and swipe open my phone.

"Is everything okay?" Paige asks.

I click on a message and see the headline – **Italy's sweetheart heartbroken.** Great, they are painting me out to be the villain. I quickly scroll over to Giada's socials, and that's where I see it, she's tagged me in the post.

Hi guys, it's with a heavy heart that Giorgio and I announce we have gone our separate ways. It was a tough decision for us to make, but ultimately it was the right one. We realized that the love we have for each other is more as friends than anything else. Even though we made this decision to separate a while ago, we are both still healing from it. I understand this has come as a shock to my fans, but please do not troll either of our accounts during this time. Gio is not to blame, and I will not stand for anyone coming after him; he does not deserve that. I thank you for your love and support during this time.

Xoxo

Giada

"Fuck."

"Gio, you're scaring me," Paige states.

"Here, read this," I say, handing her my phone as I run my fingers through my hair.

"Oh," Paige gasps.

"I know. She did it."

"It's a good statement," she says, handing me back my phone.

My phone rings, and it's Natalia. I pick it up. "I just saw," I say, answering the phone.

"I can't believe she did it. Why do you think she changed her mind?"

"I spoke to Allegra last night. They are coming back to Rome to talk to the parents."

"Oh, that's brave of them," she says.

"It is. She wants all of us there when she tells them her secret."

"No, I'm not going. I can't support her," Natalia states angrily.

"She needs us."

"I don't care, she's a raging bitch."

I pinch the bridge of my nose with my fingers, it's too early for this shit. "Have you thought the reason she's a raging bitch is maybe because she's been trying to hide her secret?"

Natalia falls silent on the phone. "No, I hadn't thought about that."

I send a prayer up to heaven to help me deal with her. "Please, can you do this for me?"

Silence falls again.

"We should all be there to support her. I don't care if after you go back to hating her, but in that moment, she needs us to be there for her," I implore my sister.

"Fine. Message me the details and I'll be there," she grumbles. Thank heavens. "What are you and Paige going to do now that you're no longer engaged to Giada?"

I look over at Paige, and she gives me a shrug. "I don't think Paige and I can go walking hand in hand down the streets just yet."

"Where are you now?"

"Paige's apartment."

"Good, no one should know where that is. Be careful, this is blowing up everywhere already and you know the paparazzi are hunting you down as we speak," Natalia states.

"I know," I say, running my hand nervously through my hair, this is the exact situation I never wanted to put Paige in, but it's happening now.

"Good luck, Gio. Call me if you need anything. Say hi to Paige for me." And with that, she's gone.

"Shit's about to get real now, isn't it?" Paige asks.

I nod. "Yeah, it is." I can't sugarcoat it for her.

I watch as Paige takes a deep breath and looks down at her phone as it starts buzzing. "Callie and Sav just saw the post."

Shit.

"Come here," I say, pulling Paige into my lap. "I love you," I tell her as I cup her face. "I will not let anything happen to you. Do you hear me?"

She nods.

"Once I leave this apartment today, I'm not sure when I'm going to be able to get back. I will not lead them to your door, do you understand me?"

"Yes."

"We are free of one prison, but we've entered another. I'll understand if …"

Her brows pull together. "If what?"

I suck in a steady breath. "If you don't want this anymore, I understand. Things are about to get crazy, and I will not let them drag you into this mess."

Paige reaches out and wraps her arms around my neck. "You tried to protect me from this happening fifteen years ago, and yet here we are."

My stomach sinks.

"I'm glad you are giving me the option now, unlike back then," she says, those dark eyes narrowing on me. Because I would have given you the same answer then as I am now. I'm all in because I love you," she says.

Fuck, I don't deserve this woman.

"I love you, too," I tell her as our foreheads meet.

"Good, now take me to bed and show me how much. If we have to be apart for a bit, I want you to fuck me so good that I'll be able to feel you inside me even when you're not there."

"Fuck, P," I curse.

How the hell can I say no to that?

33

GIORGIO

Leaving Paige sleepy and sated was the hardest thing I've ever had to do. Thankfully, we'd fucked each other's brains out for the past twenty-four hours, not knowing how long it would be until we saw each other again. The only reason I'm leaving her now is because Allegra and Giada have arrived back in Rome. And today is the day Allegra comes out to our parents.

"Sweetheart, are you okay?" My mother asks as I had to dodge a paparazzi scrum out the front of their villa. Thank goodness for tinted windows and the undercover garage.

"I'm fine," I tell her as I kiss her cheeks.

"Vultures," my father hisses as he comes to welcome me.

"They are," I agree, hugging him before they escort me into the living room where Luca is seated.

"Where's Lilly?" I ask, usually they are joined at the hip.

His face tightens. "Thought it would be safer if she stayed at home."

Oh.

"I'm sorry," I say quietly.

"It's not your fault," he says, shaking his head.

"Has the party started yet?" Natalia asks as she struts in, giving us a hug.

"You're early, so it hasn't started yet," I tell her as one of the staff brings us some drinks.

There's a commotion and moments later Allegra walks into the living room.

"Hi." She waves nervously as Natalia huffs and Luca nods. I'm the only one of the siblings to get up and hug her.

"It's going to be okay," I reassure her as I take my seat back down on the sofa.

"It's so good to have all my children together again. You have been missing for far too long, Allegra," our mother states as our father takes a seat.

"I know, Mamma, just there's been a lot happening," Allegra starts.

Mamma waves her comment away. "It can't be more important than Luca and Lilly's pregnancy or Giada breaking your brother's heart."

Allegra twists and turns her hands in her lap as he looks over at me for help.

"Actually, it is," I say for her.

Our mother stops fussing and stares at me, then back to Allegra. "What is going on? We already have one scandal to contend with, we don't need another."

Allegra's face falls, and in an instant, I see her deflate. "I can't do this. I'm sorry," she says as she gets up and rushes out of the room.

I'm disappointed in Mamma for not thinking about her words as I rush out after my sister.

"What did I say?" I hear Mamma question as I leave.

"Allegra, wait, please."

When she turns around, there are tears streaming down her face, and she looks so broken. My heart breaks for her and nothing else matters more than comforting her. I reach out and pull her into my arms and hold her tightly as she breaks down. "It's going to be okay," I try to reassure her, but she just breaks instead.

"What's going on? Your mother is fussing in there," Papà asks as he walks out into the hallway. His face falls when he sees how distraught Allegra is. "My sweetheart, what happened?" he asks as he pulls her out of my arms into his. He gives me a concerned look over her shoulder as he hugs her tightly as she breaks again. "Whatever it is, we can work it out. I promise, my girl. I love you," he says, kissing her head as she squeezes him tightly.

Moments later, Mamma walks out, grumbling about everyone disappearing, and as soon as she sees Allegra, she loses it. "My baby, what's the matter? Who did this to you? Do I need to kill him?"

I try to stifle a laugh because she couldn't be further from the truth. She slaps me in the chest. "What is wrong with you laughing when your sister is going through something? Come, my love, come sit down and talk to your mamma," she says, pulling a reluctant Allegra from our father's arms and back into the living room.

"Is she okay?" Papà asks me.

"She will be, but you have to try to make Mamma listen. I can already see she is going to steamroll over it all."

Papà nods and walks into the living room.

When I join him, I look over at my siblings who are staring at the scene in front of them, not knowing what to do.

"Sweetheart, let the poor girl breathe," Papà suggests to our mother.

"I'm worried about her. I haven't seen her in months and now she returns from Greece in tears," she states.

"I'm sure Allegra will tell us when she's ready. You know she hates fussing, sweetheart," he tells her.

Mamma's brows pull together at my father's words. "It's my job to be sure my children are okay, and Allegra isn't," she says, rubbing her hand on our sister's back.

"Mamma, maybe give her a moment," I suggest, giving Allegra a reassuring smile.

"I'm sorry, my love, I just want to make it all better, okay? I love you," she tells her.

Allegra looks up at her with watery eyes. "I don't think you can make this better, Mamma."

Our mother's face falls and concern etches into her skin. "Whatever it is you can tell us. We will always be there for you."

Allegra takes a deep breath. "Do you really mean that?" she asks softly.

"Of course, my love, I'm your mother. I will always love you. Some days you may drive me crazy, but I still love you even then," she reassures her.

Allegra looks over to where we are all sitting and the three of us give her a thumbs-up to push her on to tell her truth. She nods and centers herself. "I'm gay," she says, and the room falls silent.

Mamma blinks a couple of times as she stares at her. "Gay?"

Allegra bites her bottom lip as uncertainty hits her. "Yes."

"I thought you were going to tell us something bad like you had killed someone." Mamma sighs and falls back against the sofa, looking relieved.

"Wait, you thought I came here to tell you I killed someone?" Allegra questions them.

"Kind of." Papà shrugs.

"You thought I was capable of killing someone?"

"Yep." Natalia chuckles.

Allegra's eyes narrow on her before returning to our parents. "And you don't care that I'm gay. That I like women?"

"We don't care. We love you," Papà tells her.

"Two women can still have babies, right?" Mamma asks.

Allegra turns to me, and I just shrug. "Yes."

"Great, you can still give me grandbabies. You know, Sylvia's daughter is lesbian. You would like her, she's very beautiful. She's an artist, very talented."

And just like that, Mamma is back to interfering in our lives.

"I'm not single, Mamma," Allegra states.

We all still at her admission, each one of us for different reasons.

"You have a girlfriend?" Mamma asks.

"Yes."

"Is it serious?"

"Yes," Allegra answers, and I can see the nervousness is back.

"Would I know her?" Mamma continues to question.

"Yes," my sister answers shakily.

Mamma's eyes widen with that bit of information. "Will she be coming to Sunday lunches?"

"I don't know if she will be invited," she answers.

"Why would she not be invited?" Mamma huffs.

"Because it's Giada."

My heart stops, my stomach sinks, the entire room stills in slow motion as Allegra drops the news that her new girlfriend is my ex-fiancée.

Next thing I know, all hell breaks loose, and everyone starts yelling. It continues until I can't take it any longer, and I let out a loud whistle silencing the room.

"Enough," I yell at them all. "This is probably not what you wanted to hear that Allegra's new girlfriend is my ex-fiancée, but if I'm okay with it, then you should be okay with it."

"We are in shock, son," Papa tells me.

"How long have you known?" Mamma questions me as her eyes narrow.

"Since the engagement party, I found them together." I shudder at the image.

"And you have forgiven your sister for stealing your fiancée?" Mamma asks.

"It wasn't like that," Allegra tries to answer, but Mamma holds up her hand, and she shuts her mouth.

"She did me a favor. I was never in love with Giada."

Mamma gasps.

"That's because he's in love with someone else," Natalia adds.

My eyes widen as my head turns to where she is standing.

"What? It's the truth," she says with a shrug.

"My children have been keeping secrets from me," Mamma says as she clutches her chest, stumbles backward, and takes a seat. "Where did I go wrong?"

I roll my eyes at my mother's theatrics. "You don't need to know every little thing that goes on in our lives."

"It seems I don't need to know any big things either," she snips.

Okay, she might be right there. Fine, I'll change that. "I've fallen in love with Paige," I confess to her.

"Paige?" My mother gasps.

I can't quite tell if that is a happy or angry gasp. "Yes," I answer hesitantly.

"My prayers have been answered. Thank you God," she says, waving her hands in the air.

What is going on? As I turn to my siblings for help, they all shrug and look equally confused.

"I always knew she was the one for you. Lucia and I always prayed for you to find each other again. Even when she was married, Lucia never gave up hope that her good-for-nothing husband would mess up and she would finally leave him. I just wished she was here to see it all, she probably has a front-row seat in heaven."

That is ... I don't know what to think.

"Then when you brought her to Sunday lunch, and you told me she was divorced, I was so happy. And the fact that she had moved back to Rome was even better as if Lucia was planning it herself. I prayed every single day from then on that the two of you would fall in love and you have." She smiles triumphantly as if she had planned it all.

"Mamma, that's messed up," I say.

She seems genuinely shocked by my comment. "What? Lucia always said that the two of you would get back together again. She believed that you were soulmates. And you know Lucia wasn't one for the warm and fuzzies."

"That's not good karma, Mamma," Natalia warns.

"What? Wanting my children to be happy?" she responds.

"I think I'm going to go now. This has been fun," Luca says, standing up.

"Luca, wait," Allegra asks. He pauses and raises a questioning brow at her. "I want to apologize to you and Lilly. If I hadn't stuck my nose into your business, then the two of you wouldn't have spent all that time apart, and ... she wouldn't have been kidnapped. And I wish I could go back in time and stop myself, but I was so angry at the world, and I took it out on you. I'm sorry."

Luca's eyes widen at Allegra's apology. "Thank you," he says stiffly.

"I know it won't happen overnight, but I want to be the best aunty I can to your little man, if you let me?"

"No, you don't get to come in here on your apology tour and try to take favorite aunty status. That is mine," Natalia states.

"I ... I wasn't trying to step on your toes, Nat," Allegra says.

"Well, you have. You have been missing from our lives for years and now suddenly you want to be back in as if all the shit you have caused never happened."

"I'm trying to make amends," Allegra explains.

"You're not the only one that is hurt, Allegra. For years I wanted to be a part of your life and you never once let me in and now you're demanding we bring you back into the sibling fold as if nothing happened."

"That's not what I'm asking. I know it's going to take time. But I do want a relationship with you, Nat. And I'm sorry I pushed you away all these years."

Tears well in Natalia's eyes. "I just wanted my sister." And with that admission, Natalia walks out of the room in tears.

I go to chase after Nat, but Allegra halts me. "I'll go, we have a lot to sort out."

"I need a drink. Today has been a lot." Papà chuckles as he sits back down in his seat.

"I've got to go, and get back to Lilly," Luca says, giving his good-byes before exiting the room.

"Are you really okay about all this?" Mamma asks.

"About Allegra and Giada?"

She nods her head.

"Yeah, if it hadn't happened, I wouldn't have found Paige."

"God can work in mysterious ways." Mamma chuckles.

Unless God has been watching too much Jerry Springer, I don't think he could have thought up this mess.

"You really love her, son?" Papà asks.

"I do."

"If she can stand by you through all this, then it's going to last." He smiles.

34

PAIGE

"Give us a twirl," Savannah says through the computer. "You're going to knock Gio's socks off looking like that."

"You look like a princess, Paige," Callie adds.

"You think?" I ask, twirling again, trying to catch a glimpse of myself in the mirror. I was worried about the dress as it is a little more daring than I would normally wear—with a high neck, low back, and high thigh split. The dress is a deep scarlet color, and it compliments my complexion perfectly. The hairdresser pulled my hair up into a gorgeous high bun, and I raided Lucia's diamonds and found a stunning long necklace that I could wear backward so the diamond falls down my spine. The makeup artist went for a smokey eye, darker than I would normally wear, but it suits the dress. I look like a completely different woman. *Maybe even a countess.*

"You're going to be the belle of the ball," Callie adds.

"Thanks for the confidence boost, ladies. I can always count on you both to lift me up," I tell them.

"We miss you." Savannah groans.

"I miss you, too. Wish you girls were my date for tonight."

"I'm sorry I can't come over. I'm so upset." Callie moans. She's been given a big career-making case that clashes with the dates she wanted to come over. I'm sad but I understand.

"We can celebrate when you win," I tell her.

"I'll be over soon, just dealing with the red tape for this new bar." Savannah groans.

"Maybe I can come back to New York instead."

"No," they both say.

"Michael's moved on, I'm sure it's safe," I tell them.

They both shake their heads. "Smith would have a heart attack," Callie reminds me.

"When isn't he?"

She chuckles because she knows it's true.

"Speaking of heart attacks, have you told him about you and Gio yet?" Callie asks.

"No. There's no point until we can go public. You know he's not going to understand."

"True, but you know he's going to get butthurt that you hid it from him."

He will be hurt, but I don't need him worrying. I'm hoping it won't be for too much longer.

My phone dings, letting me know my driver is here. "I have to go, otherwise I'll be late. Talk to you both soon." They wish me luck, tell me to have fun, and we wave goodbye to each other. I double-check one last time in the mirror that I don't have lipstick on my teeth, and grab my clutch and head downstairs to where my driver is waiting for me. I'm so nervous; I'm arriving at this event by myself. I've never walked a red carpet before or had my picture taken by the paparazzi and it's freaking me out. When I jump in the car, I'm surprised to see Mackenzie, Zoe, Matteo, and Tomas.

"What a lovely surprise." I smile, greeting my new friends.

"Gio thought you might want to arrive with us instead of alone," Tomas explains.

"That's great. I've been freaking out all afternoon about it," I confess, which makes them laugh.

"I'm a professional on red carpets, follow my lead and you'll do just fine," Matteo explains.

"Ignore him, he's a media whore, we will use him as a distraction to get inside without having to talk to anyone. Stick close to me, I've got you," Mackenzie whispers which makes me feel so much better.

We join the long queue of cars, waiting our turn to arrive at the red carpet.

"This is the worst, waiting for your turn," Matteo grumbles.

When it arrives, a man opens the door and helps me from the car, and I'm assaulted by the flashing light bulbs, which blind me momentarily.

"You guys go on ahead, I've got her," Mackenzie tells her family. I watch as the three of them comfortably walk the red carpet together.

"Sending in the throuple first usually distracts the media long enough for us to sneak right past them," Mackenzie jokes as we step onto the red carpet. We take the first couple of tentative steps and her plan is working, they are all trying to get Matteo's attention. *I can do this.* One foot in front of the other. It's not until we are halfway up the carpet that I hear people screaming my name.

"Countess Paige over here."

How did they know that?

"Guess you can't sneak by." She chuckles as she steps away from me, letting the photographers get their photo. I try to channel my inner supermodel, but my eyes are blinded by all the flashes; this is intense. I smile and pose and move along as quickly as I can, trying to catch my breath as soon as I step out of the spotlight.

"See you did it. You did good," Mackenzie tells me."

"That was petrifying," I confess to her.

"I still hate red carpets, even though I've been to so many," she explains.

Moments later, there's an ear-splitting roar and the cameras go wild —the paparazzi are in a frenzy. Who the hell has arrived? Whoever they are must be super famous. I wait around the corner, peering out just enough to see who it could be, and then I see him.

Gio.

He strides along the red carpet confidently, but I see the tension on his face and the way he grits his teeth. He stops and chats to some of the networks covering the event, giving them a fake smile. I know it's fake because I've seen his real ones. He chats about the charity, keeping the interviewer on task by talking about the event, not his personal life before stepping away and posing for the cameras. I've never seen him in his world before and if I'm being honest, it's terrifying.

He turns to look for the exit, and that's when he sees me, his face lighting up, and the real Giorgio breaks through the façade. He cuts short his red carpet walk to stride over to me. My heart thunders in my chest as I look around to make sure no one has spotted the change in his disposition.

"Mackenzie, so great to see you again," he says, greeting my chaperone warmly.

"Nice to see you, too. Have you met my friend? Countess Paige," she says, joining in on the charade.

"How nice to meet you," he says, pretending he doesn't know me as he leans in to kiss both my cheeks. "When we go inside, follow me," he whispers before stepping back and striding into the ballroom.

"I ... just ..." I turn to Mackenzie.

"Go," she says with a grin.

I go to follow Gio, but his strides are so much longer than mine, especially in these heels, that I lose him in the crowd. Where is he? There are so many people here and everyone looks the same dressed in their tuxedos. I move away from the crowd and to the edge of the ballroom. How has he vanished? My phone buzzes inside my clutch. I pull it out and read the message.

> Giorgio: Look up.

When I do, I notice him right above me on another level. My phone buzzes again.

> Giorgio: Take the stairs on your left to this level. There is a door marked office. Meet me in there.

When I look up again, he's gone. My heart pounds in my chest as I nervously look around, feeling like everyone is going to notice me going up the stairs and following him. Ignoring my anxiety because I need to see him, I head toward the stairs and slowly walk up them, looking out over the opulent ballroom, and notice no one is paying me any attention. When I make it to the top, I scan the mezzanine for a door that says office. There, at the far end. I rush toward it as quickly as I can in these heels and turn the brass knob. I push the door open, thinking I'll see Gio on the other side, except it's dark, only the streetlights filter through the window.

"Gio," I whisper yell as I close the door behind me. Do I have the right room?

"You look so fucking beautiful tonight," he says, stepping from the darkness. I whirl around and smile, seeing him standing in front of me. "It's killing me not being able to walk up and kiss you, making sure every single man in that room knows you're mine," he says as those dark eyes run over my body, taking in every inch of me.

"I'm glad you like it." I smirk.

"I fucking love it," he says, reaching out and sliding his finger along the slit of my dress. "Are you wearing any underwear under this?"

"Why don't you find out?" I answer, quirking a brow at him.

The next thing I know, he is on his knees and pulling my leg over his shoulder. His nose runs up my inner thigh, and an animalistic growl vibrates between my thighs when he discovers I'm certainly not wearing any underwear. He licks from the front to the back in one long, hard lick, groaning against my skin. His words are muffled, but I can imagine it's a slew of cursing. He pulls me harder against his face as he starts to devour me in a needy frenzy as if the last couple of hours since he was last inside me was too long.

I'm unable to hold off the orgasm that comes hurtling to the surface, surprising me as I stifle my screams, not wanting to alert anyone within hearing distance to what we are up to. Gio triumphantly removes himself from beneath my evening dress, looks up, and smiles.

"I'm addicted to you," he declares.

I can see myself glistening on his lips as the streetlight catches it. I'm addicted to the way he looks at me after I've come as if he's making sure I've found my satisfaction before he can move on to his.

"I'm addicted to you, too." I grin.

"Good, because we have to be quick. People will be looking for me and I can't go out there and plaster on a smile when my dick wants to be inside you," he says, still on his knees. "I need you to put your hands on that sofa, and I want your ass out, legs spread for me."

Yes, please, I think, and do as I am told. I place my hands on the sofa, arch my back, and spread my legs. I look over my shoulder and see him stand up, using a handkerchief to wipe his face before stalking over toward me. A shiver slides down my body as anticipation rushes through my veins. His hand grips my hip as he pulls up the hem of my evening dress over my hips, exposing my bare ass to him.

"Fucking perfect," he mumbles as his hand grips and pinches my ass.

I bite my bottom lip as I hear his zipper slide open, my skin prickles, my pussy aches as a throb begins between my thighs, and wetness starts to pool with each agonizing moment I wait for him to fill me. "You ready, babe?"

"Yes," I moan, feeling him tap my ass with his dick.

"Good, now be a good girl and guide me into you," he asks.

I reach around and grab his cock and rub the tip of it through my wetness, coating him and teasing the tip before pushing it and out of me. Gio's hands grip my hips as I slowly torture him until he has enough and takes over, pushing all the way in. We both moan at the connection as he fills me.

"This has to be quick, but I needed you to know that you're mine tonight even though I can't show it … yet."

I understand. Seeing him arrive and the frenzy it created, *I get it.*

He starts to furiously slide into me, his fingers digging into my skin as if he's trying to burn his fingerprints on my skin, marking me.

"That's it, babe, fuck," he growls as I try to squeeze him while hanging on for dear life. My fingers dig into the velvet sofa as I meet him thrust for thrust. "I'm not going to last. I'm close, babe, so close." So I squeeze him tighter, loving how my tightness drives him wild. "Fuck, fuck, fuck," he curses, and I feel him pump into me, filling me.

Oh shit, that's the first time he's come inside me.

A hand lands on my ass, which makes me jump, and he groans. "Fucking perfect, babe."

"Shit." He stills, realizing what we've just done. "I ... shit ... we haven't talked about this." He usually comes all over me, marking me, but he couldn't do that tonight with this evening dress.

"I have an IUD," I awkwardly explain.

"Here," he says, handing me his handkerchief. "When I pull out, you should be able to clean up my mess."

Taking the handkerchief, I slide it between us, then he pulls out, and I plug myself with the material. Turning around awkwardly with my hand between my legs, I look up at him and he smiles down at me.

"Probably not the right time to say this, but it's hot knowing that while you're walking around this event, I'll still be inside you," he says, licking his lips.

He makes me laugh at his dirty thoughts. "You really have a kink about marking me with you."

I pull the material from between my legs, it's still very wet between them. It's going to be uncomfortable all night, I hope I don't stain my dress.

"Here," he says, grabbing the handkerchief from me, rolling it up, and placing it in his pants pocket. "You going to be, okay?" he asks, noticing me moving uncomfortably.

"It feels like you're dripping down my leg," I tell him.

"Show me."

Pulling the split to my dress open, I show him the mess he's made.

"My dick is getting hard watching me leak out of you, Paige. I'm sorry if that's gross, but fuck it's hot," he says, adjusting himself.

The way he is looking at me is hot.

"Hold on, I have an idea," he says, dropping to his knees again and running his tongue along my thigh, cleaning himself up off me. He then does the same on the other side and toward my center, licking and sucking me clean until I'm wriggling beneath him and climaxing again. "That feel better now?" he asks, standing back up.

"Yes," I splutter as my cheeks burn from the heat of what he just did. Did I just unlock a new kink? Feels like I did.

He then leans forward and kisses me gently. "Don't want to mess up your makeup," he explains. That might be suspicious if I walk out there with my lipstick smeared across my face. "I have to go, people will be looking for me. I'll see you after this circus, yeah?"

"Yes, back at my place."

"Good. And I promise after tonight, we can go somewhere, just the two of us."

I like the sound of that. He kisses me one last time before disappearing from the room.

35

PAIGE

"Hey, where have you been?" Natalia calls out to me as I descend the stairs.

I still; did she see Gio do the same thing moments before me? I thought I'd left enough time between us to not be suspicious. "I was looking for the restrooms."

Natalia smiles as if that sounded plausible. "I wanted to show you where you're sitting. You're at the table next to ours with Mackenzie and her crew." Of course, why did I expect to be on the family table? No one knows you and Gio are together. Natalia leans into me and whispers, "You and Gio are side by side though."

That makes me happy. I let her guide me through the ballroom, stopping every so often to say hello to people and introducing me to other members of society until we get to the family table at the front of the room.

"Paige, you look spectacular," Lilly says, giving me a hug and stepping away from her conversation with Mackenzie.

"As do you," I say, looking her over. She's dressed in a stunning black evening dress that is sexy and accentuates her bump.

"Yvette's dresses are amazing, I feel beautiful in this." She rubs her stomach, and her face scrunches up.

"Are you okay?" I ask her, worried something is wrong as I try to look around the busy ballroom for Luca.

"I'm fine. This little thing has started kicking, and it hurts," she says, rubbing her belly. "Do you want kids, Paige? Before I start complaining about pregnancy and scare you." She chuckles.

"She's started to scare me, and I've helped deliver babies," Mackenzie jokes.

"Yes, I'd love kids, *one day*."

"Okay, well then being pregnant is the most amazing thing in the world," she says sarcastically, making us all burst out laughing.

"You make it look good," I compliment her, and her eyes get a little teary.

"Hormones, a little overwhelmed." She moans, dabbing her eyes.

Poor thing. "Do you want me to help you with anything? I don't really have anything to do with my days."

"Besides Gio," she quips before placing her hands over her mouth and her eyes widen. "I'm blaming that outburst on hormones."

"Well, you're not wrong." I giggle, which makes her gasp before she starts laughing. "I'm serious, if you need any help with Lilly's Place, let me know."

"Really?" Mackenzie adds.

"Yes, not being able to see him, my days are spent not doing much. I'd like to be useful if I could be. I've gone from working twelve hours a day in our restaurant to nothing," I tell them.

Lilly and Mackenzie look at each other and smile. "That would be wonderful," Lilly says.

"You owned a restaurant?" Mackenzie asks.

"Yeah, back in New York. I have a degree from Italy in the culinary arts."

Mackenzie's face lights up. "We could get her to help teach some of the women how to cook."

"Or even offer culinary arts in the school," Lilly adds.

I'm excited, this sounds fantastic, I want to be able to do something and from what I've heard about their charity, it really helps turn those women's lives around. If I can help them return to as much of a normal life as I can, then I'm all in.

"Does that mean you're staying in Rome, not going back to New York?" Lilly asks, her question catching me off-guard.

Hadn't thought about that when I offered. "I don't know."

Lilly shakes her head, reaches out, and squeezes my arm. "It's okay. We don't need to make any permanent plans. You've been through a lot recently and had a lot of upheaval."

She's right. Everything has been a whirlwind and I haven't stopped and thought about anything long-term.

"I still would like to help."

"And we would love it. Let's talk about it after tonight." Makenzie smiles as someone calls out to her and pulls her from the conversation.

"Everything will work out. You'll be where you're supposed to be, eventually," Lilly adds.

Maybe. As I stare out over the ballroom and catch sight of Gio walking through the crowd, my heart skips a beat.

Lilly nudges me. "I'm glad you found each other. In all the years I've known him, I've never seen him this happy, since you've walked back into his life."

Gio is standing with his brother and parents, and I sigh, gosh he is handsome, a shiver runs down my spine remembering what we did earlier. "We have a lot to sort out before any happy ever after can happen."

"I know, be patient. It will all work out in the end," she reassures me. "What the fuck?" Lilly's eyes widen as a buzz starts to filter through the room; people's whispers get a little louder, and heads turn. It's like a wave of activity. "It's Giada," Lilly warns me. When I turn around, I see her striding through the ballroom as if she owns the room, looking like she's enjoying the attention she is getting. "I didn't know she was coming. Oh, I see, she's Allegra's date." That's when I notice the other stunning woman walking behind her. "What the hell is she thinking?"

"They thought this would shut down the media attention if they saw Gio and Giada hanging out as friends," Luca advises as he gives his wife a kiss on her temple, as he joins us.

"Don't you think you should have warned us?" Lilly glares at her husband.

"Babe, I didn't know. Gio got a phone call five minutes ago about it. You know both of them would be relishing the attention."

"It's your family's big night," Lilly adds.

"She cleared it with our parents before arriving," Luca declares, as I watch Gio make is way over to where we are standing.

"Oh," Lilly reacts.

"Sorry, Paige. I hope this isn't going to be awkward or anything. I know Gio would have told you if he had known," Luca tells me.

I wave his concerns away, there isn't anything I can do about it. No point in getting angry, just nervous.

"Mackenzie, how are you?" Gio says, greeting her.

"Great, thanks," she answers.

"Oh no." Lilly gasps.

We watch as the two girls make their way over to where we are all standing.

"Gio, it's so lovely to see you," Giada states loudly as she kisses his cheeks as photographers go crazy, catching the shot of the two exes reuniting. He stiffens for a moment but greets her warmly before turning his attention to his sister. Giada is even more beautiful in real life. She's dressed in a white crystal evening dress that dips low, showing off her largest assets; it molds to her curves like a glove, her olive skin shimmers under the lights. Her dark brown hair cascades around her shoulders and she's dripping in diamonds. She looks up and her eyes catch mine, she stills for a moment and then a wide smile falls across her plump lips, she leans over to Allegra and says something that draws her attention to me. They both move away from Gio, who tries to stop his sister, but she shrugs him off. His mother grabs him, stopping him from following, and I can see the worry on his face as he watches the two women head for our group.

"Lilly, you look so beautiful. I can't believe how much you have grown since I've last seen you," Allegra says, greeting Lilly warmly.

"It's been a while," Lilly answers.

"Luca," Allegra acknowledges her brother.

"You better not have come over here to cause a scene." He glares at his sister.

Allegra stiffens at her brother's warning tone and shakes her head. "I would never do that here."

I catch that she says *here*, not that she would never do it.

"You must be Paige, we've heard so much about you," Allegra greets me.

"You are stunning, this dress, wow." Giada smiles as her eyes run down my body as if assessing me, as she moves around behind me to see the back. "And this back," she murmurs as she runs a manicured finger right down my spine, sending goosebumps across my skin. What is happening?

"Are you flirting with her?" Allegra chuckles.

"Maybe." Giada grins as she gives me a wink.

What is happening?

Lilly bursts out laughing while Luca groans.

"I see why he's fallen for you." Giada grins as those dark eyes slide over me again before she leans forward. "If you want to come over to the other side, call me." She smirks before walking away and chatting with someone else, Allegra follows her laughing.

"What the hell was that?" Luca asks.

"I don't know," I say, shrugging.

"I think your new man's ex wants you. You can't make this stuff up," Lilly says before bursting out laughing.

"It's going to be a long ass night. Come, let's take our seats." Luca groans as he escorts Lilly toward their table.

I go and find my seat, joining Mackenzie and her family. I'm sitting right in between Mackenzie and Tomas. A waiter comes by and pours water into our glasses and I hastily take a sip, trying to calm the swirling nerves inside me.

There's a tap on my shoulder, and when I turn around, it's Gio, he's taken his seat and it's literally right beside mine. "Are you okay? What did she say to you? You looked shocked," he questions me.

"She was fine, other than that she started flirting with me." I smirk.

Gio is lost for words as he stares at me. "Flirted with you?" I nod my head. "This night keeps getting stranger by the moment," he says, shaking his head. "I'm sorry about her. I didn't know she was coming. Allegra asked at the last minute and then our PR teams got involved and thought that it would raise awareness of the event and hopefully squash the gossip out there."

"I think that's a smart plan." His brows raise high. "People will be talking about the two of you at the event. Which then means people will investigate it and maybe they might see some worthy causes and donate money to them."

"I just want to kiss you right now. How the fuck did I get so lucky?" he says, looking at me heatedly.

"Later, now go do your thing," I tell him as I turn around and join in on the conversation at my table.

"Here, have this," Tomas says as he hands me his handkerchief.

"Thank you," I say, taking it and dabbing my eyes. I probably ruined my perfect makeup as the tears flowed while I watched Lucia's tribute. It was beautiful. I miss her so much and wish she was here with me so we could enjoy this night together. We would be having the best time; she could introduce me to all her friends, we would drink champagne and dance the night away. I wish she had pulled me into this world earlier, I would have loved to have been a part of all the good she was doing in the world. Gio is standing to the side of the stage with his family who gave the opening speeches for the event, and he is rubbing his mother's back as she, too, is dabbing her eyes watching the reel. Once the tribute is over, I excuse myself and head to the bathroom to freshen up. I look a mess, but thankfully, my makeup has held, just my eyes are puffy.

"Hey, are you okay?" Gio asks as I step out of the bathroom. My heart blossoms seeing his handsome face.

"It was nice seeing her again. I miss her," I tell him.

He looks around quickly before he pulls me into his arms and kisses my forehead as he squeezes me. We are hidden behind a pillar, so no one can see us unless they go to the bathroom. Gio looks down at me, and I see fire and lust swirling behind those dark eyes before he kisses me softly.

"Tonight has been torture. I have to go. I love you and I'll see you later." With that, he's gone.

I lean back against the pillar and suck in a deep breath. This man takes my breath away. I'm smiling when I leave our hiding spot and stop abruptly as a chill slides over my body, my stomach sinks, and that same feeling I used to get before I saw Michael hits me. Nervously, I look around the room but don't see anyone. I pull out my phone from my clutch as panic starts to grip me and I dial my brother.

"Hey, how was it?" Smith says, answering the phone happily.

"You're still following Michael, aren't you?"

"Yes. Why, what's going on?"

I shake my head and a sense of unease fills me. "I don't know. I just had a strange feeling, that's someone was following and watching me. That couldn't happen, could it?"

"No, I've had no alerts that he's left the country. Where's Gio? Find him and stay near him. I'll call around and see what I can find out," he says frantically before hanging up. I shake my head, there is no way he is here, yet I scan the space around me again.

There's just no way.

Collecting myself, I step back into the ballroom and take my seat again. I grab my glass of champagne and notice how unsteady my hand is as I raise the glass to my lips.

"Are you okay?" Mackenzie whispers, noticing my hands shaking.

"Guess I'm still a little emotional about the tribute," I lie, which seems to be enough as she encourages me to try the steak.

We get through the rest of the gourmet meal, then the MC announces it's time for dancing as he starts encouraging everyone to the dance floor. When I look around, I notice Gio isn't at his table anymore, neither are Luca and Lilly. His parents have gotten up to dance. Where has he gone?

"You coming to dance?" Tomas asks as Matteo and Zoe stand beside him.

"I'll wait until Mackenzie gets back from the bathroom and then come join you," I tell them as they head off. I watch the three of them laughing as they disappear.

"Hey, Paige," Allegra says as she comes and takes a seat beside me, Giada joining her on the other side. Why does this feel like an ambush? I'm already stressed enough as it is with this stupid gut feeling to worry about these two. "This might be a strange request, but Gio has asked us to help you leave the event with him," Allegra explains. He what?

"He sent you a message," Giada adds.

I frown as I pull out my phone, and sure enough, I have one. I open it up and read it.

> Giorgio: Allegra is going to help you leave. I'll be waiting in the car outside for you.

Oh.

"Are you ready?" Allegra asks.

I nod.

"It was so lovely meeting you, Paige. Hope to see you again soon," Giada says, standing up and giving me a hug. "Gio deserves happiness and I think he's found it," she whispers into my ear before flitting off into the crowd.

"Come on," Allegra says as she escorts me out of the gala. It's easier to make our way through the crowd now that most of them are up dancing. She walks us outside back along the red carpet, and I can see cars pulling up and collecting the departing partygoers. A car flashes its lights as it pulls up before us. "This is your ride." She smiles, opening the door for me.

"Thank you," I say, still confused.

"I look forward to getting to know you," she adds as I get into the car.

"Me too," I answer before she slams the door.

"Thank fuck you're safe. Fuck, I can't believe they can't find him," Gio says as he pulls me into his side.

I go still at his words. "Can't find who?"

Gio looks down at me, and I can see the barely contained rage on his face. "Michael."

36

GIORGIO

Watching Paige's face pale when I tell her they can't find Michael feels like someone has stabbed me in the guts. It's my job to protect her. I told her she was safe with me, that I wouldn't let Michael harm her ever again and now I've failed. Her body shakes as I hold her tightly against me. "Smith called me and told me you had called. When he looked into it for you, they realized he's missing."

"He couldn't possibly be here, could he?" she asks, looking up at me with those dark doe eyes.

"I doubt it, but I'm not taking the chance. I'm bringing you back to my villa. You'll be safe there."

"What about the paparazzi?" she asks quietly.

"Most are at the event, trying to get the scoop on us there. Security has advised me that no one is at home," I reassure her.

"Why would he be here? I don't understand. Why would he follow me here? He hates Italy," she asks as tears slide down her cheeks.

I wipe them away, but each new teardrop is like a dagger to my stomach. "I'm sure he isn't here. We are just being cautious."

"I thought this nightmare was over. Why won't it be over?" she asks before burying her face in my chest as she starts to break down. She cries all the way home.

I carry her exhausted body from the car and up the stairs. I'm thankful for my underground garage in case there is a lone photographer out there waiting for his scoop. I carry her up another flight of stairs to my bedroom and lay her on the bed. She looks so beautiful, so fragile, there is nothing in this world I wouldn't do for this woman. I slip her shoes off and place them at the side of the bed, then reach around, remove her necklace, and lay it on the bedside table. I walk into my closet and pull out one of my T-shirts for her before I remove my tuxedo and slip into something more comfortable. When I walk out, she is softly snoring. Knowing she's not going to be comfortable sleeping in that evening dress, I help her out of it, and she grumbles as I move her around. She's like a rag doll as I slide the material from her creamy skin. She's lying naked on my bed, and as much as my dick twitches to life, now is not the time. I slide my shirt over her head and repeat the process. Then I remember the lingerie I bought her that was going to be a surprise, and I grab the lace bottoms and slide the silky material up over her thighs, covering her. I know how much she hates not wearing underwear to bed. I place a kiss on her forehead as I tuck her in.

Grabbing my phone, I close the door to my bedroom behind me and call Smith.

"Do you have her?" he asks in a panic.

"She's asleep at my home. She's safe."

"Thank fuck. This fucking asshole, hasn't he done enough?" he curses down the phone.

"What do you know?"

"Nothing. No one has seen him. Apparently, he's been missing for a couple of days. I thought that her leaving for Italy would be the end of it. I don't think it is," he explains.

"I've called in favors to see if he is in Italy, but I don't think we will know until morning."

"Yeah, same here. As long as she is safe with you, that's all that matters. Thank you for looking after her," he says.

"This probably isn't the right time to tell you, I know Paige wanted to wait, but you need to know that we're together. I love your sister, always have, always will. There is nothing I wouldn't do to keep her safe."

Silence fills the line between us.

"You're together?" he asks slowly.

"Yeah."

"How long?"

"The entire time she's been here," I confess.

"The entire what?" he shouts.

"I know. The situation with my engagement was complicated, and I didn't want to bring her into the media frenzy. We thought the fewer people that knew, the safer she would be."

"I'm her brother. Does she not trust me?"

What do I say to that? "She does. I think she didn't want to worry you."

"Which is just code for she didn't want a lecture," he mumbles. "I don't have anything against you, Gio, but that's my sister. I'll protect her until my dying breath, you understand me."

"I'd do the same for her and my own sisters," I tell him.

"Good. Well, I'm glad she has you to keep her safe when I can't. Stay in touch and let me know when you hear anything."

"Will do." And with that, he hangs up.

I'm woken by my phone ringing beside me, and I pick it up without even checking who it is and answer it.

"Shit's going down, Gio," Natalia yells down the phone.

"What?"

"That asshole has gone live and has told the world that you and Paige have been having an affair."

My stomach sinks.

"He had the two of you followed. He has pictures of you in New York, Paris, and here. He is telling everyone who will listen that he's the victim. That she left him for you. He's trying to ruin her."

"Fuck, I'll call you back," I say, hanging up on her. There's no way. I tell myself this has to be a bad dream as I pull up my socials and see the numerous tags.

"What's happening, Gio? Is it Michael? Have they found him?" Paige asks, sitting up in bed.

How am I going to be able to tell her about this? I scan my phone and it doesn't look good.

"What? You're scaring me, Gio?"

My shoulders slump. "Michael went live overnight and told the world that you and I were having an affair."

Her eyes widen as she gasps. "No, no, no, no," she says, shaking her head. I hand over my phone and show her what's been happening. She jumps up off the bed. "Fuck. Fuck. I'm ruined. He's ruined me," she yells as she frantically paces the room, looking distraught. I jump up and try to reassure her that it's all going to be okay, but she isn't interested and pushes me away. "I have to go. They can't know I'm here," she mumbles as she tries to grab her things.

"No, it's safer for you here."

"Clearly not," she yells at me and her words are like a slap to the face. "I want to go home. I can't be seen with you."

"Paige, please, security surrounds this place. You are safest here," I try to explain to her.

"What don't you get? I can't be with you," she shouts as she gathers her things in her arms.

Does she mean can't be seen with me or does she mean she can't be with me? *She's panicked, she doesn't know what she's saying.*

"I think it's better for you to stay here, Paige. Please, I promise I will sort this all out."

She looks up at me, the fear clearly written all over her face. "I want to go home."

My heart aches, my stomach twists. "I'll take you home."

She shakes her head. "Not you, someone else."

"I'll organize a driver for you."

"Thank you," she says, and I disappear out of the bedroom.

I'm like a bear with a toothache as I yell at my staff, unable to control my anger over the situation. I'll make it up to them later, but for now I want to punch something. I grab my phone and dial Smith, maybe he can talk some sense into his sister.

"How is she?" he asks.

"She wants to go home. Nothing I can say will change her mind. She doesn't want to be anywhere near me. I don't know what to do."

"Fuck."

"The look on her face …. She's devastated and afraid, but she won't let me protect her. I can't keep her prisoner," I tell him.

"She's scared and panicking. It's not about you, she's probably going into self-preservation mode. You know the whole fight-or-flight thing. Will she be safe at her apartment?" he asks.

"Yes, it's secure."

"Good. Look, Michael is here in the States. We found him in Vermont with some woman. She's safe from him." Thank God for that. "Paige will feel like everything is spinning out of control, and I'm guessing the only way she feels in control is in her own environment. If there is no way the media can get to her, let her go home."

When he explains it like that, I get it.

"I'll ask my sister if she can take her, at least I know she's not alone."

"Call me if you need me," Smith says before hanging up.

I dial my sister. "I need your help?"

"Anything," she says.

"Paige wants to go back to her apartment. She's scared, and she doesn't want to be anywhere near me. Can you take her?"

"Do you think that's a good idea?" she asks.

"No, but it's what she wants, and I can't force her to be somewhere she doesn't want to be," I say, raking my hand angrily through my hair. I'm ready to put my fist through the wall. That fucking snake doing this to her like that. I'm going to make him pay.

"I'm on my way."

37

PAIGE

Natalia sits in the back of the car with me.
"Call me if you need anything," Gio tells her. I can't look at him. It's not his fault this is happening, it's Michael's. But I feel so betrayed by everyone and everything right now, I'm shutting the entire world out to protect myself, and that includes him. He sadly closes the door, and we drive out of the underground garage and as soon as we are above ground, I can see all the media standing out the front of his gates. Blinding flashes start to go off when they notice the car, and cameras are pushed up against the glass as we leave. People are shouting and screaming horrible things as the car drives through the media crush. They are savages as I scream, trying to get away from them banging on the car, as Natalia hugs me tightly. Maybe it was a bad idea to leave Gio's home.

"It's going to be okay," Natalia reassures me as we huddle until we are away from the scrum.

"I'm going to try and lose them," the driver says as we rush through the already chaotic Roman streets. We look behind us and see a cavalcade of paparazzi on bikes. We are flung back in our seats as the driver tries to lose them down narrow streets, all the while, these parasites are trying to take photos of us. Why? I'm a nobody.

"Gio, we need the police. They are chasing us. We're scared. They have lost their minds," Natalia screams down the phone at her brother.

I shouldn't have left. I should have stayed. I've put us in danger. Gio is used to this, he knew this would happen, and I stupidly thought I knew better.

"Take us back to Gio's, please," I yell at the driver. "I'm sorry, Nat. I'm so sorry I got you into this mess. I should have listened to Gio. I should have stayed where it was safe." I cry.

"It's never been this bad before. They've lost their damn minds."

And that is the last thing I hear before everything goes black.

38

GIORGIO

"She's going to wake up soon," Smith says, squeezing my shoulder to reassure me. I flew her entire family and her friends out to be with her. It's been three days since the accident, and she's still not opened her eyes. The doctors say putting her in an induced coma is the best thing to help her brain heal. She hit her head hard when the car tried to avoid one of the paparazzi on the bikes; their car was clipped by another car, which spun it into a wall. Luckily, it hit the passenger front corner first, taking the full brunt of the impact, but Paige was sitting behind that seat and was flung forward, resulting in her brain injury. One of the driver's legs was crushed, and Natalia walked away with a broken arm and a hell of a lot of bruising. All our cars are installed with cameras, and they caught the entire chase on video. Paige had asked the driver to come back to me because she was scared. It broke my heart, hearing her and Natalia's fear as the assholes chased them. The paparazzi have been caught and are currently sitting in jail waiting to post bail which I was able to get set for one million euros, thanks to my connections. If I had gotten to those assholes first, I would have murdered them.

"Come back to me, Paige, please. This is not how our story ends." I cry as I kiss her lifeless hand.

"You look exhausted, Gio, come have a coffee," Luca asks.

I look up at my brother from the hospital bed. "I can't leave her. I need to be here when she wakes up."

His face falls. "I know, and you will be, but she doesn't want you falling asleep on her as soon as she wakes up now does she?"

I've spent every waking moment beside her since the accident.

"Let me take over for a while," Smith offers.

Right, yes, I'm sure he is worried, too, it's his sister. "Okay," I say, reluctantly leaving my spot beside her. Luca places a welcoming hand around my shoulders as he drags my weary ass toward the café. Thankfully, we have a private area of the hospital with our own café area, so no one can bother us. Luca orders our coffees at the window and comes back and sits down beside me.

"I can't lose her," I say as my head falls into my hands and tears splash against the linoleum floor.

"You're not going to. She's a fighter, that's what the doctor said; she's just not healed enough to wake up yet. Her body will tell her when the time is right.

"What happens if she wakes up, and she doesn't remember me, us? What if she is a different person?"

"Then you will deal with it. There is no point worrying about the what-ifs. She's alive. And her brain function is good. She just needs time," my brother states, trying to reassure me.

He's right. I know he is, but I'm so fucking scared. I lost her once, I can't lose her a second time.

"I love her so much, Luca. She's the one. I want to marry her and have babies, lots of babies for Mamma. I want to grow old with her."

"And you will. I promise you."

"Holy shit," Natalia curses as she stares down at her phone when she joins us in Paige's room. It's a full house today with her best friends, Savannah and Callie here, swapping out for her parents, who had done the morning shift. "I can't believe they did that." Her eyes widen and a big smile falls across her face.

"What is it?" Luca asks impatiently.

"Giada and Allegra released something," she declares. They did what? Why would they do that?

"She can't stand not being the center of attention," Luca snips.

"I'm not her biggest fan either, but I don't think they were being self-centered for once," Natalia explains.

"What are they saying?" I question her.

"Okay. Giada's statement says ... *I'm ashamed to be Italian. The disgusting pursuit of a story has gone too far this time. The actions of unscrupulous people in the media have put three people in the hospital. Three innocent people. Three lives nearly destroyed because of the delusional lies of one unhinged French man. If anyone had cared to ask more questions than print one man's delusions, you would have found that the countess was never married to him. That it was he who was caught cheating while she was laying to rest a family member. That this individual has a protective order against him for stalking and physical assault of the countess. That she had to escape halfway across the world to get away from this man, and yet he continues to stalk her, and you all played a part in it. This man has shown you photos of Giorgio and the countess together. Giorgio was a single man in all those photos, they were doing nothing wrong. I know this because Giorgio and I broke up the night of our engagement party because he found me with someone else. I'm not proud of how I handled the situation. I should have been honest, and if I had, maybe none of this would have happened. But the reason why I had lied was because the person I was seeing behind Giorgio's back was his sister, Allegra. My best friend. It was never my intention to fall for my best friend, but I did. She is the love of my life and I've been too scared to admit my feelings. I pushed them aside and made the biggest mistake of my life and started dating her brother, hoping that it would make me forget the feelings I believed I shouldn't have had for my best friend. I couldn't run from them, they only got stronger. I asked Giorgio to give me time before announcing our separation, trying to stave off the media fallout. That didn't work. And as the selfless guy that he is, he gave Allegra and me the time we needed to sort out our feelings toward one another. What Giorgio wasn't expecting was to reconnect with the countess again. You see, he has known her and her family for most of his life, each of them finding a supportive shoulder during a difficult time. The villain in this story is me, not her, not him. Me. I'm taking responsibility for this incredibly twisted mess I've created because I was too scared to tell the world I was in love with a woman. I was worried that I would lose everything if I was honest with you all. None of that matters when three people could have lost their lives. One is still fighting for hers, the innocent bystander in this tale, the countess. I'm asking the media to do better. If you would like to help, then here is a link to a funding page that we will be using to raise money for the countess's favorite charities. Maybe we can make some good out of this tragedy."*

The room falls silent.

"That was ballsy," Savannah states, breaking the tension.

It was. I can't believe she said all that.

"Fuck, she's raised two hundred thousand euros for the charities since posting it," Natalia states.

"That's amazing," Lilly adds.

"What's amazing?"

The room stops when we hear Paige ask the question.

"Paige," I call out as I rush to her.

"Get the doctors," Smith calls out.

"You're alive," I say as I grab her hand and kiss it.

She blinks a couple of times as she stares at me and then around the room. "Why is everyone here?"

"You were in an accident," I explain gently, and she turns to look at me.

"You look like shit," she says, and I burst out laughing. That has to be the best thing I've heard all day.

"He hasn't left your side," Smith tells her as he comes and sits on the other side.

"You're in Rome?" she questions him. At least she knows where she is. "Sav, Callie, you're here, too?" she says once she notices her best friends who are crying as they move toward her slowly, not sure if they should touch her or not. "What about your case?" she asks Callie.

"There will be others, but there's only one you," she tells her as she tries to control her emotions, and Smith wraps his arm around her for support.

Paige then looks around the room and clocks Luca, Lilly, and Natalia. "Your arm?" She asks my sister.

"I know, I was lucky," Natalia answers.

Paige touches herself to see if she has any injuries. "No broken bones, you were lucky. They think because you hit your head first and were unconscious that your body relaxed and didn't tense up. You have a lot of bruising. It looks like you've gone a couple of rounds with Mike Tyson," I tell her.

"Have I been asleep for long?" she asks, a frown etching deeply on her forehead.

"Three days," I tell her.

"Miss Johnson, you're awake," the doctor states, interrupting us.

"Looks like I am."

"I'm going to have to ask you all to give us five if that is okay?" the doctor asks. "Your friends and family haven't left your side the entire time." He winks at Paige.

We usher ourselves out of the room as more medical staff come.

She's alive.

39

PAIGE

"It's good to be back in New York." I groan as I roll over and snuggle into Gio's side.

It's been a month since the accident and this man hasn't left me for a minute. I know he never left my side in the hospital either. I don't know if I will ever tell him, but I heard every little thing he whispered to me while I lay there lifeless, the many promises and prayers he asked for to make me come back to him. The wedding he has planned, how many babies he wants us to have, the house he wants them to grow up in, and everything he wants in the future with me. And I want it all, too. Maybe not the five kids, three might be enough. The reason it took me so long to come back to him was because I was hanging out with Lucia in some sort of limbo.

"Why the hell are you here? You're early," Lucia asks as she sips on her champagne glass.

"There was an accident."

She rolls her eyes as if annoyed by that bit of information. "Hmm, I need to talk to someone about that," she says. "They said you need to wait here for a bit before going back, there's a queue."

"A queue?"

"Yes," she answers sternly as if it all makes sense.

"So, I'm not dead?"

"No, my sweetheart, it's not your time," she explains.

That's good to know, I think. "What do I do now?"

"You wait."

"Wait?"

"Yes. I know your generation doesn't have patience for things, but you have to wait," she snips at me.

"Why did you leave me?" I blurt out.

Her brows raise on her face. "It was my time."

I rub the tears away from my eyes. "But I wanted more time with you."

Lucia's face softens. "I wish I had more time with you, too, but it wasn't so."

"But I miss you," I tell her as my lip wobbles.

"I miss you, too, my love."

"Everything fell apart when you left. I was so alone."

"I know you were, that's why I sent Giorgio to you," she says, flashing me her devilish grin.

"You what?"

"You two should have always ended up together, but you're both too damn stubborn. I knew it was only a matter of time before that Frenchman would mess up. Wish I was alive for you when it happened. I'm sorry about my timing."

"You're telling me you've been up here playing cupid?"

She nods as she raises her glass at me.

"Hey, I have a bone to pick with you. Why did you hide so much of your life from me? The charities, the businesses; it was a shock finding out about them."

"You know me, I never wanted to be a burden. How do you like being a countess, kind of cool, isn't it?" She grins.

"I can't believe you did that to me."

Lucia chuckles. "It was amusing to watch from up here. But I knew you would rise to the challenge. I think offering your culinary skills at Lilly's Place is a wonderful idea.

"Haven't had a chance to help thanks to my life imploding because of my asswipe of an ex." I sigh.

"Don't worry, I gave that man the shits for pulling that stunt."

We both burst out laughing.

"I miss our chats." I suddenly feel sad.

"You can chat to me anytime you like. I just can't answer, but I'll always be listening."

"Am I making the right decision with Gio?"

"Yes, you two are going to have the most wonderful life together."

"I'll never get sick of waking up next to you," Gio says, wrapping his arms around me and pulling me to his side.

This man makes me giddy, and I can't believe he is all mine. We're back in town to pack up the last of my things and move them back to Rome. I made the decision that my life is in Rome now, and as much as I will miss New York, most notably my girls, Gio has said that he will always have a jet ready to go anytime I need to see them, or they need to see me. *This is what happens when you fall in love with a billionaire.* When we get back from New York, I'm going to join Mackenzie and Lilly at their charity and start teaching women how to cook, as well as training them how to be chefs. I can't wait, I will be making a difference in the world through food.

"Looks like someone is happy to see me this morning," I chuckle as I slide myself over him, rubbing my nakedness over his hardening length.

"Is my baby's pussy feeling empty?" He smirks.

"Yes," I coo as I lift myself over him.

"If you want it, take it, it's all yours."

That it is. He is all mine.

I wrap my fingers around his cock and run it between my wetness as I line him up. Gio thrusts his hips, not giving me a chance to sink down on him as he impales me on his dick.

"Impatient much?" I chuckle.

"Yes, now fucking ride it and show me how much you fucking love it." He grins as he places his hands behind his head cockily.

Does my man want a show this morning? I'll give him one. As I start to ride him, I run my hands all over my body, as my fingers pluck my nipples, pulling a moan from my lips.

"Fuck, I love listening to you moan." Gio growls as he pushes my hands from my breasts and starts playing with them.

I bite my bottom lip as I watch the desire on his face as he watches me fuck him.

"Bounce those titties for me." He grins, letting his hands fall away and I do, giving him what he wants. "I'm so fucking lucky," he curses as he sits up and devours my breasts with his mouth, his teeth tug on a nipple sending shock waves between my thighs. I throw my head back and stare out over the Hudson and Manhattan as I continue to ride my man. I'll never get sick of the view from his apartment. His fingers dig into my hips as he decides to take over and meet me thrust for thrust, hitting the perfect spot inside me, and I start to scream. "Tell the world you're mine," Gio growls as his hand moves to my clit, and he pushes me further toward the edge. "Give it to me, show me whose pussy I own." He pushes every single button that he knows detonates me, and moments later, I am screaming his name and he is cursing to the gods as he finds his release. We fall into a messy heap, and I can't help but giggle.

"I fucking love you," I say as I lean forward and kiss him.

40

GIORGIO

"Hey, babe, I have to rush out for a couple of hours for a meeting, you good here?" I ask as I walk over and give her a kiss.

"She's fine," Callie answers.

Paige has invited her girls over for lunch before we leave tomorrow.

"Okay, have fun," I say as I walk out of my apartment and head down to the lobby where Smith is waiting for me.

"Thanks for letting me tag along for this. You can consider this my Christmas present." He grins as we walk out of the lobby and into our waiting car.

Paige doesn't know what I'm doing today and I'm not sure if I'll ever tell her. I know you shouldn't keep secrets from your partner, technically this is a business meeting, not a secret, and I told her I was having a meeting, so technically, I didn't lie. We pull up out the front of the building and walk right in.

"Hi, we have a meeting with your boss, Michael Nelson," I tell the hostess.

Her eyes widen as she looks over me in my custom-made suit and Smith in his NYPD blues he wore for show. The young girl does the right thing and takes us back to the office. She knocks on the door, and he tells us to fuck off.

"Now, now, Mr. Nelson, I don't think that's how you speak to your new landlord."

Michael's eyes fly open when he hears my voice, and he chokes on his spit seeing Smith and I standing in front of him.

"I told you that I would ruin you and now I've come to collect on that threat. As of an hour ago, I am the proud new owner of this fine building you are leasing for your restaurant."

Michael pales.

"In case you are thinking of doing something stupid, we have a couple of police cars waiting right outside, eager to deal with a bitch like you," Smith tells him.

"What do you want from me?" he asks.

"Nothing. As of five minutes ago, this place is shut down," I tell him.

"You can't do that. I'll sue."

He still doesn't understand who I am.

"The health inspector has found numerous code violations, and he's writing you up as we speak," Smith advises him.

He's speechless as he stares at the two of us in shock. Guess my work here is done.

"This is all because of Paige?" he calls out to me.

I turn around and stalk toward him, he backs up, looking scared. "Yes. I told you to leave her alone. I made you an offer, and you refused, then you continued to harass and stalk her. I warned you I would destroy you and now I have. I've taken away everything that you've held dear to you, this restaurant, and Paige."

"She isn't worth doing all this," he spits at me.

"See, that's where you're wrong. There is nothing I wouldn't do for that woman. If you ever come near her again, it will be the last breath you take," I warn.

"Did you just hear him threaten my life?" Michael asks, turning to Smith.

"Sorry, I was tuned out." Smith smirks.

"You fucking Italian bastard," Michael swears as he launches himself over his desk toward me, except Smith stands in my way and catches the full brunt of Michael's anger and fists. It takes a moment before Smith has him under control.

"Assaulting a police officer wasn't a smart move. The boys in lockup are going to have fun with you." Smith chuckles as he cuffs him.

"Guess my work here is done?" I ask Smith.

"Sure is. I'll catch up with you later for dinner." He grins.

I walk out of the establishment with a pep in my step.

EPILOGUE - GIORGIO

"I'm so nervous," I tell Luca, who currently has my nephew strapped to his chest as he bounces him to sleep.

"Don't be. She's going to say yes."

Rationally, I know this is true, but irrationally, all kinds of scenarios are running through my mind.

We're having Christmas at the villa in the vineyard. It's Paige's first Christmas without Lucia, so she wanted to have her close by with her family and friends, including her parents, her brother, and her two best friends.

Paige's friends, and Nat and Lilly, have helped me recreate our first-ever date as teens tonight, decorating the old tree in the vineyard. Thankfully, Paige's parents have kept her busy going through the attic all afternoon so I could set up this proposal.

"I was wondering if you wanted to go for a walk through the vines with me," I whisper in her ear. Back in the day, that was code for *let's get it on*. Paige turns to me and smirks, her cheeks already flushed and I can see the dirty thoughts running through her mind.

"That sounds nice. Let me grab my jacket," she says, rushing out of the room.

Her family all give me the thumbs-up and wish me luck, then push me out the door. When Paige joins me, we link arms and head off into the darkness.

"This is turning into the best Christmas. I can't thank you enough for letting me have it here this year. I know your mamma likes to have it in Rome, but thank you for understanding," she says, curling into my side.

"I'd do anything to make you happy," I tell her, kissing the top of her head.

"How many times did we come down here when we were growing up for some nookie?" She chuckles.

Snow starts to fall as we wind our way through the already snow-covered vines.

"It's a lot colder than when we used to come," I say.

"True, don't want your dick getting frostbite. I like it too much." She giggles. That's good to know.

When we come to the end of the vines where our tree is, Paige gasps as she sees what is laid out before her. All the branches are lit up with tiny globes, there's fur and tartan rugs on the frozen ground, and a bottle of champagne stuck in the snow.

"Oh my gosh, this is gorgeous. How?" Paige asks and as she turns around, I'm already down on one knee, opening the ring box. "Oh," she gasps, staring down at the flawless three-carat diamond—it had to be flawless, just like her.

"Sixteen-year-old me fell in love with you right in this spot, all those years ago. We both took the long way around to get back here, but my love for you hasn't diminished since that first day. Will you marry me, Paige?"

Without hesitation, Paige jumps up and down, then into my arms. "Yes, yes, yes!" she screams, wrapping herself around me as we fall onto the snowy ground and roll a few feet, bursting into laughter.

"I take it that is a yes, then."

THE END

Click here for to continue on to Book 3
The Sexy Enemy - Natalia's book.

ACKNOWLEDGMENTS

Thanks for finishing this book.
Really hope you enjoyed it.
Why not check out my other books.
Have a fantastic day !

Don't forget to leave a review.
xoxo

ABOUT THE AUTHOR

JA Low lives on the Gold Coast in Australia. When she's not writing steamy scenes and admiring hot surfers, she's tending to her husband and two sons and running after her chickens while dreaming up the next epic romance.

Come follow her

Facebook: www.facebook.com/jalowbooks
TikTok: https://geni.us/vrpoMqH
Instagram: www.instagram.com/jalowbooks
Pinterest: www.pinterest.com/jalowbooks
Website: www.jalowbooks.com
Goodreads: https://www.goodreads.com/author/show/14918059.J_A_Low
BookBub: https://www.bookbub.com/authors/ja-low

ABOUT THE AUTHOR

Come join JA Low's Block
www.facebook.com/groups/1682783088643205/

JALow Books Website
jalowbooks@gmail.com

Subscribe to her newsletter here

ALSO BY JA LOW

The Dirty Texas Box Set

Five full length novels and Five Novellas included in the set.

One band. Five dirty talking rock stars and the women that bring them to their knees.

Wyld & Dirty

A workplace romance with your celebrity hall pass.

Dirty Promises

A best friend to lover's romance with the one man who's off limits.

Bound & Dirty

An opposites attract romance with family loyalty tested to its limits.

Dirty Trouble

A brother's best friend romance with a twist.

Broken & Dirty

A friend's with benefits romance that takes a wild ride.

One little taste can't hurt; can it?

If you like your rock stars dirty talking, alpha's with hearts of gold this series is for you.

ALSO BY JA LOW

Spin off from The Dirty Texas Series

Under the Spanish Sun Series

Hotshot Chef - Book 1

ALSO BY JA LOW

Spin off Dirty Texas Series

Paradise Club Series

Paradise - Book 1

Lost in Paradise - Book 2

Paradise Found - Book 3

Craving Paradise - Book 4

ALSO BY JA LOW

Connected to The Paradise Club

The Art of Love Series

Arrogant Artist - Book 1

ALSO BY JA LOW

Playboys of New York

Off Limits - Book 1

Strictly Forbidden - Book 2

The Merger - Book 3

Taking Control - Book 4

Without Warning - Book 5

Also the entire series is now available in Audio

Book 1 - Off Limits Audio

ALSO BY JA LOW

Spin off series to Playboys of New York

The Hartford Brothers Series

Book 1 - Tempting the Billionaire

Book 2 - Playing the Player

Book 3 - Seducing the Doctor

Printed in Great Britain
by Amazon

46887832R00185